TRAILER Trash

Scott T. Goudsward

DarkHart Press
Peterborough, NH

Trailer Trash
by
Scott T. Goudsward

2nd Edition

Library of Congress Control Number: 2012940765

Paperback ISBN 13: 978-1-61807-058-6
Mobi (Kindle) ISBN 13: 978-1-61807-059-3
ePub (Sony, Nook, iPad) ISBN 13: 978-1-61807-060-9
Generic .pdf ISBN 13: 978-1-61807-061-6

Interior Design & Book Cover:
Pam Marin-Kingsley, Briona Glen Publishing LLC

DarkHart Press
an imprint of Briona Glen Publishing LLC
ATTN: Customer Service
PO Box 3285
Peterborough, NH 03458-3285
Email: customerservice@brionaglen.com
Web site: www.brionaglen.com

For Mom and Dad,
and all the things that go
bump in the night.

Acknowledgements

I guess this is sort of the 5th anniversary of *Trailer Trash* the novel being out in trade paperback. So it's been roughly fourteen years since the short story first saw print in The Design Image Group's (RIP to a great small press) *The Darkest Thirst*. Like the short story being my first published work, the novel was my first published novel; I still have a few trunk novels that someday I'll go back and edit, or maybe just print out and burn in sacrifice.

Some of the same people still need to be thanked from the original printing of the book, Kelly Gunter Atlas for the edits, Gregory Norris for the back cover synopsis, Pam Marin-Kingsley for doing the cover (and accepting the book, twice). Briona-Glen Publishing for taking on the second edition and of course, the original crew that made it all possible: Brien, Pete, John, Jim, Eryk and Ray.

The main character's name in this novel is Elvis—he is ***still*** in no way, shape or form, related to or based on Elvis Presley.

— Scott T. Goudsward
July 2012

1
Elvis: Now

"Damn it, Shaun, you know I can't live this way—your way." Lenore stared at the window through the lightning creased sky and hammering rain. The crash of thunder shook the room.

Shaun turned away, wiping a bloody tear from his eye that left a slight, crimson trail down his cheek. "Lenore, I can't promise you perfection, but I can promise you immortality and life filled forever with my love." He brushed a lock of black hair from his shocking blue eyes and focused on Lenore.

Outside, the storm pounded mercilessly against the cottage, the rain sounding like metal pellets hitting the gutters and running in rivers from the mouths.

Lenore crossed to the center of the room, took Shaun's cold hand in hers and smiled weakly. "You just don't understand, Shaun. I can't be with you. I can't be like you." She turned to hide the tears running down her face.

Shaun forced back a bitter laugh, grabbed her shoulder, and violently spun her back to face him. "Can't be like me? Just what the hell does that mean? I can give you anything."

"You're a cold blooded killer, a murderer, and now, my darling…" she said running her hand across his cheek.

Shaun pressed his face into it, greedily stealing pleasure from the warmth of her soft skin.

"You must die!" Lenore said.

"Wait, cut! Hold it!" Shane Douglas stomped onto the movie set, pushing his hair back into place. "Where's the damn fog? Someone cue the fog machine!"

A flurry of people ran in back of him, and after some incoherent shouting, the set began to fill with a gentle mist licking at the actors' feet.

"All right, on my mark, take it from *now you must die!* Three, two, mark!" Douglas rushed off the set as the cameras rolled again.

"Now, Shaun," Lenore hissed. "You must die!" She pulled a wooden stake from the folds of her evening gown, raised it high overhead, and brought it down.

"Damn it! Cut! Where's that makeup idiot? Look at her face. She has a giant crater in her forehead. What's with the lighting? Vampires don't sweat, do they? Everyone break for lunch. We'll pick it up in an hour," Douglas barked, and the set emptied immediately.

The rain and wind machines were powered down, and the stormy landscape faded into a painted country backdrop.

"Can you believe that shit, Shane?" I looked at him quizzically.

"Oh, so the great actor speaks," Shane snarled at me.

"Don't get yourself in such an uproar, Shane. Go with it baby."

"Listen to me, Elvis. Jesus I wish you'd take a fake name. Bob, Harold, maybe even… I don't know, Howard or something—just not Elvis."

"This is my name, Shane—only God himself can make me change it."

"Look, kid, we're late in finishing this beast of a movie, we're over budgeted, and in three days, they take back this set to start shooting another movie."

I fidgeted in my chair while all the extras and prop hands bustled about us. It was like being in a weird little corner of the universe, one ruled by chaos and impatience.

"You keep going like this, Mr. Director, and you're going to give yourself an aneurysm."

Shane stomped over to me and dropped a clipboard on my lap. "You think you can do this film better? Then *you* direct it!"

"I ain't ever said anything of the like. It ain't my damn fault you rewrote the thing. I was just an extra."

"So you admit you're not a screenwriter or a director and, inadvertently, it is your fault."

I shook my head way too much, even made myself a little dizzy, trying to get a smile out of him. Man, it looked like the stress was just going to make his damn heart burst.

He just reached down, never taking his bloodshot eyes off mine, and picked up his clipboard. "It's my damn movie and I don't need your input!" He stalked off the set, knocking over a table loaded with sandwiches, cans of soda, and cookie trays.

A crowd of extras and stunt doubles cleared a path for him, and he disappeared into a small side office, slammed the door, and started throwing stuff against the walls and kicking things in there. Momma would have said he was throwing a screaming hissy fit.

My personal assistant, Rachel, rushed over to me. She was wearing a dress that paid no compliment at all to her cute little figure. She had black hair with a shock of blue in the front and these big, black-framed glasses on that almost seemed to swallow her nose right up. I was still personally amazed I even needed an assistant. She had her arms full of all sorts of important looking stuff—papers, folders, clipboards, and whatnot. Rachel tripped over a cable and nearly sprawled out face first in front of me.

I hadn't moved from my chair. I didn't need to. It was comfy and all, one of those folding wooden ones with your name on the back. I know they used to call them director's chairs, but Shane didn't have one, and I was only an actor and didn't have a big part at that. This was my first movie, and I didn't even think I deserved it. If it weren't for that dickhead attacking me, this wouldn't even be going on.

"You have to stop upsetting Shane like that."

"It wasn't nothing I did, Rach, honest. I was just saying some stuff. It's not my fault he's all stressed out."

She handed me a croissant wrapped in a napkin and plunked down a bottle of water near my feet. She was still holding onto a clipboard, folder, and a whole stack of papers. I took a bite of the pastry and nearly choked on it. She handed me everything but the clipboard.

"What's all this?" I asked after spitting out the pastry.

"The folder has publicity photos the big shots need for press kits. The envelopes are some fan mail, which the movie people thought you should answer personally."

"You mean letter writing? Why can't we just bring in some of the fans for a lunch or something?"

Rachel rolled her eyes at me and then pushed her glasses up her nose.

"Come on, Rachel, think of the publicity—a *lunch with Elvis*."

"Okay, I'll start to book that, and you can explain all the new added costs to Shane."

"Just a thought—you always say when I have an idea I should spit it out."

Rachel went back to shuffling the papers in her arms. "That second folder there is a schedule of magazine and radio interviews, talk show appearances, commercial tryouts, and casting calls."

"Could you please say that in English?"

"Take them back to the trailer, Elvis, and read them. Get back to me before midnight."

"What happens at midnight?"

"My coach turns into a pumpkin. Now get going, kid."

I sat back in my chair and took a long swig of that water. I didn't know what all the damn fuss was about. Just some dumb ass movie I got all caught up in. My stunt double, Arnie, walked by, waving to me. That was the most shocking thing I guess. They actually paid this skinny fellow—maybe thirty or so who stopped growing at thirteen—to fall off buildings and dive in front of cars and such, mostly because it was too dangerous for the actors to do. Shit, if they even knew about half of the stuff I've seen and been through. Didn't make any damn sense to me, none at all. Maybe this frigging movie wouldn't be so expensive if they got rid of all those damn people. *Redundant*, that's something Erik would have said—that all these people doing the same thing, being consulted by their bosses who do the same thing, is redundant.

I packed up my mass of papers, folders, and envelopes and headed out. Arnie had his ear pressed against Shane's office. From inside I could hear Shane yelling at someone. I hoped it was over the phone. One thing Shane knew how to do was be loud and get in your face. He said you had to do that, being a director, because everyone was always telling you what to do even though you were in charge.

There were guys pushing these giant cameras on wheels down mini train tracks—guys with cell phones wandering all over the place in a huff—more guys fixing microscopic problems with the set. Shit, there was even one guy washing down the backdrop that five minutes ago was being sprayed with water.

Coming out of that giant warehouse building they called a set, I bumped into one of the makeup guys. He was carrying a giant case that looked like a toolbox—only it was full of makeup, brushes, and other assorted gizmos. I asked him about the tear thing.

He said in a very flat voice, "It's simple. In the old days, we would have to cut the scene, take out an eyedropper, and put a physical drop on the guy's cheek. These days there are two ways to do it—with CGI, on the computer where the actors have to pretend it's there, or prosthetics."

"You mean them women who do stuff for money?"

"You're new to this, aren't you?"

I nodded and kept on listening.

The guy's name was Ken. He had long hair, four or five days-worth of stubble, wore camouflage pants, and a ripped Black Sabbath concert shirt. "These days we just paste on a piece of latex, fake skin, run a tiny plastic hose under it, and attach the hose to a bladder in the actor's hand. He palms it, turns away from the camera momentarily, and gives the bladder a squeeze. Inside is fake blood. It runs up the tube and down the actor's face. Understand?"

"I think I like it better the old way, and you confused the ever-loving shit out of me."

"That's my job, man." Ken packed up his gear and walked off after hitting what was left of the catering table.

All the extras were grouped around a shed where this hot little number was sitting, smoking clove cigarettes and signing autographs. She wasn't in my movie but in the next one starting in a few days.

Out in back of the "warehouse" was a lot where all the trailers were kept. There were two big rows of them. Since I came into the film so late, mine was at the very end. Sleeping alone in a new place always seemed creepy to me. At least when Erik was around, I knew there was someone else there to talk to. The truth is, no matter how many times you see things, they can still scare you and freak you out—especially the bloodsuckers, man. They do it all the time. Seemed every time we went to a new place, there was a whole new type of them bastards waiting for us.

I started down the back lot after adjusting all the papers Rachel gave me. Behind the trailers was an old service road that was used mostly for deliveries. When the trucks weren't coming up and down, those damn paparazzi were parked out there, trying to get a glimpse of the stars or directors. I always wondered how the public would react if I mooned them. But that agent fellow of mine would have shit himself twice over if that ever happened. Separating the trailers from the road was a giant chain link fence. Must have been at least twelve feet high, and I can't tell you how many times it called to me to just climb up and down and be done with all this movie BS.

I have to admit my trailer was cool. A lot cooler than the one I had come from back in Kentucky. Walking to the thing was like going full circle from back home—but even though I was *still* in a trailer, this one was fancy. Being with Erik for all those months had sort of spoiled me, but in reality, it all comes down to where you're from and where your roots lie.

I unlocked the door and stepped in. As the door closed, I heard all the *clicks* and *pops* as those photographer fellows snapped their shots. On occasion, I'd go out and talk with them, but after a while, they'd all get to shouting and hollering, trying to be louder than the next guy. If they all weren't in so much competition, I'd stay and talk it up all day. I set down the paperwork on the small desk and then locked the door.

I had one key for the outside, but inside, I had the movie guys install five more locks especially for me. I didn't want anyone sneaking up on me in my sleep or finding their way into the trailer when I was taking a shower or wanted some downtime. I picked up the phone, called the catering truck, and ordered lunch.

Shane really hated when I did that because it cost him more money. "Why can't you just eat off the damn buffet like everyone else?" he'd yell at me.

I didn't like other people touching my food, plain and simple, no fingers on it but mine. You never know when someone has slipped a mickey in there.

The trailer was essentially one long room with different areas in it. In the very back was the bedroom, and in the middle, the kitchen and living room. There was some furniture in there. The bathroom was just off the kitchen, and you had barely enough room in there to take a healthy shit. The front of my trailer was the business end—my desk, phone, makeup table. When they let me do it myself, or when they were in a rush to shoot a scene again, those makeup guys would just pile in, do their thing, and disappear.

I waited for the food to arrive before starting anything. I hated to work on an empty stomach, especially all the business stuff. When you hunt vamps, you're better off being hungry for most of the time or else you end up retching your guts out from the smell of the bodies lying all around. Lunch finally showed up—nothing special, just a meatball sub, fries, and a couple cans of soda. After the door closed, the delivery guy went over to the fence and talked up the reporters. Saw one of them hand him some cash. I can only imagine what he told them. But then again, I'd probably be reading about it in the papers in a few days.

I sat at the desk, moved all the papers aside, and slipped in a CD. The food was sloppy but it was hot, and that's all that mattered. I never want to eat cold meat again. I went through the trailer and turned on all the lights, then checked through it just in case. You can never be too careful, especially when you're on the lam and on a mission at the same time.

Those damn sponsors put me up to this. If they weren't in such a God-awful rush to have this place screened and cleaned, I'd be hidden away safe someplace until all this crap blew over.

I sat down to eat, got back up, opened all the blinds letting in the sun, and then finally had my food. I went through a stack of napkins, slopping that stuff all over the place. When the napkins and food were gone, I curled up on the couch to read. I didn't have any scenes in the movie today, but I still liked being there to watch how things ran. Might help me out later on if I stayed in this business. But I didn't really know what was worse, vampires or Hollywood, because in a way they both were the same. Both of them were bloodsuckers—just of a different nature.

I signed the press photos with this silver marker that Rachel had mixed in with the paperwork. There must have been about fifty of them. Didn't need anything clever written on them, just my signature. According to Rachel and my agent, I was one of the more aggressive marketing campaigns in years. The schedule was unnerving—Howard Stern, Oprah Winfrey with the rest of the cast, and E! There was talk of getting on "The View," and apparently, someone had started an unauthorized biography.

Everyone in Hollywood knew I was an orphan, but they didn't know the conditions or why. Erik had been my guardian for the time I was with him, and I miss the crazy bastard every damn day that goes by. Now I have no one.

According to the papers, I had a photo shoot for Levi Jeans in two days and then I would have to eat some kind of cereal, making a fuss about how much I like it. When I came here just a few months ago, I was no one, and now, everyone and their damned sister knew my name. That's the press and wonders of media, getting me plastered everywhere and on everything.

I read through the fan mail, and there were some pictures of the girls in there who wrote them. Putting pen to paper, I scribbled a few letters, threw in a personalized picture, and got them off to the mail truck. Nothing left to do now but nap. I shuffled around the papers and uncovered what seemed to be a daily rewrite. Sitting on the desk were three copies of the script, already rewritten since I had been there.

Outside some guy on a motor scooter went by. The paparazzi yelled to him to take some photos of me, the trailer, whatever he could get. But he didn't stop. I grabbed a quick nap and then went back to the set. Everyone, even Shane, was there doing their things. He seemed to have calmed down quite a bit. There was bottle of Valium on the catering table next to a glass of water. He smiled and winked at me.

I took up my spot as the fog started rolling into the room. Lenore raised her stake again, Shaun shrunk back in terror and then…

2
Elvis: Before

It was the beginning of August and hottest damn day I could remember. Back in the trailer park, rotating fans covered each stoop. Everyone was dressed in shorts and T-shirts, trying to beat the heat. The women would cool themselves with artificial oriental fans, and all the men would drink beer and eat popsicles. It was your typical day in the Starry Night Trailer Park.

I was up in the game room with Jimmy Riley, my arch nemesis and "best friend." Jimmy had this mop of red hair and freckles all over his body—I mean *all* over. Rumors floated through the park, how Jimmy was the product of a passing UPS delivery man, which was why Jimmy's dad beat on him so much. Both his parents had dark hair and blue eyes. Jimmy had green eyes and a bush of red hair that curled up every time it got humid out.

The game room also doubled for an eatery. There were four red picnic tables with chipped paint, three pinball games, and six old video games with faded screens from where the images got burnt into them.

The three walls facing the outside were big sheets of Plexiglas with wood bases. The fourth wall, the one attached to the kitchen, was more of a half-wall where to order your food you had to shout over the drone of the old air conditioner.

We were playing Asteroids, and I was going for my all-time high score. Just when I was about to hyperspace into a clean spot, Jimmy went off and belted me upside the head. It was like this giant flash of white light, and when my vision cleared, I was looking up at him from the floor. Jimmy was all smiles, and I could see the gap in his teeth from where his father knocked out the front two.

I thought the bastard had smashed me with a rock, but he was standing over me with clenched fists. Me never being much of a fighter, I did what Daddy showed me. I pulled back my leg and kicked up as hard as I could. All the air left Jimmy's body, and after grabbing his privates, he crumpled to the floor. Jimmy and me were still good friends. This is just what we did to pass the time. I still had one life left on the machine, so I played until the ship got destroyed by one of those little flying saucers.

Stepping over Jimmy, I decided to help him up to one of the tables. There were tears rolling down his cheeks and he wasn't moving real fast. I kicked him square in the bits, and the only way anyone would be seeing his nuts again would be to look up his nose.

A long road, all cracked and scarred with rubber, ran from the game room all the way to the trailer park. By the time I had walked it, I was soaked with sweat, and being so close to the river, it seemed that every damn mosquito in the state was there with me.

The first trailer I passed belonged to Mrs. Kotch, who we nicknamed *Mrs. Crotch* on account of the way she smelled. She was a dear old lady, who liked to bake cookies that you could never eat 'cause you never knew if she washed her hands or not. But on a hot day you could smell her five trailers over. Her trailer was what Momma called "cute." It was green and white, had a canopy over the stairs, and all around were wooden sunflowers, wind chimes, and faded pink flamingoes. When Jimmy and me were on a tear, we could trample every damn flamingo and not break stride. With Mrs. Crotch around with her chimes, we didn't need any weathermen, just listened for the chimes and waited for the smell of rain.

Her trailer was the first of many. There must have been maybe a hundred or so in there, and by car, we were just maybe fifteen minutes outside of town. When we wanted anything, we would just send Daddy—if the truck was working and the state checks had come in. Jimmy called us *trash* 'cause neither one of my parents worked regular like his. Momma couldn't work on account of her feet being so bad, and Daddy was a truck driver and refused to do anything but. Sometimes he'd catch a break and get to ride shotgun on a delivery, but ever since the accident, he didn't do much driving.

Momma was out in the front yard, her hair up in curlers, listening to the 700 Club on the radio from her lounge chair. Daddy was under the truck cussing, trying to change the oil. All I could see of him were his oil-stained hands and his old greasy ball cap. Momma was in her sundress. She had her little paper fan and was drinking iced tea laced with Daddy's homemade gin.

I hopped up the stairs to the trailer and ran to my room. I stripped down and changed into my swimming shorts. I grabbed a towel from the bathroom, one that wasn't crunchy, and headed for the river and the cold waters therein. Not much had happened since my changing, except Momma had fallen asleep, and there was a new empty beer can lying near the front bumper of the truck. I ran out of the park and straight to the river, getting as sweaty and nasty as I could. Besides, running kept some of the mosquitoes away from me.

I wasn't the only one out there though. The river was roaring with its usual fury. All along the banks were these giant trees. The river had eroded away most of the dirt so the roots were exposed. When the river was really high, you could climb in the roots, sit there, and not worry about getting washed away.

Jimmy was out in the middle, wedged between a couple of slick rocks. His clothes hung over the branches of one of the trees. He always went in bare-assed whenever he could. I never had the guts to show all and stroll into the waters.

"You suck, Taggard! My damn nuts still hurt," he yelled out.

"Why'd you slug me so hard?" I asked, staring at the water.

"It seemed right at the time," Jimmy shrugged.

"How's the water?"

"How do you think it is, Taggard? It's cold."

I slipped in, wincing as my skin went all goose bumps. I found a rock big enough to sit on and took my place in the frigid river. You go a few miles downstream, and there's one hell of a fishing hole formed by runoff from the river. There's this big mansion down there too where old man Norris used to live by himself. Everyone says that Norris killed his first three wives and buried the bodies in the basement. Crazy bastard kept a house full of cats around to cover up what he called the sounds of ghosts.

I stayed in until the sun started going down. My fingers pruned up and my teeth chattered. When I crawled from the river, I heard Jimmy calling over to me.

"Getting out already, Elvis? You're such a pussy."

I had to cover a snicker 'cause of Jimmy's lisp from missing them two teeth. "I can't feel my nuts anymore, Jimmy, and I think my feet are numb."

"Well you shouldn't feel your nuts. You'll go blind."

I beat the towel against a tree a few times to get the kinks out and wrapped it around my waist. Jimmy was still perched out on that same rock, leaning back and staring at the sky as if waiting for a sign or something.

"You up for something later, Elvis?"

"Like what?"

"Midnight meeting with fate."

"Such as, Jimmy? Something new, something original? None of the same old shit?"

"How about a late night tour at old man Norris' place?"

I swallowed deep. Jimmy heard me and laughed. Not what I had expected from Jimmy. I learned from experience he usually meant sneaking into town, or stealing sodas, or pulling pranks in the park—not old man Norris' place.

"You sure about that, Jimmy? What about all the stories?"

"You chicken shit, Elvis?"

"Meet you at the game room at midnight, Jimmy." I slipped on my shirt, and headed back for the park and the warmth of my trailer—before the heat and humidity melted me. Now, after sitting in that damn river, I was near frozen.

Momma had dinner waiting for me when I got back—a big plate of noodles and some kind of meat. Sometimes Daddy would hunt, sometimes he would fish, but more often than not, it was something Momma had gotten from my grandmother.

The trailer was wide-open in hopes of some sort of breeze. Of course, my room was closed tight. It was like a sauna in there. I started sweating again just opening the window. I got changed, and Momma yelled at me for being naked near the windows where the whole world could see my business. I ate dinner in my room, regardless of the heat. I "borrowed" the fan from the kitchen and pointed it at my head. Dinner was tasteless, as usual, and through the window, I could hear Momma's radio and the *clink* of Daddy's tools. Now Daddy had been under that truck for almost two weeks, and it still didn't run. Momma just let him keep on fixing it because it kept him out of her hair.

Daddy was no mechanic by any means, but being under that truck not only kept him away from Momma, it gave him a shady spot to sleep, drink beers, and not be seen by everyone. I closed my door and turned off the light. Outside my window, I could see the park lights and hear the television sets playing. Farther out still, I could hear the peeper frogs and crickets.

When the mosquitoes came out, Momma came in to watch TV, and Daddy went off to talk to his buddies about guns, trucks, tits, and beer. I had my headphones on, listened to the radio, and tried to get a look at the stars through the window slats and glare of the trailer park sign. The sign was a giant cactus with “Starry Night Trailer Park” on it in blinking pink and blue letters. Underneath was a smaller sign that constantly read, *NO VACANCY*. The park hadn’t accepted any new people in almost a year and no one had any ambitions to leave.

When Momma went to bed, I snuck out. The night had cooled off—at least some of the humidity had gone off, anyway. I walked to the game room, got a frosty can of Coke from the machine, and waited for Jimmy to show up. Jimmy had his own signature prank and was a legend through the whole park for it. He would sneak from trailer to trailer and turn off the gas to the trailers so there was no hot water or coffee come morning. He was never caught. My legacy to the park was when one night I collected all the lawn ornaments and locked them in a car.

At eleven, Mr. Crawford kicked me out of the game room, and I had to wait outside sitting on the grass. The glare and lights from the park wasn’t so bad, and I could see the stars pretty well from up there. Mr. Crawford came up from behind and put another can of soda on the ground next to me. He was dressed in denim overalls, a Lori Morgan concert shirt, and cowboy hat, stained with sweat around the headband from where it soaked through.

“Hell of a night tonight, eh, Elvis?”

“Sure is, Mr. Crawford. You can see the whole park from up here.”

“You want to know a secret, Elvis?”

I looked up at him through one eye, keeping the other on the road for Jimmy. “Sure.”

“On nights like tonight when the moon is full and high up in the sky, if you stand up on the roof of the parlor here, you can see the moonlight reflected off the river going all the way to old man Norris' place." He took off his hat, wiped his head with his sleeve and then put it back on. Underneath, the hat was mostly skin and scalp, but Crawford still had a ring of gray hair all around the edge.

"Now I told *you* and not that Riley boy because there's something I see in your eyes, Elvis. That Riley boy, he ain't right in the head. Why you hang around with him baffles me. Well, it's getting mighty late. I better be going and get Mrs. Crawford to sleep."

I watched him walk down the hill, avoiding the road like it was bad, and then disappear among the trailers.

Around back of the game room was an old wooden ladder missing a rung. After propping it up against the back of the building, I climbed to the roof. All the constellations seemed to be out, at least ones I knew anyway. I heard Jimmy coming up the road before I saw him. I jumped off the roof, threw the ladder into a pile of trash, and went around front.

"How long you been waiting here, Taggard?"

"Maybe a half-hour."

Jimmy reached down and started drinking the can of Coke Mr. Crawford brought out for me.

"You sure about this, Jimmy?"

"Either that or we're going to sneak into the game room and play games all night."

I wondered how long he had thought about this and planned doing it. "How we going to get inside for the games?"

He held up this big ring of keys and jingled it in front of my face. "Coming up the hill, I lifted these from Crawford. Still got a chance to back off, Elvis—run, tail between your legs, back to your trailer."

"Let's go, Jimmy, and don't go getting all mental on me. I heard how you're scared of the dark."

Jimmy dope-slapped me upside the head and started down the road. Mr. Crawford was talking to his wife inside his trailer, and an ill wind blew from someplace inside the park that smelled like backed up sewage and chocolate chip cookies.

We followed an old worn path to the river's edge. Jimmy wanted to slip in and follow it downstream—said it would cut an hour off our trip. I told him he was fucked if he thought I was swimming for his dumb ass idea. Jimmy picked up a stick, whistled best he could with those two missing teeth, and dragged the stick, letting the moon light the way. Jimmy, when not whistling, kept talking about this legendary pile of spank magazines his daddy had hidden under the baseboards of the trailer. These magazines were *too* legendary. Every now and again Jimmy would produce one just to keep me and the other guys in our places, but we knew he was lifting them from town. Shit, if his old man ever found out he was stealing his girlie magazines, he'd knock out another two of Jimmy's teeth.

About thirty minutes outside of the Norris place, Jimmy stopped walking. We were near the old fishing hole where we swam more than we fished. From here we could see the house silhouetted against the moon. We heard the sounds of cats. At first I thought it was Jimmy and smacked his head, then I heard it clearly myself. It drowned out everything else, the peeper frogs, crickets—even muffled the river a bit.

We skirted by a bend in the river by walking across an old fallen tree. On the other side, Jimmy crouched real low and started heading in, checking up on me every few feet to make sure I hadn't turned tail. I was close on his heels, trying to walk softly, but kept stepping on pinecones, needles, and leaves.

Clouds crept past the moon, dousing us in pools of dark deeper than the Atlantic.

The tree line broke at the base of the hill. A thin dirt road, big enough for a car, wound up the side to Norris' place. High atop the hill was the outline of a car sitting next to the house. There was no other noise, just the cats and our breathing. Jimmy started up the road, his feet crunching on the dirt and gravel. The tree line got farther away from us, and I wanted dearly to run back to it. With the passing clouds, shapes and images swam in and out of focus. I didn't know what was real and what wasn't.

We were more than halfway up when a shadow broke free from the trees and came charging up after us. Screaming, I turned and fell back on Jimmy. The cats got quiet. The shadows crept closer and closer. Jimmy pushed me off and then the shadow just vanished. Another cloud crawled across the moon and Jimmy punched me.

"Asshole!" he hissed at me.

Still though I was scared and there wasn't anything to make that feeling go away—that nervous tingling like a thousand spiders all over you or when you hear and see stuff that's not there. Every damn shadow seemed to move on its own, and every time something didn't look *quite right,* I got a little closer to Jimmy.

We lay on the road, waiting for a light to go on, but none did. I kept my eyes peeled on the woods, waiting for something else to come charging out. I was about ready to run back when Jimmy grabbed my arm and started dragging me up the hill. Whenever I turned around, I saw something else walking through the woods, something else running towards us, or other shapes and unidentifiable phantoms waiting and watching.

The car was an old Cadillac. The headlights were broken, the shards in the dirt near the hood. There were no windows left, they were smashed in and the fragments covered the seats.

The license plate had been pried off, and the keys still hung on a small chain that dangled from the ignition. Jimmy reached in, gave a turn, but the engine didn't even *click*. The bitch was totally dead.

No lights in the windows, no sounds of radio or television, no voices—just the cats. Bats darted from the trees surrounding the house. Somewhere off in the distance, I heard an owl and the shrill cry of something it had just caught.

Jimmy eased up onto the porch. There were big holes in the boards of the stairs. When the moonlight hit just right, you could see spider webs through the gaps and the egg-sacks, waiting to burst. The porch groaned with each step. The windows were either boarded or painted over, some both. The door was slightly ajar and the cats were even louder now.

Jimmy was first to the doorway and peeked through the crack. A small chain hung limp from the base of the door. The hinges were rusted in place, and when Jimmy pushed on it, flakes fell off. A cloud of dust erupted from the foyer when Jimmy got it all the way open. All I heard was about a million cats, scratching the floorboards and trying to get hidden from the intruders.

Man, that place totally reeked of cat piss. All over the floor were piles of shit, old dried hairballs, and chunks of little dead animals that never got eaten. Even though I couldn't see any of the cats, I could feel their eyes on me—even hear them walking around upstairs, mewling and growling. Jimmy reached for the light switch. It sparked when he flipped it, and two or three light bulbs exploded overhead, freaking out them cats a little more. He took a first step in, looked back, and for the first time I remember, I saw fear in his eyes.

Just past the foyer was a set of stairs leading to the second floor. We didn't have any light and could only see about five stairs up. Beyond that, a small hallway devoured what was left of the moonlight, leaving everything else in pitch darkness.

Even during the day, it must have been dark with all the windows boarded up. The house had been deserted for years—ever since the trial, which was more of a hanging than anything else.

Norris' third wife had eight brothers, and they were all good old boys who lived on the farm with Mom and Dad their whole damn lives. One night, Norris got drunk, beat up the sister, and she died from it. Him being such a recluse and never really letting her leave the house, no one noticed her missing for about two months—until she stopped visiting her parents. As the tale goes, six of the eight brothers went inside, found a shallow grave in the basement with her in it—only the cats had started eating the body. After killing about a hundred or so of the cats, they brought her body out. They also found two other bodies, Norris' previous wives who were in much worse condition.

The six of eight brothers dragged Norris out of the house, strung a rope over the strongest branch of the only tree in his yard, and hung the bastard up. The brothers took their sister's body back home and buried her on the farm, leaving Norris dangling from the rope. A whole week went by and finally the sheriff checked it out. Norris was cut down, brought in for an autopsy, and it was all ruled a suicide. End of the story? No sir. Norris' body disappeared two days later and was never found. And the rope that he was hung with still hangs from the tree. About five years ago, some kids made a tire swing out of it, until one of them fell off the swing and bashed his head against the tree, killing him instantly.

"Damn it, Jimmy, let's come back when we at least have a flashlight."

"I knew you would fold first, Taggard."

"I just said that so you could save face, you stupid bitch. Let's skin out of here."

Jimmy took a second step and a third and a fourth. He was swallowed by the darkness beyond the foyer. I heard his breathing and small furtive steps. "You coming, asshole?"

I followed the sound of his voice, stepping over the piles of shit and broken glass everywhere. I waited and my eyes slowly adjusted just a little bit to the point where I could see murky outlines. Jimmy wanted to kick some of the boards off the windows, and I almost let him, until I thought about being brought home in a police cruiser.

Jimmy kept going down the hallways until I heard him walk into something. "Damn it, Elvis, someone put up a wall. There's holes down the bottom. I guess that's how the cats get in and out."

"What now? Back to Crawford's?"

"No chicken shit. We still got them stairs to check out."

I reached for the wall, and my fingers brushed against the peeling wallpaper. I could feel a spot of moisture or mold, didn't know which. I imagined the phantom spiders running across my fingers and pulled my hand back just in time as something skittered past my feet. I screamed, jumped back, and stepped on a cat. The wall in back of me gave way, and I tumbled down a set of stairs.

"Taggard, you dumb fuck, are you dead?"

I sat up at the landing, saw nothing but blackness and smelled something worse than road kill. The stink was everywhere. I coughed, brushed myself off, and the lights snapped on overhead. I saw Jimmy staring open-mouthed down the stairs at me, his fingers poised on the switch.

I spun around so damn quick I nearly fell over and came face to face with what was left of old man Norris. He was hung from the rafters. I felt the scream building in my lungs and choked on the vomit coming up before it. He was missing from the waist down. Everything that was inside had spilled out—not that much of it was left.

The floor was littered with shotgun shells, bullet casings, cat skeletons, and among the remains, was Norris's lower half. His legs had been broken. I don't know by who or what, but they lay twisted on the floor. Jimmy bolted out of the house. Thankfully, he left the light on.

It didn't feel right playing games and being in the arcade so late, but Jimmy was in the lead. We left the lights off, no matter how much I protested or bitched. He turned on the video games and the air hockey table. Last year someone stole the other blocker so now we used an old soup can with some felt glued on the end of it.

We hadn't spoken a word about what happened since leaving Norris' house and most likely never would. Another urban myth squelched out before even being born.

Jimmy pulled out Crawford's key ring, found the right one, and opened up the door on the first machine. "Okay, Elvis, play you at Space Invaders. Best three of four games."

"What does the winner get?"

"Nothing. Now just shut up and play." Jimmy put a dozen or so credits on the beast.

We could have taken all of the quarters out. Shit, most of them were ours anyway. The picture was faded, and the aliens in the bottom row sort of leaned to one side. It seemed almost unnatural how Jimmy kept looking over the hill, waiting for someone to come after us. But as long as he didn't mention it, neither would I.

Nervously, I tapped the controls. I was about to clear my first screen when the room went awash with lights. Jimmy dove under one of the tables, and I hid to the side of the machine.

"Jimmy, we're screwed! We're busted. I told you I saw someone out in them woods with us."

"Shut up, you moron," he hissed.

The lights went down the access road towards the park. I peaked out from behind the machine to see an RV stop at the first trailer. Mr. Crawford came out in a robe, talked to the driver, and sent him around to the temporary lot for people staying one or two nights only. Usually, only the truckers stayed in there when they were between states and had too far to go before their next stop. Mr. Crawford went back to his trailer, and Jimmy headed for the door.

"Where are you going?"

"To spy, you dickhead. Let's go check it out."

"What about this place? Shouldn't we lock up or something?"

"Leave it. We'll come back in a few minutes. With what we've seen and done tonight, Elvis, how could we be in any more trouble?"

We talked in rushed, hushed whispers. I turned off the arcade machines before we left though, just in case. I followed Jimmy down the hill. No need to sneak because of the damn moonlight. I kept telling him we should just go back, but after he called me a pussy for the hundredth or so time, I had to stand my ground. I kept looking into the shadows, waiting for Norris or some of the wife's eight brothers to come out—or worst of all, a damn cat.

We found the RV in the temporary lot. The driver hadn't plugged in the water, gas, or electricity yet. Jimmy snuck right up to the front of the camper and peered in the front window. A blanket hung from the ceiling right behind the driver's seat. I could hear noises inside but couldn't make them out. The noises must have been talking or a television set. Jimmy crept along the side of the camper and reached for the door. I hissed at him not to do it, but he tested the door and it was locked tight.

The noises inside stopped for a few seconds and then started up again. I felt the shadows move around me. It instantly got cold, the chill going straight through me to my soul. If shadows had fingers, they were wrapped all around my neck. It's then I noticed the mist creeping in low, thick, and cold. When I put my hands in it—it felt like death, cold and clammy.

Jimmy stood up on one of the tires and looked in through a side window. I heard a noise escape his lips, like a whine or a cry or something. He let go, fell to the parking lot, and took off, never looking back. The camper started rocking, like someone was walking inside and moving fast. Jimmy flew off into the trailer park, not stopping. I hopped up on the tire and looked in. I couldn't see much and had to wipe off the steam from where Jimmy breathed on the glass.

The doorknob turned and I strained my eyes to see. The fog was high as the tires now, and clouds swallowed the moon. The door eased open, and my arms exploded with goose bumps. Through the window screen, I could see something on the floor—lying there, not moving. I looked closer and saw my second dead body that night.

I leapt off the tire and slid under the camper. Two pairs of legs stepped down from the RV and started walking around through the fog, stirring up miniature eddies. The two inhabitants became frenzied and started running from truck to truck and camper to camper. They talked in a language I didn't know, one a lady and one a man from the tones. I felt my bladder go loose and the hot sting of piss on my legs.

I buried my head under my hands and prayed for them to go away. The moon came out from the clouds, and I saw something I couldn't at all believe. Those people weren't normal. Without looking or caring, I crawled out from underneath the RV and ran as fast as my legs would carry me.

3
Dorian: Whole New World

More for companionship than warmth, we huddled in the belly of that metal beast, waiting for the time when we would again see the stars. We numbered thirteen in all, including Deirdre and myself, the last of a breed from Ireland, the homeland. The last of a way of life feared, shunned, and reveled. Deirdre slept next to me curled into a ball. The others, the elders, talked quietly trying to disguise the fear and concern in their hushed whispers by adding in badly-timed, artificial-sounding laughter.

For those long weeks across the ocean while the tanker slowly chugged, spitting up its fowl clouds of putrid smoke, our only companion was the constant metallic beating of the ship's engine, a giant heart made of iron and steel that lived off oil, coal, and fuels. While the crew feasted on fish, fresh bread, and meat, we lived off rats and whatever vermin crawled into the hold. Other times, the crew would wander in drunkenly to stare at the freaks in the hold. For those poor souls, I prayed, feared, and yearned. Sometimes we would drink each other's blood, just to sustain us for another day.

The cold, stale blood did little to help. It kept our minds and spirits going while our bones and muscles atrophied. When Deirdre cried, I would chew open my wrists and force blood onto her pale lips.

Deep down inside, we all felt the frenzy coming. The time when we would revert to our most animalistic forms in the quest for blood and a new influx of fresh life. The sweet succulent gush of hot blood, streaming and steaming over our lips, into our mouths, through our cold dead hearts in an attempt to weave some temporary life back to our frozen souls.

There was even talk of sacrificing one of us so that we might find enough old blood to keep us going for the remainder of the trip to America, to the new land full of hope, blood, and promise. What were we to do? What were we to do? Would our escape be our deaths? The trip had cost far more than material possessions. If it continued as such, it would cost us our lives, again.

We landed on the shores of Ellis Island under the cover of night. Even though it was the night that embraced us, the air never smelled so sweet. A man with jet-black hair, eyes the color of coal, and the slightest hint of a beard met us on the rocky shores. While Lady Liberty watched from above, we were given new names and new identities—at least for when we walked among the mortals. The man, Jonathan Kane, greeted each of us in turn, speaking in our native tongue and giving us instructions where we could stay temporarily to hunt and feed.

Three of our party were sickly, near death. Our first duty was to them, to find them safe passage to haven and leave behind a few of us to watch them while the others all hunted, brought back blood, or the vessels that carried it. Kane brought us through the island to a smaller dock where a tugboat waited for us. We all climbed aboard and no questions were asked. Deirdre clung to the rail of the boat and marveled at the city, the lights, and all the fresh blood waiting.

"Is it not a grand sight, Dorian?"

I turned to my sister's sweet voice. "Aye, Deirdre, it is."

Kane walked among us. Named after Adam's son, one had to wonder if he really was a descendant of the mythical man who was our creator. He had a sleek elegance to him, almost as if you were watching a panther on the prowl. Kane kept himself wrapped in a flowing, ankle length coat that concealed most of his body save for his hand that grasped a walking stick.

Although Deirdre and I had the appearance of children, we were both over a century old, twins in life, death, and the immortality that followed. Taken from our homes to work on the roads in Ireland in the time of the great famine, we succumbed to hunger and plague, and finally, were stripped from that world into this new one.

No longer would we be forced to bloody our hands, fight for scraps thrown to us by wealthy landowners, or stay hidden in the shadows while the world revolved around us. We were in America, and now, the food that we needed walked the streets in abundance. No more would we be forced to hide for fear of discovery. As long as we were careful and did not call attention to ourselves, we could be with the mortals. Once settled into our new haven, we were, for the most part, on our own. The ones we came over with, the elders, would keep track of us in their own subtle ways.

The tug docked in the harbor. Unidentified men scurried to secure the boat to the pier, lashing the ropes around posts. Kane walked through them and handed men small rolls of cash. Then they disappeared. The captain of the boat led us off the ship. Our footsteps echoed hollowly off the wooden slats, swaying on the tides.

We were directed off the docks, and I took Deirdre's cold hand in mine. I offered her my wrist, but she turned away. Her lips were starting to turn pale blue, and I could see violet colored veins starting to bulge in her cheeks and forehead. Kane brought us down the streets through the masses of mortals. I heard each heartbeat as if it were my own. I could smell the life coursing through their veins, and it took all I had not to lose control and feed openly.

The depths of the subway were our final stop. Standing on the platform, the tunnels became the veins of the city—the trains that traveled along them were the white and red cells. Lady Liberty, although far away, still watched us, and I believe she was and is the *eyes* of the city. Even though inanimate, made of steel, carbonized from weather and time, she still had a special consciousness known only to her. The metals assembled here from the French absorbed the essences and dreams of those who touched and worked on her throughout the years.

A giant steel snake came into the tunnels. The last of the riders piled off the trains and headed for the exits, like the damned walking to the hangman's noose or a chopping block with Kane holding the axe and rope. When the tunnels were deserted, and the drivers left with their trains devoid of precious human cargo, we marched into the tunnels and followed the rails. Jonathan vanished into a side service tunnel where there was no light. It was the deepest part of the subway, long abandoned, and Kane walked through the tunnel like it was a well-worn forest path.

The hallway ended at a thick oaken door reinforced with steel. As if to show us what could happen to us, he punched through the door, ripping it from the hinges, and flung it out into the tunnels as if throwing away a baseball. In our current state, we were no match for Kane should we even want to try anything. I doubt that even if healthy, we would survive a battle with the man.

"Behold my friends—*sanctuary.*" With outstretched arms, he spun in a circle and our eyes took in the wonder.

Instantly the thralls were upon us, offering up their arms and throats for our feeding. We drank deeply of them, enough to sustain us, but not to cause them any permanent damage. Living on the rats and refuse of an ocean liner gives you a taste for something sour and fetid. Finding this fresh blood was like falling into a wine cellar filled with ancient vintage.

Deirdre drank first, until the color came back to her lips and the veins that scarred her face faded beneath the newly refreshed flesh. Her pallid eyes took on their natural green color. She wiped her mouth, licked her pointed teeth, and savored the last drop of life when it dripped onto her tongue. She smiled and took her place on one of the many chairs with the others of our kind.

The next breath of life was my own. A new vessel came over to me and lifted his wrist to my lips. His eyes were hollow and sunken. There was an air of excitement and expectation about him. I took his arm, licked the soft tender skin of his wrist, saw the scars of those who fed before me, and bit in. He gasped with both pleasure and pain. Our eyes closed in that moment of shared time. His blood was exquisite and thick. I felt my long dead heart beat once again with the rejuvenating flux of this man. Deirdre watched from her chair. I soon joined her, and we all waited for those of us on that ship to feed.

Kane talked to the others. Even here, it was evident that all the factions had gathered. In Ireland, there was one controlling faction. They had many names and were known to us as Changelings, the chameleons of our race. Those who could transform and take the shape of those they have fed on. The more experienced had the abilities of animal transformation.

Deirdre and I had the ability to walk in sunlight for short durations. It was our birthright, but we also had the powers of the chameleon within us. We were an experiment in combining the races to form one, an attempt to unite the factions in the same manner that William Wallace brought together the clans of Scotland to fight against King Edward. We were the only two to survive a sharing of blood from many factions. Any mortals we chose to bring across would have our gifts—if they survived the ordeal.

We were in a sitting room, the walls lined with heavy wooden chairs. Set into the wall, another doorway led deeper beneath the city. There were no portraits on the walls. The cinder blocks that composed them had at one time been painted green, but the paint chips now mostly lay in piles beneath the chairs.

"My children," Kane announced. "This is your new home. Through this doorway you will know haven. This place is, for lack of a better term, sanctuary. All the factions in the city are welcome. There is no fighting here. If you do, you will be expelled to the city streets and hunted. Have no doubt, newcomers and all others, I rule this city and I know everything that goes on in this underworld."

Kane went through the opening, and all the others followed him into the next room. Deirdre and I sat for a moment. I pushed a lock of her thick red hair from her eyes and smiled. She looked like our mother—strong chin, gentle eyes, and a petite frame. Even there in her eyes, she always kept something hidden. I stared at my own reflection. I resembled my father in almost every way. Red hair, slender in face and build, predator eyes with a hint of green, and constantly flushed cheeks.

"What troubles you in this new land, Dorian?"

"I'm worried about the future and about the past. Look at us. We have the appearances of children and we've lived more than the oldest mortal I know of has. We've escaped the island to come here to a land ruled in chaos."

"You fret entirely too much, brother."

Our voices were thick with Irish brogue. She took my hand and led me through the passageway. Kane stood in the center of the room. The walls were covered in thick rich tapestries depicting biblical scenes. Short oaken bookshelves, over-stacked with ancient volumes, sat beneath the tapestries. A grand crystal chandelier lit the room and hung low over a mahogany table set with linen napkins, the finest of china, and golden goblets.

As we watched, each of Kane's mortal followers slit their wrists and bled once more into the goblets. We were instructed to sit, and the rules of feeding were laid down before us.

Jonathan referred to other factions of which I was not familiar. Introverts, who stayed hidden in forests and underground, only fed from animals and almost never touched human blood. Another small band of hunters were indifferent about that on which they fed—man or animal, nothing was safe from them. They even hunted their own kind for sport. They were indiscriminate to the rules of Kane and banished from the sanctuaries.

We drank from the goblets, and those in the enslavement of Jonathan Kane seemed to wither in his presence—until he left the room.

4
Elvis: Breakfast

I ran so damn fast I thought my frigging head would implode. I carried my clothes under one arm and a towel under the other. It was the brink of dawn and I got up, before Crawford and even before Momma. I had already promised God and myself that no one would find out what happened—least not from my mouth anyway. There was no way of telling what the hell Jimmy would say if anything at all. I had a good idea though that the first time he uttered a damn word about it, his old man would just wallop the shit out of him until he stopped talking.

My clothes reeked of piss and I did too. Last night, I didn't sleep after getting away from the camper and what I saw. If the shower had been turned on, that would have woke Momma and Daddy. If the washing machine were put on, they'd hear it too—not to mention that they would see all the stuff outside on the line when they got up.

My first plan was to hitch a ride into town and use the laundromat. Who in their senses was going to give a piss-stinking kid, half out of his mind with panic a ride? I could still picture the freaky people from the temporary lot. Still envision the body on the floor of that RV. They saw us too. I was sure of it. Those folks knew all about Jimmy and me, and they'd be coming for us, no damn doubt in my mind.

I did the only thing that came to be of any sense—started running balls for toes for the river. The dew-slick grass kept making me slip and I rolled a few times too. By the time I was in the woods near the park, I was panting so hard you could have mistook me for a wild dog.

I heard the river even though it was still kind of far away. I found the path that Jimmy and me wore into the ground and followed it like a baby through the birth canal. It got louder with each step, sounding like the roar of a big cat on the plains. I half expected to see Jimmy still out there perched on his stone in the middle of the river, but he wasn't there. No one was. Just me.

There ain't no polite way to say this. I stripped down to the suit that God gave me and hauled ass to the roots along the bank. I stuck one toe in and felt my dick shrivel from the cold. I can't imagine Jimmy sitting out there on those damn rocks for so long when I could barely get my foot in. I left my towel on a branch close to shore so I could just jump my ass out when the time came. Normally I'd never be naked out here, but today reeked of being discrete, after being naked of course.

I dragged my clothes in from the roots, soaked them in the water, and rubbed wet sand from the bottom all over them, and if that wasn't enough, I filled them full of stones and then rubbed the hell out of them again. I didn't bring any damn soap, so I hoped that this was enough. Then it was my turn. I scrubbed the hell out of my skin with some sand and roots until I was red all over.

I climbed from the river frozen to the core, and for a minute, nothing mattered. I couldn't remember anything, except for the fact I was all shriveled and blue-lipped. The woods were strangely quiet, and I had to keep looking all around to make sure no one was near me. I figured that maybe Jimmy was hiding someplace out there, but maybe not. Wrapped in the towel and sitting under a tree, I waited for the sun to come out and maybe partially dry my clothes.

Someone started up the path. I heard sticks breaking. They were coming up fast. I ducked in back of the tree and grabbed a stick and a rock when Jimmy came busting out of the woods.

"Did you tell anyone?" he screamed.

"No, Jimmy, no one. Never going to tell anyone either."

"We just keep our damn mouths shut and we'll be fine, Elvis."

We walked back to the trailer park. I never did drop that stick though. I carried my clothes, still wet, wrapped in my towel. All I had to wear was a spare pair of shorts and my sneakers. Jimmy kept punching me in the arm until it bruised up. I followed his attack by hitting him in the back of the knees with my stick.

I couldn't believe my eyes when I got back to the trailer. The truck was off blocks, and Momma and Daddy had gone out for a ride. Jimmy waited outside while I changed. We went up to the game room, and Mr. Crawford was outside scratching his head over his key ring being in the door's lock.

He waved his hat at us, took his keys, and went into the kitchen. We ordered take-out chili and eggs, hash browns, and maple grits. We sat outside on the lawn and ate in shifts, keeping an eye out for anyone that might be coming over the hill or up the road.

"We have to check out that camper again, Elvis," Jimmy said through spoonfuls of grits. "Have to go there and see what's what."

"That's crazy talk, Jimmy. They're only there temporarily. Soon they'll be gone, and things will come back to normal again."

"Man, shit ain't never going to be normal again until we can prove what we did or didn't see."

Jimmy's old man hollered for him, and Jimmy went pale like he was going to the chair or something. He packed up the last of his grub, handed me the Styrofoam food box, and slinked down the hill towards his trailer.

"You meet me at three, Taggard, right in from of Mrs. Crotch's trailer."

I swallowed hard, feeling the food start to come back up my throat and nodded to Jimmy.

"Don't be late and make damn sure you don't tell no one."

"You sure this is the right thing, Jimmy?"

He started walking backwards down the road nodding back at me. He held up three fingers and that was the end of the conversation. I choked down the last mouthful of food, rolled over, and threw up.

5
Dorian: The Wardrobe

Kane smiled slyly, for the first time showing us his wicked pointed teeth. He drank from a thrall until she was empty and tossed the body aside like a discarded coffee cup. "Now, my children, go forth into the city." He wiped the crimson from his chin and licked each of his fingers, savoring the taste of blood before it cooled.

I saw the hunger in Deirdre's eyes as Kane approached us.

"You two don't wish to feed?"

"I'm afraid this is all so overwhelming for us…"

"No, we'll feed, but we wanted to invite you for the hunt," Deirdre blurted out, cutting off my words. Kane raised an eyebrow, bowed his head, and then kissed her hand.

"It would be my pleasure to join the twins in their search. Shall we meet outside in about ten minutes? I have some business to finish up here."

Deirdre nodded and actually blushed, a strange contrast to her pale skin. We rose from the table, and Deirdre suddenly looked ashamed at our threadbare clothes and ragged appearances.

"Dorian, we need to change."

"Where, and into what? We didn't bring anything with us. It's all back in Ireland—that was our payment for coming over here, or have you forgotten? If it wasn't for Mr. Kane, we'd be in a sewer tunnel feeding off the rats."

As if sensing our predicament, Jonathan came over and handed me a business card.

"Go there and tell them I sent you."

Deirdre looked away as if more ashamed to take his charity.

He took her chin in his hand. "Fear not, girl, for in this city you are all my children. I'll meet you at the store in an hour. Find some suitable clothes to your liking and be happy." Without another word, he strolled off, head held high, slicked hair never moving an inch, his predator eyes taking in every corner, every shadow, his ears hearing the sounds of the blood coursing through our dead veins.

We found an exit behind one of the lush curtains. The passage way was lit by lanterns, flames contained safely behind panels of leaded glass. There were no loose stones in the walls or the walkways, no cobwebs or signs of insects or vermin. It was cleaner than most churches, at least the ones I could remember. Deirdre hummed softly holding the business card tightly in her hands. We emerged near the tracks and found ourselves on an empty platform. The stairs leading up were lit dimly, and the graffiti-tagged walls brought back memories of Dublin.

"Do you think we'll be safe here, Deirdre?"

"Safe as safe can be. We have a guardian angel, so to speak. We have a home, a provider, and hopefully a friend, maybe more so." She pushed past me into the city.

It was very late and almost all of the stores had closed. A few twenty-four hour variety stores and sex shops were still open. Theaters advertised live nude girls, their neon signs burning incessantly into the morning sky.

The streets were still crowded for so late. *I want to wake up in the city that never sleeps.* Taxicabs lined the sides of streets, waiting for their next fare. Theaters let out, sending a fresh new buffet into the streets before us. I could hear them breathe, hear their hearts beat, and smell the emotions. Strangers looked at us hungrily as if we were for sale, another product this city could so easily provide.

We made our way carefully down the streets, around sleeping drunks and crowded outdoor sidewalk cafés, still serving coffee and pastry. I had not tasted food since the moldy bread shared in the cabin with Deirdre, and I yearned for the taste against my lips. How I missed the sweet taste of wine or ale. But our bodies could no longer digest the food, no longer process it.

We arrived at the clothing store, stuffed between a coffee shop and restaurant. There were no open signs or business hours posted on the door. There was just a buzzer, which Deirdre rang before I could say a word. Inside, the lights snapped on, showing racks upon racks of suits, dresses, and other clothes.

A tired-looking man, dressed like he had just stepped from the pages of a Victorian novel, greeted us at the door by talking through a speaker. "Yes, how may I help you?" His voice was nasal and an octave too high for his frame, sounding artificial.

Deirdre pressed Kane's card against the glass of the door, and a broad smile swept across the man's face. He had a thin moustache and thick brown hair, braided with golden ribbons draping over his shoulders. The lock *clicked* and turned. He repeated the action twice more before we were shown in.

The man, introducing himself as Adrian Sneed, told us to take as much time as we needed and to call out when we were through. Deirdre went towards the gowns, shrugging off my arm when I reached for her shoulder.

"Don't you suspect Kane of anything? Why is he being so pleasant and charitable?"

"Because he cares. Remember what he said back there? We're all his children. Do not forget how we became this way, Dorian."

"I haven't forgotten at all. I'm reminded of it every time a drop of blood passes these lips. We must be careful or end up his slaves. Did you forget everything from back home? The wars and fighting? Forget the damn mortals. What about the conflicts among our kind?"

She picked up a dress from a wall hook and went into a changing room without speaking to me. I listened to her undress and the gentle whir of the ceiling fans. Sneed was just behind a door to the back room. I could hear him breathing and smell his fear. I didn't know how much control Kane had over him, but I knew for certain he was not one of us.

I looked through the men's clothes, found some shirts, pants, and a pair of shoes with no holes and I tested the heels and seams to ensure they would not tear or break. It would be a long time again before I went without proper shoes. Deirdre emerged from the booth looking a changed girl, or should I say, woman. Trapped in these bodies, with the appearance of sixteen-year-old twins, there was nothing we could ever do to look more grown up. She twirled in front of me and brought a smile to my face.

"You look beautiful, sister."

"Still having doubts about our savior?"

I shook my head, changed into my fresh clothes, waited at the counter for Deirdre to finish, and read a sports magazine. The clock on the wall read 3:00 am. We still had some time to spare, but not much. If we were going to be out past the sunrise, we would need to hunt and feed soon.

"Are you two kids all set? I know how Mr. Kane likes to have his flock inside before dawn." Carrying bags, Sneed slithered from the back and began packing away our new clothes. He held up my old clothes with a look of disgust.

"What should I do with these?"

"Burn them." I said. "It doesn't matter what you do."

"Such a lovely accent, where are you from?"

"Ireland."

Sneed bit the end of his finger, a droplet of blood slowly pooled out and he offered it to me. When I shook my head he seemed quite dejected.

"Deirdre, hurry it up. We have to be back soon."

There was a soft rap on the door. Both Sneed and I turned to see Kane waving at us from the street. Sneed practically fell over me rushing to the door.

"I take it Mr. Sneed has been helpful in your acquisitions?"

Adrian looked at me pleadingly, like he feared what Kane would and could do to him.

"Yes, very much."

Kane looked deep into my eyes searching for something, a lie maybe or perhaps an excuse. He smiled and turned as Deirdre came again from the booth in a suede skirt and silk blouse.

"You look ravishing child. Shall we?" He held up a gloved hand towards the door, and Sneed packed away the last of our clothes into the bags.

As Sneed handed them to me, he pulled me in and whispered urgently "Get out while you can!"

I broke free of his grip, looked at Kane nervously, and left the store. Deirdre took his outstretched hands and joined me on the street. Sneed, sweating profusely while dodging Kane's glare, locked the store.

"You'll have to excuse Adrian. We've known each other for such a long time and he still gets nervous—despite promises I have made to him. The hunt awaits us. Let's be off."

"But how can you withstand the sun, Jonathan? We have our ways. But you, you're not of our faction."

"Don't fret, my dear."

An old man dressed in tuxedo and top hat sitting in a horse drawn carriage stopped beside us. The horse whinnied softly as the man tugged on the reigns.

"Now, if you please? We have little time left."

The horse moved ahead, causing some bells on its harness to *ring*. I shuddered at the sound and almost collapsed in the street.

"Do you still remember the bells, Dorian?"

I nodded absently, hoping, maybe praying, the memories had been buried deeper than they actually were.

"But tell me, Deirdre, are they the bells of wagons or churches?"

6
Elvis: 3 pm

I sat on the crabgrass in the shade of Mrs. Crotch's trailer, watching a passing truck make one of the wind chimes sway in the breeze. It was hot as sin and old Mrs. Crotch was reeking up a storm. Every time I turned to look for Jimmy, she'd be right there next to me in her summer moo-moo dress, offering me a cookie from a tray shaped like Elvis's head—not me, the real Elvis, *The King*. I had to take one occasionally, say thank you, and when she went back to her beach chair, throw that damn cookie hard as I could over the next trailer while pretending I was eating and enjoying it.

Jimmy finally came up the road, hitting rocks with an aluminum baseball bat. He plunked down in the grass next to me, and when Mrs. Kotch got up to offer him a cookie, he just waved her off, shaking his head.

"You all geared up for this, Elvis?"

"How come we're doing this in the damned afternoon? Why can't we tell anyone?"

Jimmy raised that bat and brought it down on the back of my hand. "Now shut up for a minute, trash-boy, will you? We do it in the afternoon, you damn fool, because at night someone would see us snooping around. Same thing if it was the morning."

I looked all around at the park, at all the people milling about, playing ball, hanging clothes, working on their cars or washing them. Over in the temporary lot, there was some family having a picnic while their kids played on the swing set and jungle gym.

Then I looked back at Jimmy—the scowl on his face and him bouncing that ball bat in his hand. "Okay, Jimmy, you're the damn boss. Just don't get us killed."

We snuck away from Mrs. Kotch, trying to be as stealthy as we could out there in the open with no cover except for the occasional trailer that we passed. Seemed everyone was outside, and they all stopped to say hello to us on our mission for the truth. I still didn't know why Jimmy had that bat. I had an idea but didn't want to risk another shot upside my head or someplace else, depending how he was feeling about my kick yesterday.

We got to the temp lot and there was that camper just sitting off to one side. The gas and water had been hooked up—sometime after we left last night no doubt. Jimmy lay down on his belly, slithered across the gravel, and turned off the gas, leaving the water on. There was no noise coming from the inside though—like they had gone off for a walk or were still sleeping something off.

He waved me over, and I crawled to him on hands and knees. He gave me the bat and told me to stay right there where I was and not to move a damn muscle or he'd kick the crap out of me.

"What are you doing, Jimmy?"

"Shut up, you jerk. I'm scouting. If I ain't back in two minutes, you come after me."

I lay flat on my belly and watched him walk around the RV. Every now and then he'd step up on tiptoes, looking for a glimpse of what we saw last night. But the curtains were drawn tight from the inside.

Jimmy went around front. The windshield had a spider web from where something had smashed into it. There was one of them cardboard things that blocked out the sun obstructing his view inside. I decided that I looked and felt like an idiot lying there in the gravel—not to mention I was scared shitless too. I was sweating, but I still had goose bumps all over my arms and legs. All the little hairs on the back of my neck were sticking up. I was waiting for something to come, that didn't, and waiting is the worst part. Jimmy was back up on tiptoes when I went to him. That sun blocker had actually slipped down and there was now a crack big enough to see through on the driver's side.

Jimmy tried to maneuver himself in there for a peek, but couldn't quite do it. "Elvis," he whispered. "You get in here. I'm too tall."

I handed him the bat, and he got ready to use it if the need arose—against me or anything else. I had to climb up on the wheel, and Jimmy hissed at me to be quieter and more careful, but there wasn't any other way this was happening. I used the side mirror for support and pulled myself up.

It was totally dark in there. Nothing moved, least not that I could see anyway. I crooked my head to one side and then saw it. Hanging in back of the driver's seat was a big heavy blanket. It was taped to the ceiling and floor from the other side or stapled or something, I couldn't tell. I dropped off and told Jimmy.

He went silent, like he was trying to devise another plan. "You got anything, Elvis? Only thing I can think of is sneaking in. But I don't know how and swear I really don't want to either."

"I think we should tell someone, Jimmy."

"We tell anyone and we're screwed. They're going to want to know what we were doing up so late last night and why we snuck out."

"What do you think will happen when they see us sneaking around this RV? They're going to call the damn cops."

Jimmy reached back and popped me one on the side of the head. I retaliated and hit him hard in the ribs—gave him another shot to the gut and then the face. He knocked me down, climbed on my chest, pinned my arms with one hand, and started beating my face with the other. I saw blood on his knuckles and didn't know if it was his or mine.

Suddenly the camper rocked, like someone was walking in there. Another shot to my face—blood spattered my cheek and forehead—and something cracked. The footsteps got louder, ringing out like cannon shots. I kicked out and Jimmy tumbled off me. He rolled for the baseball bat. I ran up, planted my work boot upside his head and made a break for it.

I only had one place to go before Jimmy caught up. That bastard would be pissed as hell at me too. I made tracks for Mrs. Kotch's trailer, which wasn't my salvation, but a stop along the way. I weaved through the windmills, wind chimes, and flamingoes, trampled some tomato and bean plants, and dove under the trailer. I could hear Mrs. Crotch walking over me. I waited till I saw Jimmy run by, heading up towards the game room. When he was clear, I ran for the woods and the river.

I thought I was safe, maybe even out of harm's way for a couple days. Jimmy would ignore me, throw rocks and spit at me for a while, before he came slinking back like he always did. That's when I heard the footsteps coming fast and hard up the path in back of me. He was shouting incoherently, and I dove into the river. Jimmy went whipping right by where I had jumped in. I climbed into the roots and waited.

About an hour into it, the water stopped being refreshing and started getting cold. At two hours, my fingers pruned and my teeth chattered. By the third hour, I couldn't feel my toes. Jimmy was still up on the banks stomping around like a wild man, breaking sticks, and tossing rocks. He climbed trees, did some scouting, jumped down, and then started breaking stuff again.

Somewhere deep inside, I heard something. A deep guttural sound—I felt it. The sound overcame the roar of the river. I saw fear in Jimmy's face. That gap in his teeth stuck out like a damned eclipse. The sound crashed through the trees and Jimmy panicked. He couldn't control his emotions. Did he want to stay and try to kick the shit out of me or race home before his father yelled again? Jimmy started off down the trail at a slow jog, stopping, running backwards, and then finally he just booked it.

I pulled myself from the roots and the cold water. I knelt on the ground, hugged myself, and began to shiver. I was soaked and chilled right to the damn bone. I started down the path, not knowing what was making more noise—my damn teeth chattering or my footsteps. Jimmy could be behind any tree or rock waiting for me, but I didn't give a good goddamn.

Then like a gunshot, the forest went quiet—no sound except for my breath and the river. It was like someone had turned off the volume—no birds, no frogs, and no crickets. Through the trees, I saw what was left of the sun drop behind the horizon. All I could do was sit there for a couple minutes, watching and waiting.

I heard a footstep—a stick broke under someone's boot. My skin froze. The breath got choked in my throat and I gagged on a dry mouth. Another step, and I reached down to the forest floor for a stick, one big enough to knock the bejesus out of that little bastard, Jimmy Riley.

I spun around and started cussing up a storm—the way Daddy showed me how to. I let loose with a stream of vulgarities that would have made Jesus blush. I froze dead and then turned and dropped my stick. Standing right there in front of me was a woman—most beautiful woman I ever saw.

7
Dorian: The Bells

You two do what I say or you'll be feeling the back of my hand!"

"But, Father, I..."

His hand was strong, solid, and swift. He bloodied my nose and lips. "Don't make me hit you again, boy. This is already hard enough. We've no other choice."

"Just do as he says, Dorian. All of the fields are dead, all the crops rotten. I've dug until my fingers bled, but there's nothing edible left out there."

I watched the tears start to roll down her cheek. Deirdre bit down on her lip and got up from the table. The cottage was cold. The clay and stone walls did little to keep what was outside from seeping in. The three of us, Deirdre, Father, and I stood huddled around the small stove, wrapped in a blanket.

"When do we go?"

Father looked down at the floor while Deirdre cleared the chipped dishes from the table. The only window faced out upon rolling fields of green with roots blacker than death.

I asked him again, hoping to get a response other than the back of his hand. "When do we go?"

He wiped at the traces of my blood on his fingers. "First thing in the morning, a man will come with a cart to take you away."

"What will we do?" Deirdre asked.

"Build the roads. They pay you by the basket loads of stone."

"And what will *you* do?"

Father looked away when Deirdre's posed the next question. He stood up, shrugging off his part of the blanket, and headed for the door. "I'm leaving to work the docks, wherever that will take me. When I have enough money, I'll send for you both, and we can go to America. Over there, we can build the rails until we have enough for another farm, one without the rot. There's nothing left for us here now."

Through the cottage's eye, I watched him going down the path to Mother's grave. He stopped briefly at the white cross that poked out of the rounded pile of stones and dirt. He ran his hand along its surface. Then he kept going.

Deirdre came over, shivering. I wrapped the blanket around her shoulders.

"Do you think we'll ever see him again, Dorian?"

"No."

The wind and rain whipped against us. We all stood or knelt in a massive line, unloading pieces of broken stones for the roads that would never be used or finished, roads that for decades to come would be monuments of sorts to all the lives lost in the attempt. I watched Deirdre make her way down the treacherous hillside, shivering and coughing, carrying another one of those damned baskets filled with stone. My fingers were bloody and numb from the cold, but we kept building. My hands and cheeks were decorated with purple and black patches, and I could feel the cold down to my soul. She dropped the basket near my feet and fell over, almost on top of me.

"Are you all right?"

"Leave me be, Dorian. Get the basket and go up the hill. Just over the rise is a pile for you."

When I reached for her shoulder, she pulled away.

"Just go, Dorian. Please." She fell forward in a fit of coughing, straightened herself out, and went back to piling stones on the road's surface.

From all around us came the sounds of misery and anguish—crying, coughing and those damned bells—the bells on the cart driven by the faceless man who hauled away the dead and dying.

I climbed the hill, feeling mud and cold water from the rain puddles oozing through the holes in my boots. My feet hurt and I could not feel my toes. I slipped on that hill more times than I could count, and it had brought me to one knee more than I care to remember. Just over the rise, like Deirdre had said, was a mound of broken up stones, enough to fill up the large, flat basket.

I piled them in. The weather broke for a moment showing a glimpse of the sun, a touch of God's warmth. I turned to see Deirdre looking up to the sky and smiling for the first time in months—since our father had deserted us.

"Can you see the sun, Deirdre?" I called out pointing to the sky.

I took a step forward to stand in a ray of light, slipped in the mud, and rolled down the hill in a flurry of grass and broken stones. The tumbling and rolling seemed unreal, the stones collided with my head. Just imagination? It was an illusion, all a giant dream—until I heard and felt my leg snap just below the knee.

Deirdre rushed over to me. She was the first and only one to offer any help. The others rushed to gather the stones that I had dropped and dislodged when falling down that damned hill.

"Lord Jesus, Dorian, so much blood! It's broken."

I heard the clanging bells of the cart coming as Deirdre

tore a sleeve from her dress and tied it around my knee. She handed me a stick from the side of the road.

"Bite down, dear brother. I have to set this." I tasted mud and bark. I screamed out as the rains started again, the bones in my leg scraped against one another. She set my leg, and I watched her work until consciousness left me.

When I awoke, I was lying prone in the corner of a small hut with no door. Missing bolts, the shutters of the only window hung from hinges. Deirdre sat huddled in the corner, hugging herself for warmth. Full of holes, a ragged blanket that used to be the door covered my legs. The right one was cold and clammy, the left, numb below the broken knee. I lifted the blanket to make sure my leg was still in place.

"Back to the world of the living, are you?" my sister asked.

"Aye, Deirdre. Where are we?"

"Small abandoned hut—no lantern or stove. No wood for fire. I managed to get some carrots and bread without too much mold."

"What I wouldn't give for a cup of hot tea or a warm smile from my sister. I've never been so cold."

Deirdre came over and sat next to me on the earthen floor. She leaned in close and we shared our body heat. "Jesus, Dorian, it'll be a miracle if we last another night."

"Is there any word from Father?"

"No," she said, tearing off chunks of the flat bread and picking off the pieces of mold. "No word at all."

"Do you think he'll sell the farm?"

"And everything with it. Should be enough to buy him passage for one to America, if he can sell it."

I ate stale bread while outside the weather crept in. Wind and cold rain blew in while we shivered. I noticed the purple and black blotches running up her arms as we shook from cold. She was right. It truly would take a miracle to live through this night.

CLANG, CLANG, CLANG.

I awoke to the sound of bells and horses. The blanket that covered my legs was soaked with rain, sweat, and urine. I was sweating so much it hurt. Breathing hurt and leaning up to get a look through the doorway was agonizing. Sun streamed in through the entrance, and the trembling began. Next to me, Deirdre gasped as I reached for the sunlight. My fingertips passed through it, and for the first time in months, I felt warmth.

An expressionless man wearing a long coat and pulling on heavy leather gloves came into the hut. For a moment I thought he was an angel, the way he was bathed in sunlight. Next to me, Deirdre sighed, a soft, sickly wheeze. He was strong and stunk of sweat, horses, and tobacco. He carried us out to the cart and laid us in the back. Thankfully it was empty.

"Wake up, Deirdre. We're being taken home."

She stirred briefly, and I could tell that she was slipping away from me. It was too much for us to fight. The struggle had gone on too long. Our father, curse him and his black soul, had left us to die on the roads while he fled across the ocean to freedom. Freedom from his family and this country. Now we were in the cart used to haul away the dead and dying. What I didn't tell Deirdre is that we were going home to be with God.

Our journey ended in front of a cave set into a sheer cliff-face. The road we traveled was rutted from wagon wheels and pitted from shod feet. Despite the rain and cold winds and the darkness that oozed from that cave, the grass around it was thick and green with life.

"Where we going?" My voice was raspy, my throat sore from lack of fluids.

A drop of sweat rolled down my nose and spattered on my hand. It was cold, so very cold. When I shook Deirdre, she hardly moved. Her lips were pale and chapped, and her eyes had rolled up.

"Let her go, son," the driver said.

"She's just sleeping. Once I get some food and tea into her, she'll be fine again. Why did you bring us here?"

"You're going in the cave. Just lie still and it will be easier for you both."

I lay back down and listened to her raspy, shallow breaths. I let the sun wash over me for what I believed to be the last time. The nameless man moved each of us to the cave entrance. I was too tired to fight, and Deirdre looked like a limp rag doll in his arms. From inside the cave came hushed whispers, cold drafts, footsteps all around, and the *clinking* of coins being exchanged.

Voices swam all about me. For a moment my fingers brushed against Deirdre's hand. At least I thought it was hers. I was lifted again and carried down into the cave with my foot scraping against the wall as we went. When the tunnel widened into a cavern, I again fell prey to unconsciousness.

More voices in my head. The cave wall was cold against my back when the bandage and splint were removed from my leg. Fingers moved all over my face, chest, and leg, and there was a soft tickle of a wet, warm cloth on my cheek and neck. My eyes opened to behold an odd sight. Deirdre stood, smiled, and looked down at me. There was a terrible taste in my mouth and dried blood at the corner of her lips.

There were no lanterns, torches, or fires, yet I could see her as if it were mid-day. Then I noticed my legs. I had the feelings in both. A sudden fierce hunger consumed me and doubled me up.

"Don't fight against it, Dorian."

It was then I first saw the face of Jonathan Kane.

8
Elvis: Thrall

She was dressed to kill and had that air about her too—with straight blonde hair to her waist and pale blue eyes that caught the moonlight. She was a ten if there ever was one. She wore leather pants and boots that said she was a wild ride, and to top it off, a slinky white shirt that left nothing at all to the imagination, if you know what I mean. I recognized her instantly. From the voice and brief glimpse of her face, she was the lady from the camper—the one that Jimmy and me spied on. I didn't know where her man friend was though.

"Come with me, Elvis." Her voice was soft and soothing, hypnotic.

When she reached out her hand, all I could do was put mine in hers. I had no will to do anything but. Her hands were cold but soft, like a comfortable leather jacket left out on a spring day.

"My name is Katherine."

I nodded. Shit, it was all I could do. We started back for the park. Even though I was with Katherine and had no fear of anything at all, I still kept an eye open for Jimmy Riley. I wanted the bastard to be jealous of what I had found out in the woods. No more worn *Playboy* magazines for me. No sir, I had the real thing.

All through the woods, there was no sound. When we left an area, the noises came back—slowly though. Katherine didn't say much of anything all the way home. She just held my hand, sometimes stroking it gently with her other hand, the way a mother would when trying to re-assure you.

I was real late getting back to the trailer, but it didn't matter at all. Momma was in her chaise lounge listening to rebroadcasts of the 700 Club on the old radio. The truck was back up on blocks. I could see Daddy underneath it with a droplight looking at something. Every few seconds he'd let out with a stream of cusses or reach for his beer can. Sitting on the stoop was my dinner, cold and all stuck together, noodles and beans, 'cause that was Momma's specialty and Daddy's favorite.

When Katherine and I walked from the shadows, Momma just near damn died there in her lounge chair. Without blinking, she reached over and switched the radio off. Moving like some snake woman, she got up from her chair and got out Daddy's best belt from Sears, which she just happened to have sitting on the ground. I ran over to her. I didn't want to, but something inside my mind made me—the things sounded an awful lot like Katherine's voice.

"Just what in the hell do you think you're doing, Elvis?" Momma's voice was high and shrill.

I'm not sure what she was more shocked at, Katherine or me.

"Do you know what time it is? Jimmy Riley came over here and said he drowned you in the river. Lordy, you're soaked to the bone! Now go inside and change!"

I looked back at Katherine. She nodded, and I bolted inside the trailer, hopping over my plate. Daddy came in right after me, making a bee line for the bathroom with a Louis L'Amour paperback stuffed under his arm, muttering something about the oil pan and oblivious to the world outside.

I put on my best jeans, a shirt with only one hole in it, and got into some other stuff—the unmentionables, you know. Through my open window, I could see silhouettes of Momma and Katherine. Neither one was saying anything. Momma was trying to stare her down, and Katherine smirked with those red painted pouty lips.

I ran out again, hearing this God-awful noise coming from the bathroom. I hit the stoop, jumped back over the plate, and went over to Momma. She was still staring and raised her hand with Daddy's best belt wrapped around it. The first time that belt came down, it caught me across the shoulder and back. When Momma raised her hand again, Katherine came over. Jesus she was fast—so fast I never saw her move! It was like she just appeared right there in front of us.

"*Jesus, Mary and Joseph…*"

Katherine wound up and slapped Momma so hard her lip split wide-open. Blood trickled all down her chin and onto her chest. Katherine ran her finger through the blood and tasted it. When Daddy came out, he just about died from the sight. He looked like he was torn as to what he should do, help Momma or try and make time with Katherine. From the look on his face though I could almost tell what he *really* wanted to do.

Katherine smiled at him, that same smile she laid on me in the woods, and Daddy was dumbstruck. She slapped him—even harder than Momma. He flew back and bounced off the truck.

"Katherine," I screamed, "why are you doing this?"

"Hush now, Elvis."

She went over to Daddy. He was just sitting there on the ground dazed and trying to shake it off when Katherine knelt next to him.

"Your son saw something he shouldn't have, and now I have to fix it." She pulled back her hand and these giant claws ripped through her skin, but there was no blood. Her eyes turned this crazy shade of red. With one of the claws, she drew a line around Daddy's face, until the blood ran all over his cheeks and nose. He didn't scream though. Not one sound came from his mouth. I didn't know if it was Katherine doing something to him or Daddy realizing what was about to happen, trying to die like a man.

Momma, still on the ground stunned from Katherine batting her, started crying, cussing, and praying all at the same time. "Hail Mary, you damn bitch, full of grace, dirty whore, I hope you rot in hell!"

With Momma slowly going crazy, Daddy seized the opportunity to spit in Katherine's face, a big wad of phlegm and blood. Now that really, *really* pissed her off. She turned on Daddy, and that's when the screaming started. It's funny how no one in the park even batted a damn eyelash at all the noise. Guess they figured that it was just some other drunken asshole taking a fist to his wife and kid.

Using her claws, Katherine shredded his face. There was skin and blood all over the place, splattered up on the truck's windshield and tires. Daddy started kicking and screaming, but it didn't do any good. It was over soon enough, thank God. When I ran over to Momma, Katherine shot me a look that froze me in my tracks, literally. I couldn't move my legs at all. When she was all done with Daddy, Katherine was soaked with his blood. Her once white shirt was stained red from Daddy. Then she strolled over to Momma who after seeing that could only cry.

Katherine was quick and almost merciful on her. She just bent down and started chewing on her neck. I heard the skin break and then Momma whine softly. After that Momma moaned, like she was getting into it. Katherine certainly was. She drank everything that poured out from Momma's neck. Finally it was done. Katherine came over to me, wiping her mouth. She took my hand and led me over to the temporary lot.

When I woke up it was in a dark space, a closet or something. Didn't know for the life of me where I was. It felt like I was lying on dirt too. After trying to stretch, it was pretty clear I was in a box, only it was big—big and full of dirt. That was crazy. When I reached over in back of me, my hand brushed up against something cold. I felt all around, and it was like clammy rubber, only there was hair, and lips, and teeth. I started screaming so loud that I literally woke the dead. Katherine reached over and clamped a hand over my mouth. She didn't say a word, but in my mind, she told me to shut the hell up.

The box opened a little, and an immense man with a beard, pale skin, and dressed in an olive green suit lifted me out and set me on the floor. This was Katherine's friend from the trailer. The room was pretty plain and all. Nothing more than her damn box, which turned out to be a frigging coffin! There were no windows visible, but I could see where they had been boarded over, and there was thick material stapled over the planks. In the corners of the room were some brass candleholders and chairs. A single bulb hung from the ceiling and cast what little light was there.

He didn't say a damn thing, I was yammering away, asking questions and trying to get anything out of that fellow. He just ignored me and motioned for me to follow. He led me downstairs and all through Katherine's house. It was big and pretty but had hardly any furniture at all. We stopped in the kitchen. He sat me down at an island and fed me until I thought I would puke.

"C'mon, mister, at least tell me your damn name. I'm just a kid and I'm scared. I see that scary lady up there kill my parents and wake up in a damn coffin. *What the fuck?*"

"My name is Ben. Now eat."

That's all that bastard would say to me. He walked off into another room. I heard a television snap on.

The next week or so went pretty much the same. I'd sleep in Katherine's coffin, and twice a day, during sunlight hours, I was let out to eat. Talk about being fattened up for slaughter. I was going to be that bitch's snack, and if something didn't happen, I'd be in a pine box next to Momma and Daddy, or worse yet, in a pine box next to Katherine.

I don't know how many damn movies on vampires I'd seen in the cinema or when sneaking out after bedtime and watching them on TV. Sometimes, Jimmy and me would even watch TV through other peoples' windows in the park if anything good was on. I knew what killed them damn bloodsuckers. But how the fuck was I going to get a stake, mallet, and holy water in that box of hers?

One morning for breakfast, about ten days into my stay there, Ben left me alone when I was eating. It was the only chance I ever got. I went into the closet with a good-sized knife from the table and, after breaking the handle from the broom, made a stake. I slid it down my pants leg and slipped the pointed end into my sock. Every time I took a damn step it would dig into my foot. I could feel my blood seeping and soaking into my sneaker, helping to remind where I was and what had to be done.

Right on schedule, Ben brought me back upstairs, opened the coffin, and I crept in. I waited until I heard him walk off. Then I lay down, hoping Katherine didn't have any of her *mind stuff* going on. It always seemed she was weaker during daylight. I didn't know why. Even when I was in the coffin and freaking out, she wasn't as powerful. I could resist to a certain degree. But when the night came, I was useless, doing whatever she told me to do. If she had told me to screw a cat, I would have.

I pulled the stake out of my pant leg and held it tight in my hands. I rolled over, felt for her chest and when I found the center, brought that stake back as far as I could and pushed. It went in—not far, but in. Right from the instant it broke through her skin, she was awake and in my head—like a whirlwind of noise and pain racing through my skull. I moved around, got my foot on the end of the stake, pushed and kicked until it went through.

All the time in my head, I could hear her asking me *Why*? and *How could I*? I forced the lid off the coffin and got out. Katherine was laid out on her back, a red stain spreading across her chest. All that shit in the movies about the vamps dying when you stake them? That's all horseshit. All it did was paralyze Katherine and make her pissed off.

I ran for the window and ripped off the material. I heard the footsteps coming up the stairs and ran for the corner. Ben came in holding a shotgun. He scanned the room real quick. I couldn't believe he didn't see me as he went for Katherine. I saw my chance and took it. I slugged that fucker on the head with a candleholder. He fell in next to Katherine. I took the shotgun and kicked the cover closed.

I started tearing at the material over the boards again and ripped most of it off. Then I went to work on the planks. Man those things were on good, nails in every possible spot. I began kicking and punching. Then I tried a candleholder. I was about to quit and just make a run for it when I remembered the shotgun. I chambered a cartridge and fired. Damn kickback tossed me halfway across the room.

A corner of a board blew off and sprayed the room with shrapnel. I fired again, missed, totally and then just went nuts tearing at the boards to get them off. With the last shell in the gun, I blasted out the window and all that glorious sunlight streamed in. Below, there was traffic. One of the cars screamed to a stop outside the house. Best sight I ever saw in my whole damn life.

The top of the coffin all but flew off when Ben woke up. He saw the sunlight and must have been confused. I knew Katherine was probably in his head making him crazy. He grabbed the material and tried to cover up the window. I whacked him with the shotgun. He tumbled out of the window. There was a sickening crunch when his head hit the driveway.

I grabbed hold of that coffin and tried to pull for all I was worth, but the thing just wouldn't move. Katherine started to panic, screaming in my head, and it took all I had to block her out. I commenced to reciting prayers in my mind, songs from the real Elvis, whatever I could think of. But I was damned if that coffin was moving.

Then, in like a burst of adrenaline, I actually moved it, not much but a little. Then I inched it a little more and more until the edge of the coffin was just in the sunlight. I saw the first of many bloody tears run down her cheek. She apologized, asking and begging me not to go any farther. I ran back, jumped over that coffin, and stood in the corner. I got a running start and slid into that coffin like it was home plate, forcing it and her into the sunlight.

The scream that came out of Katherine was terrible. When sun hits vampires, they explode. Forget all that melting into ooze or drying out into sand. There was a massive fireball that engulfed the room. The curtains and everything else caught instantly. My way out was blocked, and I didn't have enough time to take apart another window. My pant legs were on fire so I jumped out the window, landed on Ben, and took off running down the street.

That car I had seen earlier stopped in front of me. This guy with long blonde hair and crazy eyes got out. I didn't know what the fuck he wanted. I was in a frenzy and had to get away. A window from the house blew out from the fire. The guy tossed me in the car, and we sped off. I sat hunched against the door getting ready to jump.

He smiled and stretched out his hand. "Hi," he said. "I'm Erik Chamberlain, and right now, you're my new best friend."

9
Dorian: The Last Show

This aspect of your abilities has always amazed me," Kane said, reaching below the seat, taking out a black umbrella, and opening it. "I am quite envious."

The driver whipped the horse into a light trot.

"No matter how many times I see it, it's a spectacle. Plus, it will be nice to see how far you two have come with your gifts."

Deirdre squeezed my hand as we arrived at the park. Even at this early hour it was full of joggers and people walking their dogs. The homeless slept beneath trees or on benches wrapped in coats.

"What shall be our breakfast, dear brother. A jogger or a transient?" Deirdre asked.

"We don't have time for games, Deirdre," Kane said. "It's getting a little too bright out."

I turned to the horizon and gazed at the crimson and gold-colored clouds.

I pointed to a bench and a prone form. "Him," I said hopping out of the coach before it stopped. I helped Deirdre out, and we sat on the bench on either side of the sleeping drunk.

Kane wrapped himself in a blanket and joined us. He took up station near the subway entrance.

Deirdre was first. She bit down hard, puncturing the voice box so he couldn't scream out. While she drank greedily of the man's life, I scanned the street. Then I finished the task. He reeked of body odor, cheap wine, and his shoes were nothing more than tape wrapped around socks. But his blood was fresh and hot, despite the slight aftertaste of the wine he had consumed.

Deirdre took out her dark sunglasses and put them on. I imitated her. We stood and walked out into the park. I watched the sun rise, it's warming light creeping across the grass. Kane inched into the subway entrance.

"Isn't it grand, brother? A new life, new land, and a new dawn."

The sun washed over us like a tidal wave. We were bathed in its wake. Kane fled into the tunnels after seeing us. Deirdre smiled and started for the entrance. I grabbed her shoulder.

"I don't trust him, Deirdre."

"It's been a hundred fifty years, Dorian. Try to be forgiving. We should have died. Would you have preferred it that way, dying out in the cold with no one to remember us? No family or belongings? Everything on us stolen and used until we died building those damned roads."

"I can't stay here, Deirdre."

"Where will you go?"

"California."

"Still the dreamer, dear brother?"

"I will stay until dusk. But then I must go."

"Have it your way, Dorian. But never regret or forget what you are." She walked away and descended the stairs into the tunnels.

10
Elvis: Another Day

It all started out so simple—another job in another dumb ass, backwater town. For months, Erik and me had been on the road hitting spots, checking them out, and then running. Each new job brought a new town, a new car, and new names. No touching the past—that was the motto. Run in, run out, and run fast.

Every time we swapped names, we switched cars, and each one was better than the one before. We were living well in the best hotels, eating the best food, wearing the best clothes. Have no doubt, Erik was whacked. Fucked in the head, but he was rich. The money made up for some of the things, but not all.

Erik called us researchers—going from town to town gathering information. But on what? *Vampires.* He had to know every damn aspect of them. Shit, he questioned me seven or eight different ways about what had happened to me. Erik wanted information. I wanted revenge. That's all that mattered. Kill all the fucking bloodsuckers for what they'd done to my parents.

Strange. Erik said they were everywhere, but the only one I ever saw was back in Kentucky. He had told me once that he had been tracking Katherine for months. For what, I had no clue. And all the time we snooped, the shots were being called by some super secret organization.

Most of the time we worked alone, in and out real quick. Sometimes we met up with other teams and went in with them. But it was the same each time. They'd look at Erik, then me, and be all worried. They had no clue what they were getting into. All they knew was that someone was waiting behind the scene with a big-ass check for them. We ended up taking a hotel penthouse in a small town in Georgia and waiting for the new team to arrive.

"I don't understand, Erik. What's so damn tough about this one? What do we need a team for?"

"Just stick with me, kid. We'll be fine. Look at where we've been and what we've done. We've seen some amazing stuff."

"We've seen a bunch of old habitats and remnants. Nothing substantial, just residue of something we can't be sure of."

"Where'd you learn that?" Erik asked, half smiling.

"I heard you talking on the phone, giving your reports."

"Look, it's different this time."

Erik had something in his eye. It looked like a little piece of fear. I'd never seen that before and that scared me worse than the damn bloodsuckers. Erik crossed to the door and looked through the peephole for the hundredth time in the last hour, only this time he was dodging my questions.

"Look, Erik, just level with me okay?"

"All right, Elvis. We have to go to a house. Could be as many as three of them in there."

"It'll be empty. It always is."

"No, it was scoped out last night. There are at least three in there."

"How many normal folks?"

"Unknown." His voice had an edge of excitement to it, and his eyes were darting all over the place. That was one of the truly weird things about him. One eye was gray, the other brown. He wasn't fat, but he was a tad on the chunky side and had a thing for tattoos. He had all sorts of strange symbols and figures up and down his arms. "Trust me, kid."

"What other choice do I have?"

There was a knock on the door, and I pulled out my .38 snub nose. Erik waved it off, but I kept it out, hidden on my lap under a pillow. He peeked through the door and then started rubbing his hands together. Four guys came in, each of them introducing themselves.

The first was Frank Drake, team leader. He was stocky, maybe six feet or so with graying hair. Next up was Mickey, who wore cammies and bristled with guns. Then Pete, a tricky-looking guy with a wandering eye and knives—lots of knives all over him, some in sheaths, some tucked in his boots. I could only imagine where the others were tucked. Rudy was a very nondescript mercenary. Rudy kept sipping from a nip bottle and stunk of whiskey. They all sort of ignored me and kept talking with Erik. That Pete fellow kept his eye on me though, like he was expecting me to freak.

"What's with the kid?" he asked.

"Leave him be. He's okay. He's had more experience than any one of you."

"What do you mean?" Drake asked.

"Elvis spent some quality time with a vampire awhile ago. He's fine now."

"He wasn't a thrall, was he?" Drake looked at me all concerned.

"No, you dumb shit. I was only controlled for a while," I piped in.

"Oh, that's just fucking great. You can count me out right now." Pete headed for the door, slinging his pack over his shoulder.

"Sponsors called for a team of four. With him leaving, the rest of you don't get paid either."

The two others, the mercenaries, just stood in front of the door. They nodded to us, and Pete shambled back over, dropping his pack next to me on the couch.

"You're calling the shots and you sign the checks, but if this little freak does anything to compromise our jobs, he's a pile of goo on the side of the road."

I lowered the pillow and pointed the gun square at that bastard's chest. The rest of the guys got a good laugh out of this.

"You even try to come near me, mister, and I'll be stargazing through your chest."

"Okay, we've had enough fun feeling each other out. Let's get to business." Drake took instant control of the party, yelling orders and such. He didn't tell me to do anything, but asked me to go into town with him for supplies.

Plan was, he was going to the town hall for recon, and I'd go off gathering what we needed. Before I left the room, Erik gave me a folded up hundred just in case. The other two had to go for vehicles with that Pete guy since Drake and me were headed into town and Erik was going to contact the sponsors and give them an update. Just once, I'd like to know who was paying the bills.

Couple hours later, we all gathered back at the hotel. I had my backpack stuffed full of gear, and that leader guy, Drake, had managed somehow to get the floor plans to the place we were going. It was an old southern mansion—the kind ghost stories were made for. The other guys came back with a black full-sized Chevy Bronco, big enough for all of us and our gear. The front had a winch, and the back a trailer hitch.

Drake spread out the plans on the table. I sat down to clean my gun. That Pete kept looking at me, glancing at the map, then at me, then back at the map, like he was plotting something.

"Look," Drake said. "We'll hit at dusk—go in guns blazing while they're waking up."

"That's your idea?" I cackled. "Hit them as they're getting up? That's horse shit, especially at dusk. If they're hungry when they wake up, there ain't no way you're getting out in one piece, buddy."

"See what I mean about the kid? He's all right," Erik spouted in my defense.

"Okay, we'll go during the day, near two, and scout out the place. Get a feeling for it. See if we can find a sign of how many norms are in there. We're there to slaughter some undead. We're not there to kill innocents."

"Yeah, but if those innocents, as you call them, have been there long enough, the bloodsuckers are feeding off them and are so loyal they'll do anything to save their masters."

"Bloodsuckers? That's cute," Pete said, wiping at his eyes.

I shot him the bird and put the barrel back in my pistol. A few seconds later it was loaded and ready to go.

"Look," I said. "What we have to do is go in during the day. Kill what and who we can and then light the house. It's the only way to be sure."

"What about stakes?" Mickey piped in.

"Good, but you only get one shot at a stake. Only paralyzes them."

"Holy water?" Rudy joined the questioning barrage.

"Really pisses them off. Burns them, bad."

"Crosses?" Drake asked.

"Okay if you have faith. But if you're a belligerent dickhead like your entry man over there." I pointed at Pete. "Then you're fucked." I pulled a simple gold cross on a chain out from my shirt. "This has always suited me fine."

"What about silver?"

I was getting tired of Drake's questions, but he was checking out what I knew, how much I knew, and what he could use from me. "Works, but I don't know how or why. Heard it works the charm on them wolf people though—if you believe in that." I tucked in the cross and put my gun away.

The others went back to pouring over the map and making notes and such on it in pencil. Erik grinned at me and joined back in with them. Deep down, I knew he would support me if

I chose to torch the house. But the problems were with the local law enforcement and Erik himself. If Erik didn't get his two seconds in the sun to scope the place, he was pissier than Momma was during that special time of the month.

I started rooting through my pack. I tossed Drake all the stuff he wanted and then scoped out mine. I got a few stakes and a new mallet, just in case. Some spare bullets, a couple road flares, a squirt gun filled up with holy water, and an extra cross. I stood up, tucked the .38 in my shoulder holster and the squirt gun in the hip holster. I must have looked the sight, but no one was laughing.

"What about garlic?" Drake called out.

"Makes them stinky."

I must have dozed off or something, 'cause when I woke up in bed, all them guys were gone, even Erik. There was a note on the table saying they were checking out the house, seeing who comes and goes. I ordered up a tray of room service and a pot of coffee. When it got dark outside a few hours later, they all came back. Erik saw my tray and got an idea in his head. He ordered up steaks and beer for everyone. The two mercs still hadn't said more than three words since they arrived, but I did see the one guy refilling his nip bottle twice.

"I called the office and got some custom equipment coming—radio headsets, flashlights, and hollow-tipped explosive rounds for the guns. When they arrive we'll be all set. If we want to be extra careful, there are three sets of starlight goggles coming in too."

We all stopped, and turned, and looked at the guy talking. It was Rudy. Apparently, he had money falling out of his ass like Erik did. He shut up and sat down to eat his steak.

That night, they went over the plan again and again. I didn't have much of a part in it so I stayed to the side out of the way, which is what I think they really wanted to begin with. They argued, talked, smoked cigars, and argued more. That other guy, Mickey, finished his nip bottle twice. When he went to refill it that last time, I spied two grenades hanging from his belt. Hired guns are one thing. Hired guns with drinking problems are another. But a drunk fuck with grenades really started freaking me out. I went to my room and closed the door.

Morning came and I stumbled out of bed to the *clanging* and *thumping* of the team cleaning their guns, loading spare clips, and sharpening knives. I sat at the table and loaded two quick-loads with bullets—after etching a small cross in each tip and dunking it in holy water. All the damn bullets in the world wouldn't save your ass when it's dying time.

Mickey and Rudy loaded the truck. Pete made sure he and only he touched his gear. Drake checked the radios, headsets, and plans again while Erik scribbled notes in his journal.

"We're cool with this gig, right?" I was a little pensive about this, and nervous as all get out.

"Yeah, Elvis, this is cool. We've rehearsed it over and over again."

"Just on paper, Erik. Just on paper."

"Look, go along with what they say even if it's stupid. When they want or need help, they'll yell. I have the checkbook, and when it comes down to it, I call out all the shots."

I nodded at him and he rustled my hair.

"We're going to have to cut that mop off soon. I've seen your photos, Elvis, and you don't look like either one of your folks. Feel lucky."

"Don't be bad-mouthing my parents, Erik. You're not so high and mighty that I can't kick your ass."

We smiled and headed out, me in front. The truck was loaded and ready to go, with the others waiting inside. There was a trunk in the back that I didn't recognize either. Must have come while I was asleep.

No one talked on the way down. The only noises came from the road and from Erik writing in his journal. Drake drove. I was way in the back with the gear. Erik was in the front with the other three jammed in the back seat.

The house looked deserted—no cars, no motorcycles, no bikes, no people. The paint was all chipped and peeling, the grass near the front porch overgrown. The porch had these giant marble columns and an old wooden swing hanging by chains. On either side of the door were panels of thick frosted glass with no number or name near the entrance.

Drake parked in the driveway, a half circle with both ends going to the street. It looked more like a drive-through at McDonalds than a driveway. The lawn was only half-mowed, not like someone just forgot to finish the front after the back. The entire lawn was cut in stripes all around it, up and down the entire length of property.

There was an old unpainted gazebo off to the side with rotted boards hanging from the inside. One of the house's side windows had a good-sized hole in, like some kid had tossed a baseball through it.

We all piled out of the truck and gathered on the lawn. Rudy passed out the radios and goggles. From that crate in the back, Erik handed Kevlar vests to us all. I took mine but didn't wear it. Those vests might stop a bullet, but sure as shit wouldn't do dick against a vampire. Erik and me took up position on opposite sides of the house. Mickey, the drunk, went around back. Pete stayed at the truck with the house plans. Drake and Rudy, the other rich guy, went to the front door. I hopped up, grabbed the sill of that broken window, and peeked in. Couldn't see a damn thing, but there was something terrible-smelling inside. There was some sort of dark material over the inside of the window.

Drake checked his shotgun and chambered a shell. Rudy cocked his pistols, one in each hand and took aim. Erik didn't normally carry a gun. He never really cared for them. All his fighting was done with words or pencils. But this time, I saw the bulge of an automatic pistol under his shirt.

Rudy took his position beside the door, while Drake knocked. The fuck actually knocked. Didn't get any response at all. It was broad fucking daylight. No way a bloodsucker could come out. And if one of them thrall guys were in there, he wouldn't be stupid enough to come down. He'd be busy guarding the snoozing bloodsuckers.

Next thing I saw was just as bad. Drake poked his face up real close to the frosted glass and looked in. Then he got pissed off and knocked out one of the panes with his gun. If the vamps didn't know we were there before, they did now. Drake reached in for the door latch without even checking to see if anything was lurking, waiting to rip his damn arm off. I guess he couldn't reach it. He pulled out his arm, took a step back, and got poised to stomp.

Drake kicked in the door and jumped aside. Ready to shoot, Rudy covered him with both guns. Pete had us all check in over the radio and then told us all to hush up so we wouldn't make too much noise. Then they went in. Drake mumbled through the radio about everything he saw. The radios were all connected to a junction box in the truck being recorded for Erik's use.

They checked in from the foyer. There was a wooden staircase right in front of them. A crystal chandelier hung from the ceiling in a small side hall. On the stairs was a worn red carpet, and at the top of the stairs, a polished wooden landing.

"I hear something, people, get ready to move," Drake whispered through the headset.

Then there was static. While we waited for the next report, Mickey mumbled from around back how he wanted to go in and was sick of being outside. The sounds of rounds being chambered filled the radios. From where I stood, I could see around the corner of the house where Mickey had assembled one bitchin'-looking machine gun.

Suddenly there was a crash of glass as Mickey's broken whiskey bottle shattered on the driveway. "Screw this shit I'm going in." His voice was slurred from the drink. Then another crash shook the house when he kicked in the back door.

Erik and I stayed outside, watching and waiting. Pete ran in the front door with the winch hook in one hand and his gun in the other.

"Erik, is this what you rehearsed?"

"No, Elvis."

"We're screwed. This is bullshit, Erik. Let's beat feet while we still have feet."

"Five minutes, Elvis. Five minutes."

"You assholes better not go anywhere," Pete said, his voice coming through the headsets.

"We need a private channel, Erik."

"Where is everyone?" Drake asked.

"In the cellar." Mickey was the first.

"Right behind you." That was Pete.

"Me and Erik are still on the lawn and we ain't moving—not for five minutes, anyway."

Mickey and Pete started walking again. Drake had Mickey meet him and Rudy on the stairs as they went up. The noises they heard sounded like a child crying. I could hear it softly through the radio. I checked my bag again, making sure everything was in place and intact—.38 in the shoulder holster, squirt gun in the hip, mallet tucked under the belt, stake in the back pocket, cross out in plain sight, and a road flair in the front pocket.

"Drake, this is Erik. No more time for subtlety. It's lost. As you explore, describe everything in detail. Keep it down to a whisper if you want. I don't think it matters anymore."

"Erik, where did you get these guys, Assholes-R-Us?" I asked, covering the mouthpiece for my headset."

"They're a team, Elvis. Maybe a novice team, but a team. On their last job, six others they went in with were butchered. These four made it out alive."

"There are four doors at the top of the stairs. You getting this?" Drake interrupted.

"Keep talking, Frank." Erik replied.

"First room is a kid's."

Erik rolled his eyes.

"What is it, Erik?"

"I hate kid vampires."

"There's a bed. Big bed covered with stuffed animals. Doesn't look slept in or anything else in. There's a closet, door open and no windows visible. One dresser and a toy box. Pete, cover the hall—Mickey, Rudy cover me. I'm going to hit the closet." Through the headphones, Drake's breathing got louder. "There's someone inside the closet, and the crying just got clearer. But I can't determine the origin of it."

Pete took the narration from there.

"Frank is approaching the door. Oh look, he's stopped at the bed and is poking his gun barrel around in the stuffed animals. All right, he's back to the closet, easing the door open."

I heard a small exchange of words between Drake and Pete—didn't sound remotely pleasant, a deep inhale of breath and then…

"Okay, the closet is clear," Drake announced. "It was the way some clothes were hanging. Made me think someone was in there."

"That's great, Frank. Just keep it up. Do what you have to," Erik said, trying to add some support.

I kept looking out to the road. Thankfully it was clear of traffic, foot and wheeled. The entire damned place looked almost deserted. This house didn't even resemble what I imagined a bloodsucker to live in. I'd always heard the stories of castles and mansions and everything. Come to think of it though, Katherine's place, wherever she had me, wasn't too posh either.

"We're coming up on the second room now. The door to the third room is cracked and the fourth looks closed tight. The crying is getting louder, too. Doesn't sound like a kid though."

"What are you thinking, Frank?" Erik asked watching the second floor windows.

"I think we have a family somehow. This has been going on for a while. That would explain the kid's bedroom. We're going to find a whole lot of bodies, sometime soon."

"A family of bloodsuckers? What kind of shit is that?"

Erik silenced my question with a wave of his hand.

"Second room is a bathroom. *Jesus* it stinks in here."

The others gagged on the stench coming out of the room. Heard Mickey say how he was going to puke if he didn't get some fresh air. A window on the second floor opened up. Erik had an eye trained on it. Mickey stuck his head out and waved to us.

"What's going on in there, Frank?"

"The entire room is full of shit. Literally. There must be no water service. The toilet and sink are full, overflowing. The tub is semi full and right now, Mickey is going through the room looking for stuff. There's no linen closet, no medicine cabinet either. Judging from the condition of the feces, we have some fresh life in this place."

"This is Mickey checking in here. Seems like this room is empty aside from all the shit. Only things I found are cans of hair spray. Mickey out."

"We're approaching the third door. It's the source of the crying. Door's not open enough to see anything. I'm signing off for a little bit."

I instantly recognized that *tone* in Drake's voice.

Erik looked over at me. I shrugged my shoulders and waited. I wanted to go and check out the cellar or see what was up with the gazebo. Maybe there was a trap door or something. But for once, I listened to commonsense and stayed put. Out of nowhere came the sounds of splintering wood, some shouting, a girl's scream, and the blast of a shotgun. Then through the radio came Drake's voice.

"Freeze! No one else move!"

"Talk to me, Frank," Erik yelled into the mouthpiece.

"Drake is a little busy at the moment."

That was Rudy's voice and only the second time I heard him speak since he hooked up with us.

"Frank has just blown the face off a gentleman, and his two lady companions are now cowering in the corner while the other two keep them covered."

"It's going bad, Erik," I hissed.

"Give them time, Elvis."

"This is Frank. Rudy, Mickey, and Pete are covering the bitches. In about a minute, you're going to have a present. Get ready on the winch."

"What happened to not killing anybody?" Erik asked.

"I got carried away. Now start reeling it in." Drake shouted an order to Pete to stick the hook in the dude's rib cage.

I can only guess he agreed. Erik stuck me on the winch detail. I put the thing in reverse, and the spool started filling up. While focused on the house, I listened to the *whine* of the gears. Erik had an eye trained on the window where he saw Mickey earlier. The gears groaned, there was an awful crash and the hook for the winch came back covered in blood and meat, a chunk of bone still stuck in the curve of the metal.

"Shit!" Pete yelled. "We lost him."

In the background you could hear the two ladies crying. Something just didn't feel right.

"The body is all fucked up. Hit the banister and broke up. And man, did Drake do a number. There's brains and blood everywhere in here."

"Pete, go outside, get the winch, hook him back up and drag him out. You two, keep them covered." Drake cursed into the headphones. What he had expected to happen didn't.

Pete whispered into the headphones how Drake was kicking and breaking up some of the furniture. "I ain't going outside," Pete yelled. "We still don't know what the hell is going on."

"You two stay here, I'll check out that last room. Those bitches move, you blow holes in them," Drake growled.

"Frank, don't be an asshole, just fucking kill them."

"Shut up, kid. I'm in charge. Pete you come with me."

There was some heavy breathing, the click of rounds being chambered, and then some strange whispering I couldn't quite make out. I looked over at Erik and apparently he had heard it too.

"We're in the hallway again," Drake said. "It's clean. No other signs of inhabitants yet. In three, two, *one!*"

I imagined Drake holding up his hand to Pete for the count down. The crash of a door being kicked open and splintering wood filled the headsets. No shots were fired.

"Room is clear," Pete said.

"This is Frank. We're in some sort of a library. Looks like it's been vacant for a long time, and we struck pay dirt."

The wall above my head opened up. Drake pushed open some sliding glass doors. There was no porch, no railing, nothing, just the doors opening up into the air. I leveled my gun before seeing Drake. He waved and I took up aim on the door again.

"There's a substantial amount of dust on everything. There are also two big leather sofas with sheets on them. I don't think anyone has been in here in months. The doors were exposed, no type of covering, no boards or paint. Don't understand why you didn't see them outside. You guys on the lawn. Get ready for a package."

The radio went silent and I started to feel the call of adventure myself. One thing Momma always said to me was that if you're going to be involved in something, be in the middle of it. I signaled to Erik, letting him know I was going in. He shook his head and mouthed a lot of bad words, but it didn't stop me. I went around back to where Mickey entered, lowered my gun and jumped in.

It was the kitchen. Mickey was so fucked up he couldn't tell it wasn't the basement. What an asshole. It was a damn mess, far worse than I ever saw. The floor was covered in fast food bags, and stacks of empty pizza boxes were propped up against one wall. There weren't any tables or chairs, either. I saw the oven in the corner, ran over, turned it on, and prayed for the hiss of gas. The bitch just started to heat up instead. The thing was full of silverware though, looked like seven or eight place settings. I took a few pieces and stuffed it into my pack. I knew it hurt the bloodsuckers—just didn't know how.

I heard a crash from the side where I had just been and ran to the window, the one with the hole. Out on the lawn was that fellow's body, without a face. I saw the white of bone, what was left of it, poking out from ragged strips of skin. Drake started swearing after the body stopped bouncing 'cause it wasn't bursting into flames like he'd hoped. He had just murdered somebody. From where I stood in the kitchen, I heard them boys walking overhead. The whispering came over the headsets again—soft, supple, and appealing.

Then I heard the strangest sound ever, the soft *tinkle* of metal like something had been launched with a spring. Drake screamed and the entire house shook with an explosion. I watched out the window as Drake hit the grass right where I had been. Glass and little bits of flaming wood showered down on the lawn around him. Smoke rose from his body and the bastard wasn't moving. Pete started screaming at the two ladies.

"Everyone check in!" Erik ordered.

Pete was first, then Mickey, Erik, and myself.

"Pete, go find Rudy. See what's up!"

"Jesus, I think he's dead. I can't tell. The bastard is full of holes! Looks like the blast got him. I'm heading back."

I heard his footsteps running overhead on the floorboards.

Some more whispering, then, "Targets are on the move! They did something to Mickey."

I ran from the kitchen, gun in hand, and saw them two ladies on the stairs, moving real fast. Fired a shot up in the air and pointed the barrel dead at them. "Y'all better stop right there!"

Momma always said it was proper to warn someone first before shooting them, and if you have to, be sure you're in the right. One of the ladies just disappeared into the shadows, pulling some of that damn bloodsucker magic. The other one raced by me laughing, a blur of blonde hair. There came a terrible crash from the kitchen. Then Mickey and Pete raced down the stairs. I ran back to the kitchen and saw that there had been a door hidden in back of the stack of pizza boxes.

Pete was first, throwing me out of the way. Then Mickey stood at the top of the flight of stairs with his machine gun pointed down. He had a long-assed silencer on it, and I didn't happen to see any of the grenades he brought hanging from his vest.

"Okay, the only thing I see down here is a shitload of bodies, maybe a dozen," Pete said. "They've been sucked dry and look mummified. There's no sign of the bitch, and I can't see any type of gas heater or oil tank." For once the bastard was thinking straight, looking for something to blow up and take the house with it. "No other doors out of the basement, and no windows. It's a box."

A thunderous crash came from the hallway. The chandelier lay on the floor, light bulbs *popping* and *sizzling* before everything went out. I withdrew my road flare and lit the walls and floor. I was hoping for the fire to spread faster, but it didn't. There was more whispering through the headsets and the gunfire started.

Pete had opened up on Mickey. Mickey had started to return fire. The only shots I heard were from Pete because Mickey had that silencer. They both were either lousy shots, or the Kevlar vests were protecting them 'cause neither one was moving. Then Mickey pulled a grenade from his pocket. That was my cue. The spoon went whizzing by my face as I shot out the window and dove through. For the second time that day, the house shook. Glass exploded from the windows, followed by a god-awful shriek and more gunfire. To me, that meant Mickey was dead, killed by Pete. I started running balls for toes back to the truck.

Drake had somehow managed to drag his blown up ass away and was sprawled out in the back seat, bleeding all over everything. Erik had the thing started and opened the door when I rounded the corner. I hopped up on the bumper and took real careful aim, just in case. Pete burst from the front doors, spraying bullets. One hit the windshield, and one the grass near my feet. I squeezed off a shot and dropped the fucker. Guess the asshole didn't have any armor on his face, now, did he.

I walked back to him to make sure, but he was still squirming on the ground. Bastard had a thick skull. I lowered the gun, pointed straight to the middle of his forehead, squeezed off one more shot, and he was gone. The only way to cure someone when he's had the whammy laid on him is to kill him yourself or kill the bloodsucker that put it on him in the first place.

I ran back to the truck, checked my gun, and quickly popped it into the holster. Erik tore out of there, leaving deep tracks on the lawn. The house shook again and the damn place exploded. Flames shot out windows, and when I looked back, Pete's body had started to catch too.

"What the fuck was that, Erik? Vampires up and moving during the day? What's going on?"

"It happens, Elvis."

"What the Christ do you mean, 'it happens?' They're supposed to be asleep in their damn coffins or something, hiding away from the sun."

"Not all vampires are like the movies, Elvis. They all have they're own unique abilities."

Drake groaned from the back and sat up. He whispered the word *hospital* and passed out.

11
Elvis: On the road again

That leader guy from the failed mission, Drake, was still with us. I guess Erik had adopted him too. Drake took a long time to heal from the fight, and things just hadn't been right with him since.

The sponsors had been running our asses ragged going from town to town "investigating" all these sites where they thought there were leads. Each time we got to a new place, though, it was either deserted or a dead end. Still, Erik would go in and examine the hell out of it, then spend an hour on the laptop typing and an hour on the phone going over everything with the check signers. We had switched cars two or three times since the mishap in Georgia. I really think that they, the sponsors, were giving us these cheap jobs so the fire couldn't get traced back to them.

Sure as hell, that house went up when that grenade exploded, but we never found out what happened to the vamps. Deep down inside, I knew Erik would do whatever it took to prove his theories and get his book out. You see, Erik, aside from working for his mysterious sponsors that he wouldn't tell me anything about, was writing what he called the *definitive* guide to bloodsuckers. I didn't see much of a market for it, except maybe the Goths and people who really thought they were vampires and went to clubs to drink blood.

I'd heard him talking a couple times, listening and pretending to be asleep when he would just go on and on about how much he wanted to see the inside of their society. He said he'd do whatever it took to get in. I really didn't know how far he would go until we went to that station in northern Maine.

"Come on, Erik, we're ready for this. Let's go in."

Erik just stared out over the steering wheel, looking at the road. It was cracked blacktop, winding all though the woods. There weren't any streetlights. What little light we had came from the truck and the half moon. Drake sat in the back reading a paperback with one of those clip-on lights.

"What do *you* think, Frank? You ready to go back into the fire?"

Drake folded up the book, switched off the light, and turned to the window. If you looked hard enough you could see the lights reflected in the eyes of roadside animals.

"Yeah, Erik, I'm ready. I need to get back to the game. I appreciate the rehab time, but all things being what they are, I'm bored as fuck."

"Pretty much says it there, Elvis, doesn't it?" Erik said smirking.

"Yeah it does, Erik." I smiled, folded my arms on my chest and watched the road, all the time trying to figure out why he was so quick to agree.

Bastard was hiding something from us. I didn't know what or why, just some feeling I had that wrenched my guts. Regardless of his own reasons, withholding our information meant he wasn't only jeopardizing the mission, but us too. I looked back in the mirror. Drake seemed to pick up on what I was thinking and nodded at me.

"What's the job, boss?"

Erik looked back through the mirror at Drake, who leaned in to hear him better.

"Abandoned site in Maine somewhere between Bangor and Caribou. I figure we have another four, five hours of driving before we get there. It used to be some mid-state train stop that failed months after it opened. If it was profitable, they would have built a town around it."

"Abandoned?" I asked, letting the disappointment show.

"Don't let it get you down, Elvis. You'll have your glory days again." Erik seemed pretty smug with the entire thing.

Drake sat back, got real quiet and even more pissed off. On some of those missions when we were just snooping around, Drake used to talk about having a red line. The shit going on must have been pushing him over that red line. Just sitting there looking at him, I could see Erik coming dangerously close to that red line.

Things pretty much went quiet after that. I kept looking at the both of them trying to catch any glimpse of emotion or anything else. Drake was looking pretty old and tired these days. He'd taken to drink and started dropping weight. Right after that job in Georgia, he began shaving his head, right down to the skin. He kept talking about getting a tattoo on his skull, but never actually did it. Even through all of it, he still managed to stay pissed off at just about everyone.

"So it's just this cabin out in the woods?" I asked trying to get some talk going.

"That it is, Elvis." Erik went silent again.

"What'd they name it?"

"It would have been Woods Hole." Erik was still the same, with those damn crazy eyes that didn't tell you anything and that cocky expression that begged for an argument. He still had long hair, and I kept telling him that if he ever got into a fight it could be used against him. But he kept on growing it.

I was way too fucking young for those stress wrinkles around my eyes. Erik said they gave me character, but that was bullshit. I was a damn kid. I didn't need anything speeding up the aging process on me. Still had a few good years left in me before I had to get a real job or start making babies or whatever. Frankly, I'm not sure what scared me more, growing up or vampires. I don't know why I bothered asking the town's name. At this point it didn't matter. We wouldn't be around long enough to explore it what was left of it.

We arrived in Maine just as the sun came up. Erik checked us into a hotel, best one we found in that no name town we came to. He slipped the guy behind the counter a wad of Ben Franklins and told him we were to be left alone. I grabbed my pack, ran into the room, and hit the sheets before Erik and Drake had time to get in.

Even though I was wrapped up in blankets, I could hear Erik talking on the phone. I heard a familiar sound too, one that hadn't been around in a while. When I snuck a peek, Drake was tipping back a nip bottle. He saw my head peeking out from the blankets, offered me the bottle, and I took it. Erik woke us up close to noontime, saying it was time to hit the road.

Unlike our usual fashion, we grabbed some take-out food on the way up. Drake was too quiet. I saw him through the mirror, loading some spare clips full of bullets. Looked like a good idea. I still had my revolver. It was a gift from Momma when I turned thirteen. She said a boy's best friends were his dog, his thing, and his gun, and since we couldn't have dogs in the trailer park, I got a gun. Besides, she said she would rather have me playing with a gun than my thing.

I took out a box of bullets, very carefully carved crosses in the tips of about two dozen of them, and then drizzled holy water from my squirt gun over them. I handed the knife and water to Drake, and he did the same.

"I don't know why you two are doing that. It's abandoned," Erik chimed.

"Better to be prepared, Erik, than dead."

Drake nodded his approval to me, and for the first time, there was this bond like he suddenly trusted me.

"You have the layout to the station, Erik, right?" Drake asked from the back. "You have the plans to this place so we're not going in blind."

"Don't need them. It's been deserted for years," Erik crooned.

"Yeah, but from what? People or bloodsuckers?"

Then Erik shot me a look like I had betrayed him or something.

"I mean, think about it for a second. Who filed the reports? Did they come from a sheriff's station or the Internet? Or was there another field agent? Who did it?"

"Fine, there was another agent in the area who didn't want to go in alone. We were sent to back him up."

"Was it so hard to give some damn information?" Drake asked. "I don't know how you and the kid stayed alive so long with you in the lead."

"You'll keep your damn mouth in check or you'll be out on the road again, riding shotgun for armored cars. You want that life back, Frank? Drinking coffee, eating donuts and reading the paper? Earning nine dollars an hour to risk your neck for someone else's money?"

"You think I'm just in this for the money? Is that it, Erik?" Drake asked.

In the mirror I could Drake's eye twitching. Guess Erik had gotten to the red line.

"Why else would you be here? Graduated high school dead center of your class. No honorable mention. Spent the time barely passing. Tried the Army, got discharged on medical after a year. Then did security work, and now you're with me."

"Pull the fucking car over," Drake growled.

"No, stop this, the both of you. This is all bullshit, Erik. Stop being an asshole. Let's do the job and get done. We'll settle all of this afterwards. Do the job, then we fight."

Erik pulled the car over to the side of the road, and Drake got out. Erik pulled away, and I watched Drake slowly get swallowed by all the woods at the side of the road.

"He wanted too much control, Elvis. I hope you can understand."

"Yeah, some power struggle between you and him."

"No, between him and the sponsors."

"Who *are* the sponsors, Erik?"

"The guys in charge, that's who."

The road ended—turned into a pitted gravel path. The car spit up a cloud of dust after us. Strung between these two concrete poles set on either side of the road was an old rusted chain. Beyond it, I saw the shadow of the station.

The road gave up to an old parking lot full of potholes and broken glass. Rusted cans and other hunks of metal were scattered all around. We got our stuff and hopped the chain. Still having a few hours left before sunset, we figured all was all right. Walking over that broken glass and hearing it *crunch* under our heels felt like stomping on bones.

The station was burnt out. That was obvious enough. There was smoke scarring all over the outside and holes in the walls and roof from where the flames had eaten through. All the windows were broken, and sooty fragments sparkled in the afternoon light. Some of the area in back of the station was all cleared out, and I caught a glimpse of the rusted, pitted tracks. Between them were more broken bottles and lots of stones.

The door to the station hung from one hinge, and the station's sign laid on the porch with the chains that it used to hang from. It was full of bullet holes. Erik headed up to the steps, and I got out my gun and flashlight. He pulled a miniature tape recorder from his pocket and started talking into it.

"Erik, get your ass back here."

"It's empty, Elvis, don't be so paranoid." Erik went to the front door and after setting that recorder on the steps, kicked it in.

There was a loud crash and a cloud of soot. I swore I heard something stir inside, but Erik just passed it off as the wind. When I looked at the trees though, there wasn't a single leaf moving. He stepped in, leaving me alone on the stairs. There was a small ramp for wheeling up luggage and such just to the right. It was covered in dead leaves and mud.

I heard Erik stomping around inside. I assumed he was talking into the recorder again. I had to run to catch up with him. Damn place was creeping me out. It just felt all too familiar. I followed Erik in, and it seemed dead. There weren't any birds or bugs, or anything else, like chipmunks or squirrels. They all should have been building homes in the timbers. Strewn all over the floor were a bunch of old stained mattresses. It looked like some fires had been built, and the benches where passengers had waited for trains, were all broken up and burned.

"It's only squatters, Elvis. Probably trying to find a safe way into or out of Canada." His words that should have reassured me didn't. The cocky smile that used to comfort didn't. "Look around. If you see anything call out or fire a shot into the air."

"I'm going out to the tracks," I said. "I'll meet you out there."

Erik started walking around the small room, I backed out to the rear exit where there was no door. The platform was covered in dirt, broken burnt boards—and bodies.

12
Dorian: Walkabout

I made my way across the country, staying in havens populated by vampires of every age and faction and heard rumors of revolution. It was so much unlike Dublin, where the factions warred as openly as the mortals. But the more I stayed on, the more I could see the problems rising here as well. The factions were not united and needed a leader. Each had its own person they wanted in place to rule the entire undead community. There would be no elections or campaigns when the time came. The representatives would battle to the death.

There were more rumors. A team of hunters going from state to state, looking for my kind to kill. In the underground world of Goths and geeks, pamphlets and newsletters circulated about these hunters and us. The Goth clubs were starting to run over. The would-bes streamed into the fetish bars where, behind closed doors, they sipped each other's blood from self-inflicted wounds.

And we, the undead, walked among them, never giving a clue to our nature or true existence. But in that underground, we had followers of our own—those who would bleed for us and those who tended to us in hopes of one-day becoming like us. We called them the thralls, the slaves and weak-willed. Those whose existences were so terrible that they longed for death and sometimes even life afterwards. As depicted in the popular fiction of the day, miserable mortals made even more miserable vampires.

I was depressed constantly. I missed Deirdre and her smiling face. She was always happier than I was. Even in the fields, digging up the inedible potatoes with rotted roots, she would be telling rhymes or humming. As a vampire, I was bored and dismal.

I went to the clubs and bars and tricked the bouncers into letting me in. It was simple—just promise them something they truly longed for and make them believe I could supply it, be it drugs, sex, or anything else.

Getting to California was taking forever, but I did have time to kill. Along the way I had built a portfolio of black and white photographs, color glossies in whatever clothes and poses I could do.

I passed them out, leaving a forwarding address to a post office kept by one of the havens. I went to modeling auditions, most of them at night, and made a few appearances during the day. There were long tunnels nearby so I could to escape if I needed to. The subways proved a haven within themselves. The sewers were filled with blindness and wrong turns, and one could get lost sometimes for days and weeks. I lived on rats, snakes, the occasional alligator, and whatever else that got flushed.

My first professional shoot was doing a department store's ad campaign for sneakers. Then I did bathing suits, where they would cover my pale demeanor with makeup, jeans, underwear, sunglasses, and soon, record stores. I often wrote and phoned Deirdre. I learned Kane had taken her in as a pseudo-daughter and began teaching her different ways.

I remember vividly that one afternoon I was sitting in a haven sipping from a blood donor's bag when one of the thralls came running from the subways into the hidden chamber. He was an older man, maybe in his late forties—one of the few who derived sexual pleasure from being bled. He didn't want servitude, didn't want to be one of us. He only wanted to be near us and for us to feed from him. His body was a maze of puncture wounds and knife scars. His name was David and he hovered on the fringes of sanity.

He trotted through the chamber, breathing heavily and wearing a wicked smile. Handing out newsletters to all of us, he then backed away and disappeared into a side chamber after his job was done. The newsletter was simple, typed and reproduced on a poor quality copy machine. Whoever typed it probably couldn't afford to send it to a printer and did this, rather then spending a dollar or so for a can of ravioli.

The front page mostly consisted of blathering about conspiracies of how the government covered up the existence of my kind and about how key persons in Congress were actually vampires with a secret agenda for total vampire domination of the States. I crumpled up the paper and was ready to toss it away when I spotted an address on the internet, *www.believe-it.info.* We had a lot of items in the catacombs, but computers weren't among them. I disposed of the spent blood bag and went to the surface.

I emerged on the tracks to bewildered eyes and glances, people who couldn't believe such a youngster would be wandering the rails in search of excitement or something else. I hopped up to the platform and quickly mingled with them until I found the exit.

I waited within the confines of the station until the sun had set at last. Had the blood that had just fed me been fresh and warm, I could have easily met the sunlight and gone to my destination. So I waited and waited, and debating about going back to the tunnels and taking a less direct route until the sun had finally set, walked to the library and sat down at a public access computer for the internet. I typed in the address and waited for the screen to appear.

It was garish, tacky and ghoulish, depicting a white-faced vampire with blood dripping from his teeth. There were no URL's or access points, so I simply double-clicked on the face. It was instant. The next screen had the articles I had just read, online only there were graphics now too. Badly-scanned photographs of men in suits on the floor of Congress. Then at the bottom of the screen was one final address: *www.vhunter.org*. I went to it. The page was simple, a one page only web advertisement with text and no pictures.

GOT A PROBLEM WITH THE UNDEAD?
CALL US QUICKLY

There was an 800-555 number listed, the kind Hollywood uses all the time in movies and on TV. I assumed it was counterfeit, but after everything else I couldn't take chance.

I printed the page and made my way back to the tunnels. When I got there, the entire place had been deserted. No one there, my kind or otherwise. The newsletters were scattered all over the floor and among them was a new magazine, *UnDead*. On the cover was a blurry photograph of a truck escaping from a burning house. There were three out-of-focus faces inside the vehicle. When I read the story, it told of the courageous cleaning of another nest of vampires in Georgia. Even though more than half of the team were lost, the house burned killing all of the bloodsucking occupants.

There was also a map showing where they had been and where they were supposedly headed. Our haven was on the map. Most times, we could have dealt with the mortals. But if they were well-known in the underground and suddenly turned up missing, there would be searching. We did not want to risk exposure.

I made my way through the rest of the state by train, in cars wherever I could find a ride, or by simply walking. I fed primarily from animals. If the publishers of the newsletters knew of our haven, they certainly would be on the look out for any clue left behind. At least by feeding from animals, most of the blame would be put on UFO sightings and cattle mutilations, the headline reading, "**ALIEN VAMPIRES COME TO STEAL THE WORLD'S SUPPLY OF MEAT AND CAUSE**

YET ANOTHER DISEASE TO CLAIM THE LIVES OF THOSE STANDING UNSUSPECTING IN LINES AT BURGER JOINTS."

The road soon became lonely. I filled my nights, thinking of songs sung to me by my mother and Deirdre. Stories told to us as children by Father and long nights in the fields—eating apples from the trees and listening to the sounds of night birds. My mind would wander to collecting fireflies and setting them free, pretending they were stars fallen to earth, and staring into the heavens in search of shooting stars.

I slept in caves, drainage ditches, and in empty tractor-trailers headed to their next destination. I dreamed of times filled with music and laughing. But thoughts of the winds, the cold—those damn jagged pieces of stone cutting into flesh, and the mind-numbing pain of frostbite and starvation.

In Ohio, I found a haven strictly for those who walked in the sun. They were thankfully unaware of the two hybrids created by Kane in the States. Havens, dedicated to one breed of us, had started moving west already. At least in New York, the factions were allowed to intermingle. I'm sure that was not allowed here, but this place would have to do.

I met people, heard names, none of which I would bother to remember. They were here, most likely for a century, waiting for their moment in the spotlight, looking for power that only comes from ruling the factions. The ruler of this haven was a pompous vampire named Christopher Jennings. He owned restaurants and apartment buildings, spent centuries acquiring wealth and belongings, and now ruled over the mortals the same way he ruled over the dead.

Jennings had cold blue eyes and thick brown hair, the slightest hint of a beard, and dressed impeccably in three-piece suits with colorful ties. I met him only once and the power he controlled was apparent. There was little underground movement out here—Jennings saw to that. But in my short time with them, I did see the occasional magazine or pamphlet. There was talk of a new hunter on the prowl, a team led by a boy younger than me when I was brought over.

He was the one being credited with the fire in Georgia that claimed two of us. They were given the accolades of the hunters, and those with theories, and hated by the Goths and our own kind. Elvis had brown eyes that were slits, appearing as if it hurt him to look fully out of them. The freckles of boyhood still had not faded, but there was an age about him too, as if subjected to too much before he was ready to handle it. Another one of the joys of technology were beepers, and mine went off again—another job and another photo shoot.

"Be careful, Dorian."

I spun in a hurry at Jennings' words. I hadn't noticed him standing behind me. Like the wind, he had crept up over my shoulders. With teeth bared and eyes aglow, I relaxed and came to terms. "Careful of what?"

"Of me—of any undue attention." He handed me a folded advertisement for the department store where I stood, holding a baseball bat and smiling at the camera. Written beneath it were the words, *I know about your sister*.

I crumpled the paper and threw it to the ground. I felt my anger and blood start to boil. When I turned to face him, Jennings was gone again like a fast summer's breeze.

I left the haven and went to the photo shoot, this time for Levis. One of the thralls in New York acted as my agent and handled all my calls and contracts. Every evening after the shoot, there would be a fresh supply of money in my bank account. The shoot was quick and easy, a simple set with a flowing black satin backdrop. I sat in a chair barefoot. I pretended to eat fruit and then ran to the restroom to vomit it out.

They got pictures of me drinking coffee and wearing a shirt or reading the sports pages without a shirt. When I was done, the photographer handed me his card with his home phone scrawled on the back. I returned to him that night, not for sex like he had assumed, but for blood. I fed and, with two thralls from the haven and a cooler full of food for them, hid in the baggage car of a train headed for Los Angeles.

13
Elvis: Deep into the Dark

"Jesus, Erik, get out here now!" I fired three shots in the air and then reloaded my pistol.

Erik came charging outside and stopped dead at the foot of the platform next to me. The entire thing had been stacked with bodies, maybe a yard tall and all drained of blood and crushed. I felt like I was at a hide auction or something. I threw up when I saw some of their facial expressions and then ran back inside.

Erik stayed out for a time longer, talking into the recorder and taking pictures. I sat on one of the beds and drained the last of the whiskey from Drake's bottle before chucking it over my shoulder. I checked my gun and started holding my cross for strength.

"You okay, Elvis?"

I nodded distractedly.

"It's all right, kid, really."

"How do you figure that? I lost it. If we were fighting, we'd be dead or worse right now. I never want to end up like that, Erik. Never want to be a bloodsucker or a pancake. Just want them all fucking dead." I stood up, brushed off my pants, and walked around the station.

"You seen all you need here?" Erik nodded and started packing up when I heard something *scratching*.

It came from everywhere, so loud it made the floors rock and the walls shake. The burnt timbers started to fall in and so did the glass that was left in the windows. "What the fuck is this? A quake?"

"I don't know, kid."

"It's simple," came a voice from the doorway. I spun around, lowering my gun and cocking the hammer at the same time. "It's the vampires. They're underneath the place," Drake said, looking smugly at Erik.

"Why don't they attack?" I screamed. The shaking was driving me mad.

"Sun is still out. Way I figure, we have maybe an hour of daylight left. Then we have to fight."

"Any other suggestions?" Erik asked.

"None come to mind. We can try to run, but it looks like someone already did a number on your car out there."

I ran to the window almost falling over my own damn feet. When I got there, the shaking stopped and fell quiet. The car, a '96 Volvo, had been gutted. The hood was up and there were wires and pieces all over the place. The windows had been smashed and the tires were all flat.

"Looks like we're fucked," Erik said.

"No. There's got to be a way."

"Don't hurt yourself thinking, Elvis. This is it. They know we're here, and if it wasn't for the sun, they'd already be on us."

"Look, Erik, if we start making a run for it, we might be able to hit some town or something before the sun goes down. We just cut through the woods at a full run and give it a shot."

"Maybe the kid has an idea, Erik," Drake said. "If we can get far enough away and dig in someplace, we can fight—at least we'd have a chance anyway."

"Yeah, Erik, come on, let's try," I pleaded.

"No." That was all he said—*no.*

"What do we do?" Drake asked, stepping in from the doorway.

"Fight, examine, and with any luck, get out alive."

"Is your research and duty to them sponsors so important you'll both risk your neck and ours?"

"Yes," Erik answered.

We sat around the station, waiting for the sun to finally set. Drake and me checked our guns and equipment. I got out my cross and squirt gun and hosed down all three of us until it was empty. While the sun began to fade in back of us, I could see the fear rising in Drake's eyes, as well as Erik's. My own fear rose like the tides.

I stared out the window, watching the last arc of the sun disappear behind the horizon. The sky was all filled with gold and crimson clouds, most beautiful sunset I'd ever seen, and I prayed with cross in hand that it wasn't my last. Erik started rooting around in back of me, getting out the flashlights. There was one low-light headset left, and Drake had it—if nothing else, the man was one hell of a shooter.

Beneath all the rubble and garbage on the floor was a trapdoor. Looked like it hadn't been used in ages. There was no lock on it, and it squealed like a stuck pig when Erik opened it up. There was this terrible stink that hit us when that door popped. Erik let go and the door slammed into the floor, stirring up the dust and shaking more down from the ceiling. Nothing jumped out at us—not a bat, wolf, or a wisp of fog or smoke and certainly not any pointy-toothed bloodsucker.

Drake was the first one down and he kept the headset up on his brow while we depended on the flashlights to guide our way. Under the station, there were iron rungs hammered into the stone that formed a chute. It felt like we were crawling through the throat of some giant beast waiting to get eaten.

The shaft went down almost thirty feet to the dirt floor of a tunnel running in both directions. The walls were smoothed stone, looking like there had been an underground river flowing through there. We could hear whispers from all around us, but didn't see anyone or anything.

"We go single file, one direction only," Drake said. "I'll make marks on the wall so we can find our way back in case we're separated. I'll lead. Kid, you're in the middle. Erik, take up the rear." Drake tossed an automatic pistol to Erik who looked baffled. Drake took it out of his hand, chambered a round, hit the safety, and gave it back. "You're all set, professor. Just point and squeeze the trigger. And take the safety off first." Drake started off down the hallway, pistol in one hand, light in the other.

I kept my hand against the wall so I wouldn't lose touch with it. The tunnel just went on and on, and we took side passages only when they went right. There was a whole maze of catacombs down there, and we were running it like rats looking for cheese. On the walls were symbols written in ancient script and torches in ornate holders that had never been lit. Erik would stop every now and again and draw copies of them into his notebook.

They knew we were here. There was no doubt in anyone's mind because they had already let themselves be known. The farther we went into the catacombs, the dimmer the lights got—like the stones were sucking the energy from them. The whispers grew louder with each step. We weren't hunting or exploring. We were being herded. The hallways ended abruptly in a wall of spider-webs, dried with age and filled with dust.

"Kill the lights."

With Drake's words came the death of the flashlights. The dark was overpowering. I whimpered a little and Erik patted my shoulder. Ever since Katherine, I hadn't been too fond of total, absolute darkness like this.

I kept my flashlight in case I needed to club something. Erik and Drake both dropped theirs.

Drake pulled on the goggles and looked into the webs. "There's barely enough light for these things to work. Somewhere up ahead is a light source. I don't see any movement."

Whispers filled the hallway with *scratching* that echoed in both directions. Something cold brushed up against my shoulder and I screamed. There was no reassuring pat on my shoulder, and I reached out for Drake. He wasn't there. I stepped back and Erik wasn't there. I was totally alone in the darkness. The *scratching* rose to a fevered pitch, and the whispers filled my head. I went to scream and the darkness took me.

14
Dorian: West

The city of Angels stretched out before me as we stepped from the baggage car. My vassals obediently followed behind. I had been trying to devise a way to set them free, but there was no way they would be safe. All they would do is find the first haven and give their servitude to those within.

I had no plan or destination in mind, but with little more than four hours of darkness, I had to find haven. The thralls were weak from the trip. I had taken too much from them. Their scarred necks and wrists were the only signs of what they truly were. I had more funds than I needed, and as soon as I found a spot to stay, it would be time for more photo shoots. Then, with any luck, I'd get into a movie set and coerce someone to give me a part.

I thought of Deirdre and that bastard Kane—how she was with him and not here with me. Even though we couldn't be a real family again, she was all I had left. The family would cease and fade away with our deaths whenever they should come. And with each night, I wondered if this was really worth it, hiding from the mortals and then feeding on them. I would never be able to fall in love with a warm-bodied woman without bringing her across or having her be a thrall to the desire for blood. I'd never have children of my own, and in this child's body, would never truly grow old.

The materials I had acquired, lost, and then begun to reacquire brought me what little pleasure there was in my life. My success as child star would be another, though being a childhood star for the rest of my existence would be my undoing.

The plan was simple—it had been done a hundred times by a hundred different superstars—appear in as many ads, commercials, and movies as I could. Then I would take any job to build my name and, at the height of my popularity, disappear into the ether. And no one could disappear better than a vampire. I'd make key appearances to keep the rumors flying, then sit back and collect the profits and interest. There would be TV movies, books, and talk shows about my disappearance.

One problem would be finding someone willing to take me on and do mostly night scenes. If I did eventually gain fame, I could transform into an adult, but I would have to feed from an adult, and keep that adult as a thrall, vowed to me for the remainder of his existence—someone with similar features and tone. If that did happen, it would have to be someone of the age I currently resembled.

My thralls and I mingled in with the crowds that embarked from the trains, the businessmen in their fancy suits, the college students, and parents dragging their children as if trolling for fish. The people dispersed as did we. It wasn't difficult finding a new place. All I needed to do was be weary of my surroundings and ever watchful.

The haven was underneath a nightclub called The Aftermath, a brick-front building with a fetish-clothing store on one side and a porn shop on the other. The buildings were so close together there was no room for an alley. Further down the street was a hotel for men with rooms at eight dollars a day and an all-night Korean restaurant. I went to the diner and fed the vassals. They ate like I had been starving them. The food from the ice chest held them, but it wasn't nourishing enough.

Still being evening, there were others in there with us who paid us no mind. It seemed as if the people in here and working here were almost used to my kind coming in. The vassals ate and I watched them. One booth behind us, a man haggled price with a prostitute for a hand job in his car. In front of us, a drug deal went down.

Inside The Aftermath, techno and electronica music assaulted us from every side. Writhing bodies filled the dance floors and the scents of sweat, sex, and blood were heavy on the air. We walked through the dancers and were led by a non-descript man in a black suit towards a back room. There, a set of wooden stairs led to a room with cinderblock walls and a cement floor. Boxes of wine and beer were stacked to the ceiling. A large black, upside down cross was painted on the wall. When the man pressed on it, a secret door opened. He led us beyond it, into sewers and tunnels, long abandoned by the subways.

Our destination was a large room, guarded at the door by a stocky man with a big mustache named Jason. He eyed us over carefully and then patted us down for weapons. After nodding his approval, we were let in. The room was filled with overstuffed leather chairs and couches. A pool table stood under a buzzing neon sign advertising the club. The cues were made of epoxy and fiberglass. Wooden cues could end up as weapons against our kind, though a stake through the heart would also kill a mortal. Lava lamps adorned small tables made of aluminum, chrome, and wood polished to a reflective finish. The floors were strewn with colored confetti that caught the light oozing from the chandelier. Wineglasses and goblets were placed next to chairs and in shadowy corners.

The room swarmed with the living and the dead. Music was piped in from speakers hidden behind artwork that hung in the corners of the room. Men, women, and children wandered about, talking and gossiping. There was one single payphone near the pool table that seemed constantly in use.

Blood flowed openly from goblets and wrists. I drank often from many different wrists, feasting upon the sweet succulence from pink and pale throats. The club-goers mixed freely about us, each one marked with a tattoo of a teardrop above his or her wrist. It didn't matter how many times they came or went. Each time, Jason dealt with them. Any weapons were placed in a locked trunk, and anyone without a tattoo or a visitor looking for something new, was turned away.

"Hi," a young girl walking up to me said.

"Hello."

Her hair was black as night and from a bottle. She wore a green crushed velvet dress, fishnet stockings with holes, a leather collar around her tiny throat, and too much red lipstick. Her skin, so pale, seemed to be translucent.

"I've seen you before. My name is Holly." She ran her hand down her stomach and thigh, lifting her dress. Then she pulled something from the bands of her stockings. Between the pale digits were folded pieces of worn paper cut from department store ads—pictures of me in jeans holding a skateboard, another in a suit, and a third in sweatpants. "I used to steal newspapers from the stores on Sundays for the ads. At home, I have you all over my walls." She blushed a little. "I'm still looking for the underwear photos."

I could hear her pulse and the blood coursing excitedly through her veins. "Do you model?"

"Me," she laughed. "My parents barely let me out of the house. I had to sneak out tonight."

"How old are you, Holly?"

"Fifteen," she said, putting the papers back into their hiding spot. "And you?"

"Sixteen. At least that's how old I was when I was taken."

"No, really."

"A lot older than sixteen."

One pale scar cut across her wrist. Above it was a small teardrop tattoo. "Even before I met you, I knew you were one. I knew in the pictures. The adults are all over the place. But I never thought I'd find you or someone like you my age." She handed me a goblet filled with blood and I sipped from it. She drank from a wineglass. "How did it happen to you?"

"During the potato famine. Do you want to go up and dance for a while?"

Holly nodded. I was grateful for an end to her questions. It amazed me how welcome we were by the mortals, at least certain groups of them.

Holly took my hands. Her warmth ignited on my cold dead skin. She smiled and led me from the haven. My vassals mixed in with the crowd and ate, drank, and bled. A man with more piercings on his face then fingers on his hands stared suspiciously at us as we emerged from the club's cellar.

The music hammered down upon us from everywhere. Massive speakers stood on wooden stands at the corners of the dance floor. Set on small shelves, smaller ones lined the tops of the walls. Lights bounced and strobed from racks overhead, and a machine hissed out smoke and fog. The twirling and writhing bodies moved when we walked through them to find our own spot to dance. Although stared at repeatedly, sometimes hungrily, no one questioned us about our ages—how we got into the club or what the night would bring. A long bar was set against the wall of the club where we came in and out. Two people, a man and a woman tended it.

All around the dance floor, benches, chairs, and couches were set flush against the walls. A wooden railing separated walkways from the dance floor. People leaned against it, talked, drank, kissed, and felt each other up. Overflowing ashtrays, rolling papers, and empty glasses covered the railing's top. Glowing stairs led to the dance floor from the front and rear. At the back, near the club's proper entrance, was a wall with a sliding, one-way mirror. Behind were the DJs. The mirror was currently open so the dancers could make requests and talk to the musical masters.

We danced maniacally, frantically, and expectantly. With each new song, our bodies grew closer together until the inevitable happened. I kissed her. She smiled and ground her hips against mine. I could see the excitement reflected in her eyes.

I wrapped my arms around her, pulled her against me, and felt the heartbeat through her dress. My hands roamed across her body. She lowered her hand to my pants. I felt pressure from her exploring fingers.

"You need some blood," she whispered into my ear.

I heard her easily above the pounding music. The moment I had yearned for and even feared was upon me again. Sex with my own kind was animalistic, raw, and cold. I longed for the touch of a warm body pressed against my own.

When Holly led me from the floor to the backroom, eyes were once again upon us, curious and envious. How many would be going home alone tonight? And how many desired the pleasure of a young girl or boy? In the basement, I stole a kiss and a bottle of wine. We walked through the tunnels. It seemed like she had traveled many times along this path into the heart of haven.

Leading from the main room, a hallway lit by fluorescent tubes ran the length of the ceiling. I could hear Holly's breaths, short and fast. At the end of the hallway was a second hall running horizontally. Set into the wall were a series of doors—some open and more closed. The sounds and scents of sex leaked out. We went into an open room and closed the door. I set the wine on a table. The bed took up most of the small room, and Holly was already upon it, slipping off her dress. Beneath it she wore a white T-shirt.

"Are you certain you want this?"

"I've always wanted this, since I first saw you in the papers and then in haven."

"Are you afraid?"

"Yes, but not of you."

I opened the wine. We drank from the bottle and from each other's mouths, letting the wine drizzle from our parted lips. Our hands explored each other's bodies, stripping off layers of clothes until we lay naked, wrapped in the sheets.

"You're too cold," Holly whispered.

I shifted my weight and rolled on top of her. Her breath was hot against my face—our lips touched gently, parted, and tongues explored. I slid my hands to cover her small breasts and bit into her pale throat. The blood flowed and my body warmed. As her life drained, mine grew. I pulled away, licking stray droplets from her cheek. The blood that fueled her excitement now also fueled mine. Our bodies merged to become one, over and over again. When the blood cooled and refused to flow, more was taken in from Holly and from those lonely souls hearing the sounds of passion through the door. With the dusk came an empty bed. The only proof of what had occurred was an empty wine bottle and blood-stained sheets.

15
Elvis: Thrall

The whispers were all around me, *scratching*, filling my head. I didn't move. I lay on the floor with my eyes and fists clenched tight. I felt them moving on me, over my nose, across my eyelids, and into my shoes. Finally, when I couldn't stand it, I jumped up screaming and swinging madly. I didn't care who I hit as long as it was a bloodsucker.

I was alone in the dark. Erik and Drake were still unconscious on the floor near me. Thin wisps of smoke quickly flowed out through cracks in the walls, floor, and beneath the room's only door.

Drake groaned and sat up holding his head. "Where are we, kid? And what the hell happened?"

"I don't know and I don't know."

"Is that door locked?" Drake asked groggily.

"Haven't tried it yet."

The door, made out of thick wood and reinforced with metal braces, was locked. I rattled it for good measure and to let them know we were awake and ready for whatever they planned to dish out. Erik rolled over and sat up. None of us seemed to know what the hell was going on. The vamps had us in their clutches. Didn't make any damn sense at all. We were still breathing and warm to touch.

"We're being stored." Erik rubbed his face and started pacing around the small room. Light filtered from under the door and a crack in the wall. The shadows clung to the walls and even to us, making us all appear like monsters.

"What the hell does that mean?" I asked.

The door creaked open. The hinges *squealed* with each inch. We stood together against what would come through the door, raised fists, and prepared to strike—at a child.

"Are you hungry?" she asked.

It caught us off guard—at least me anyway. No one else was with her, just that girl in the doorway.

She was maybe six-years-old if a day, had soft, shoulder-length blonde hair, and pale blue eyes. She looked more like a doll than a kid. "If you're not hungry, it's okay. I was once a stranger here, too." Her voice was angelic. "My name is Rose."

She extended her hand to us and I figured what the heck. If I was going to die, might as well be friendly about it. "I'm Elvis."

She giggled, but her hands were warm like mine.

"This is Frank and Erik." I was getting ready to ask her some questions when someone slid in some metal plates and bowls and tossed in a water pouch.

"Okay, I have to go now. You should eat because it will be easier if you do." Rose turned to the doorway. She started growing, and her hair shortened and shoulders widened. "Eat, or you'll die." The shape-shifter left the room, leaving the door open—daring us to escape.

Drake was through the open doorway in seconds. He came back in shaking his head. "Hallway ends in doors on either side. I can hear noises, like voices and furniture being moved. Let me tell you, there are a lot of voices."

Erik bent over to look at the plates of food filled with meat, bread, and fruit. Erik took a long drag from the water pouch like it was his last and passed it to us. "What are you thinking, Frank?"

Drake spun around and then sat in the doorway.

"Seems to me..." he said, reaching for the plate of meat. He tore off a chunk with his teeth and winced as he chewed. "It's edible, may as well be raw—and it's cold. Seems to me, if they left one door open then the others are open too, or at least one of them, they want us to eat to regain our strength. Then they kill us."

"They won't kill us," Erik said, going for the bread.

"Why the hell not?" Drake asked.

I poked through the fruit and settled on an apple. "They're feeding us, they're not killing us. We're cattle."

"We're going to bleed, Elvis."

I took a piece of meat, bit in, and blood dribbled down my chin. I forced myself to swallow. I washed it down with some of the water. Drake walked out into the hallway, humming the "Star Spangled Banner" while Erik ate bread.

"It's like I said," Drake called from the hallway. " One of the doors is locked. The other is open. I didn't go through yet, but there's a lot of noise coming from the other side."

Erik and Drake sat down to eat while I chewed on that chunk of meat.

I finally just threw it to the ground and stomped on it. "Why are we doing this? Why are we eating?" I asked.

"Because, kid, we have to eat to stay strong. If we're going to fight we need strength. Besides, if we don't eat we'll starve to death." Drake was right.

"Yeah, but all this is doing is fattening us up for the slaughter," Erik said.

"Truer words have never been spoken."

We all spun around, staring at the new voice. His hair blew as if in a summer's breeze, and as we watched, his legs formed from the mists that carried him.

"Actually, there will be no slaughter unless you provoke it. You're free to roam around as you like, but you can never leave. If you try to escape, you will be killed. Join us in the dining room." He dissolved into mists, just like I had seen in the movies.

Our footsteps echoed off the stone corridors. Drake opened the door and stepped through. The room was huge, but barren of decorations and furniture. Mats were laid out on the floor.

The "mist man" appeared in a swirl of overly dramatic smoke and paced around us. He wore a ruffled shirt and what looked like a black velvet tux with tails. "Lie on the mats, mortals."

It was the same feeling I had back with Katherine all them months ago. I had no control, couldn't fight against his voice. I laid on the mat with Erik and Drake on either side.

"Normally we feed from animals, steal them from local farms or just go to town and buy them outright. Living down here in the darkness, we had our own little city here. Until you burst in. You ruined our secrecy. You know of us. You can never leave here. The three of you will live as long as we choose to keep you alive."

"What about that pile of dried up bodies?" I don't know how the words got out of my face, but they did.

"Transients, runaways, and drunks—no one seems to care about them and no one has come looking. We prey almost solely on animals. But when we get a mortal in here, we do make best use of him."

The room slowly began to fill with beings, strangely curious at our warmth. I tried to squirm, but someone else was in charge of me now. I turned my head to see Erik and Drake completely surrounded.

"The little one has some fight."

I moved my hand, flipped him the bird—and then the undead descended upon us. Hands tore at my shirt and pants. Our clothes were ripped off. The holy water I covered us with earlier was gone and dried up. I heard Drake screaming. A pair of cold hands turned my face. Cold breath washed across my throat. I started to scream, swear, and yell. I saw our packs thrown into the corner of the room.

"The bullets were ingenious, where did you learn that?"

I heard the click of a chamber being snapped back into the body of the gun. The "mist man" walked over and dropped the pistol near my hand. I strained to reach for it.

"How's that holy water feel, asshole?" I watched him peel the skin off his fingers, and just like a snake, discard it.

"It stings a little."

The first set of teeth bit into my leg. The pain was unbearable. I started screaming "The Lord's Prayer" as more and more teeth ripped at my skin. I felt my blood running from my neck, greedy cold tongues licking it up. After the feeding, we were dragged back to our cell and left alone. I wanted to die. We were brought back night after night for the same routine. They commanded our subservience and told us to lie prone while we were bled.

One night when we were too weak to walk they left us alone. They forced the cold raw meat down our throats. I saw Erik take blood from them. Both Drake and I refused, fighting back with what little strength we had. They said it would nourish us and help us heal so they could feed from us again. After two weeks of this, we learned how to play the part. If we breathed shallow and acted as if our limbs couldn't carry us, they'd let us be. We plotted and planned, tried to figure out how to get out or die in the effort. Another few days into our new lives, we were left to wander as we pleased. They thought our wills were broken—but they were wrong.

While Drake ran cover, I snuck into the other room. The mats were all rolled up and I went for our gear. First thing I reached for was my pistol and speed loaders. I dragged the packs into the hall, tossed them to Frank and Erik, and waited.

"Come on you guys," I hissed. "We're fucking dead if we don't move. I don't even know what damn time it is."

I felt the presence before I actually saw them. The room started to fill with mist. It swirled all about me and I ran for the door. Then I heard the footsteps and laughing.

"Thought you could escape, did you?"

The mist coalesced until the room was filled with pale-faced creatures. I spun on my heels and fired a shot dead bang at the head asshole's face. The bullet tore through his skull and his flesh burned. The others were on us instantly. I fired more shots into the crowd, pulled out my cross, and prayed like I never had before.

Drake slammed the door shut and Erik leaned up against it. I got out the guns from the packs and handed them out. Drake charged down the hallway to the locked door, leapt at it, and crashed on through.

"Come on ladies, beat feet!"

I took off and jumped after him as the first one crashed through the other door. Erik damn near got his head ripped off. We tore ass down the hallway, and I picked up a couple good-sized chunks of the door just in case. My gun went empty. I reloaded quickly while running.

"You get any, kid?"

"I got the head bad guy."

"Erik, catch up, would you?"

Erik was running, though not as fast as us, like he wanted to get caught. I told him not to take any of the blood from them bastards, but the stupid fuck wouldn't listen. The bloodsuckers were right on our heels when Drake saw the first mark on the walls. We ran until the hallway ended. Even with all the marks we made, we still got lost in the maze of tunnels. Drake walked up ahead with one of the torches from the walls, and Erik pulled out a penlight. I followed behind, listening to the sound of Drake's steps and the crackling torchlight.

The hallway opened up into this massive room. Looked like it could have been a library, only it was sunk into the ground and the vamps took it over. Drake ran around the room first thing and started lighting up these torches on the walls. Vamps don't need light, and fire spooks the shit out of them. Erik came in a few seconds later, huffing away like he'd run a marathon, and we slammed the door shut. Erik locked it, and there was a big wooden board on the side that slid into place. Drake had already started knocking shit over, making cover.

I think Erik just about had an orgasm when he saw all of them books stacked floor to ceiling three-quarters around the room. There were desks and chairs and tables. Drake dragged them to the door. We piled them all in front just as the banging started. There were ladders and catwalks all among the shelves, and Erik was up the stairs in a heartbeat, glancing over titles and tossing down volumes. Drake and me got that door covered pretty well and set up shop behind some of the heavy desks he flipped over.

We set all the guns, spare ammo, and clips on the floor in easy reach. I started breaking off the chair legs and left them near the guns too. We didn't have nearly enough bullets for all the damn vamps. I closed my eyes, pulled out my cross so it was in plain sight, and held it so tight my fingers bled. I didn't know if God was listening, but I hoped he was.

The other part of the wall was filled with photos and portraits of people who must have died a long time ago. Erik stood in front of the barricade when the first clenched hand punched through the door. The fingers wrapped around his face and tried to pull him through. I grabbed one of the stakes and swatted the hand until it let go. When I pulled the stake back in, there was a flap of dead skin stuck to it.

The room started to shake and books fell from the shelves. Erik dove for his pile and started stuffing them into his pack. Mist began to creep in from around the shelves. The room filled with this crazy whispering. Long dead fingers *scratched* at the doors and the *screams* of the undead echoed through the room.

"They're in here!" Drake shouted. He picked up a pistol in each hand and got ready to fire.

I grabbed my revolver and speed loader. Erik had a pistol too. I didn't know how long the bullets would last or how long we would survive if we went hand to hand.

"This can't be right! There's got to be another way out!" I screamed, running around the room, waiting for the mist shapes to coalesce into human forms.

The shelves were set dead against the walls, but still the mist was seeping in from somewhere, and it was up to our knees now. A piece of the door splintered off, and Drake fired the first shot through the hole.

I heard an ungodly *howl* and the beating against the door got more furious. I went to the wall of pictures and started knocking them off. The glass and frames shattered when they hit the floor.

"Damn it, kid, stop playing around! We need your gun."

"There's got to be another door, Frank. There has to be."

The first vamp materialized in front of me—a woman with deep eyes and short hair. I clubbed her with the table leg until her jaw broke. She reached up and swatted me away. I could still see through her, like she wasn't full yet. I ran back over and stuck the table leg in her just as she formed full. She clawed at the leg and then fell over. She convulsed and screamed—then went silent. Her eyes darted all around the room like she was expecting her friends to come save her. I picked up another leg and beat her with it until I caved in the side of her skull.

Drake fired through what was left of the door while Erik took it all in, watching us and firing the occasional shot. I tore through the biggest painting. It went from ceiling to floor, and sure as shit, there was a door behind it. No mist was coming through so I pulled it open, stepped back, and lowered my gun. Nothing but darkness.

There came a massive barrage of bullets, and Drake threw down his gun. "I'm out!"

Erik tossed him his gun and waded through the mists clubbing anything that looked like a person.

"I found a hallway, let's go!" I yelled.

A male appeared from the fog and grabbed my arm. His razor sharp claws raked down, ripping shirt and skin. Blood flowed. Drake screamed and fell back, covering his eye. Gore gushed from between his fingers. Erik bolted for the corridor after grabbing the packs. I grabbed Drake, pulled him in, and reloaded my gun before shutting the door.

"You take this, Frank. I have twelve shots left."

"Any ideas where this goes?" Drake asked, his voice weak.

"No, but follow Erik."

The door burst open and the mist crept in. I saw eyes glowing in the darkness. More sets of eyes than I had bullets. I ripped off my cross and backed to the first murky form I saw. I let the chain slip through my fingers into the mists. Something screamed. There was a rush of wind and fire as the bloodsucker exploded. The blast knocked us halfway down the tunnel. I ran to Drake, got his arm around my shoulder and helped him walk.

"What's the score, kid?"

"Good guys at least one, bloodsuckers nothing."

"That's a good score. It was a hoot while it lasted, kid."

"We ain't dead yet, boss."

We limped as fast as we could. Something in the hallway caught fire, and the flames were catching up pushing the damn vampires right into us. The corridor exploded with sunlight, blinding us. We ran towards it. Drake stopped and pushed me out farther into the light.

"You get out."

"No, you have to come with us. We're a team—a family!" I started screaming and crying.

Drake pulled his hand away from his face, and I saw where the jagged piece of wood had punctured his eye, the splintered chunk still sticking out of the socket.

"Always remember me, kid."

Drake stood his ground and started firing into the mass of swarming vampires coming down the corridor. The first few hit the light and blew up, the explosive force knocked us outside. I stood in the doorway of the deserted library screaming, too afraid to move. Erik was down the road, running and not looking back.

I saw Drake toss down the gun and then try going toe to toe. The vampires, some missing eyes, pieces of their faces, or big holes burnt in them, jumped on him. I heard his screams, tried to turn away, but couldn't. All I could do was watch Drake get torn apart. The vampires didn't know what to do. It was like a stampede, and they were all in a panic. Face the fire or the sunlight. With the fire they had a chance. They started away from the light, dragging what was left of Drake behind them. Then I saw the lead guy, the head "mist man" or whatever the fuck they called themselves. He looked at me, even smiled a little. There was a bullet hole in the center of his skull and it healed up while I watched. He pointed his finger at me, looked me dead in the eye, turned around, and walked back into the flames.

"Damn it, Erik, slow down." I saw the crazy bastard running down the road farther into safety of the sunlight.

My breath caught raggedly in my throat as I tried desperately to breathe. As the seconds passed, it was like my arm started going all pins and needles on the way to numbness. More blood trickled from my wounds than it seemed my heart could pump.

Erik slowed, limped to the road's edge, and started heaving his guts up. When Erik was empty, he collapsed on the shoulder of the road.

"What do we do about Frank?" I asked, finally catching my breath.

Erik fished around in his pockets and pulled out his mini tape recorder. "I don't know, Elvis."

During the fight, we had lost most of what was in our packs, weapons, and what we had left for supplies. I tore off my shirt and wrapped it around my arm to stop the bleeding. Erik talked into the recorder, and through the trees, I could see smoke starting to spiral up from the train station. After it caught, the bodies on the platform would go up, and no one except for us would know about them.

"What do we do now, Erik?"

"We start walking, kid."

I was still bleeding, not as much. My shirt bandages started to soak through. My arms and chest were covered in bite marks and small pink scars from where we were fed on. It looked like we had been to war and back.

I figured out by the sun that it was early morning. We walked until it was high up in the sky, dead on noon, when a logging truck came along. The driver was hauling a load of timber from Canada to a mill. He damn near shit himself when he saw me bleeding all over the place. I looked back down the road to see a trail of small crimson dots. If any of them bloodsuckers lived, it would be like a homing beacon right to me. Erik climbed into the cab first.

"What the hell happened to your arm, kid?" He stared at me through bloodshot eyes.

The floor was littered with empty coffee cups and candy wrappers. A faded green pine tree air freshener hung from the mirror. It had obviously died in the attempt of keeping the smells away.

"We were hiking. I slipped on some rocks and fell down the hill."

Erik stayed quiet and had given up on the tape recorder for a pen and paper.

"You went hiking like that?"

"Lost our stuff on the roll down the hill." I climbed over Erik getting in.

"Your friend there sure is quiet."

"It's his way."

The driver's name was Guy. He smoked three packs a day and had given it up for nicotine patches and gum. He'd been driving since he quit high school over twenty years ago, and the more he drove, the more of his life story we found out. Guy pretty much rambled away until we hit the hospital in Portland.

Erik gave him a business card and told him to call the number on it to get reimbursed for his troubles once he was done with his log run. I sauntered into the hospital lobby, read the directory, went into the emergency room, and passed out at the front desk.

When I woke up, my arm was wrapped in bandages and a tube fed blood right into it. I freaked when I saw it and tried ripping it out, but a doctor stopped me.

"Good afternoon, young man. You certainly gave us a fright."

"Hi, doc."

"How are we feeling?" He took out a pocket light and shone it in my eyes. Then made notes on a clipboard.

"Pretty tired, I guess, and sore as hell."

The doctor took my pulse, listened to my heart, and after a few minutes of scribbling on a pad, took out the blood drip. It pinched when it came out. He put on some gauze and a pink bandage. "Sorry, it's all I had with me. You've been through an awful lot, son. We need to keep you overnight for observation."

"I can't stay in this room."

It was private, one door, open bathroom and window. A television sat on a swivel arm and there was one chair. The window had closed vertical blinds and right below it was a heater.

"You'll be fine here, son. All you need is rest. I do want you to fill out some forms so we can stop calling you John Doe."

"Where's Erik?"

"Is that your uncle or father?"

"No, he came in with me—a friend."

"Sorry, son, I don't know of any Erik." The doctor's name was Michael Glass. He was married. I saw the ring, but didn't know about kids. I hadn't asked. Dr. Glass was as tall as Erik, dressed better, and losing his brown hair.

He left a clipboard on the corner of the mattress, and I started filling out all those forms—name, address, insurance, and all that. I didn't know my medical history and couldn't remember any allergies. Since Erik and me never stayed in any place long enough to call home, I wrote down the trailer park's address.

A nurse came in with a tray of soupy, tasteless mystery food. It reminded me of home and Momma's cooking, and I started to cry. She sat with me while I ate and we talked. I handed her the clipboard, and finally during visiting hours, Erik showed up. Crazy bastard said he'd been on the phone with the sponsors almost since he followed me in, telling them about the bloodsuckers, what they did to us, and what we did right back to them.

"How you feeling, Elvis?"

"Doing okay I guess, considering."

"The sponsors are pleased with our work."

"What did you say about Drake?"

"He was killed in the line of duty."

"But how does that leave him?"

Erik walked around the room, looked out the window, and sat down in the chair. He shifted around a few times and got up again. "Due to the nature of our business, as a missing person, he'll be declared MIA."

"Doesn't seem right."

"It's all they can do without exposing us and themselves."

"It still fucking sucks."

Erik filled me in on the details of the last job, sort of debriefing me, I guess, finding out if I saw or knew anything he didn't. The sponsors, knowing I was wounded, had already scheduled us for another job. How fucking nice of them. Erik had managed to put them off a couple nights so I could rest and heal some more. He refused any sort of treatment.

"I can't sleep here tonight, Erik. If any of them bastards lived you know where they're coming to."

"Where do you want to go?" he asked.

"The chapel."

The chapel was pretty small, with three or four rows of pews—simple and to the point. There was a small podium with a microphone and a gold-plated cross hung on the back wall. After some negotiating with an intern and an exchange of bills, Erik got us in for the night. They wheeled in a couple cots, and Erik spun the silver ring the keys were on around his finger. He tossed them to me and headed for the door.

"Where are you going now?"

"Couple more calls," he said scratching his head. A scab came lose and blood trickled onto his face. "And to round up some grub." He seemed oblivious to the blood until I pointed it out to him.

I locked the doors after he left, found an old chair, and broke it apart, trying for some makeshift stakes. We would sleep in shifts so no one could sneak up on us. I'd seen some other vamp tricks before. I didn't know shit one about the mist, though. Thought that was just in the movies.

Me being alone gave me the chance to start rooting around. I found the Bibles, prayer and hymn books, some fancy robes, and nice goblets, but not what I wanted. A little more digging brought up some candles, which I lit, and then I found my prize—a locked, ornate jewel box. I beat the lock until it popped and took out the pitcher and wrapped package. Inside was the body and blood of Christ. There was a knock at the door and I damn near shit myself.

"Who is it?" I asked, scrambling for a chair leg.

"It's me, Elvis. Let me in."

I unlocked the door and held the stake ready just in case. Erik pushed in a wheeled cart loaded down with sandwiches and cans of soda. I picked up the food and felt it. The stuff was still hot. I took a sandwich and bag of chips with me, stuffed a soda into my pocket, and went back to the podium.

"The sponsors want us to stay in town, Elvis. They'll pay for clothes, passage, and the room—top floor, the way you like it."

I took a bite of the sandwich and shook my head. "Erik, I think it's nice how all these people call the shots and want to give us safe passage and clothes. But there ain't a chance in hell I'm sleeping in anything but a church tonight."

"It's all right to be a little scared, Elvis. But this is safe."

I put down the hospital food and started to chow down on the bread thingies and wine. "You best be eating some of theselittle Jesus crackers for when them bloodsuckers come after us, 'cause sure as shit stinks, we're fucked.""

Erik took the wine from me and finished it off, not that I had left much. He took a few pieces of the host and nibbled tentatively on them. I finished my snack and went digging for some more. There was a small glass bottle filled with holy water, which I set aside for later. If nothing happened, it'd be in my pack by the time we left the hospital.

That night in the chapel, I hardly slept any at all. Erik, the bastard, was sound asleep on a pew in a matter of minutes, the roll-in cot totally forgotten about. With all the business taken care of, he had nothing left to do. He talked in his sleep, reciting his notes and stuff between snores. Every now and then I'd drift off for a few minutes at a whack. I was still feeling weak so the intern that Erik had bribed earlier brought in a portable IV and plugged me back in.

After some time on the IV drip, it got harder and harder to keep my damn eyes open—like there was something else in there. The fatigue was overwhelming. The mind was willing to stay up all night and guard against the evil that goes bump, but the body had a whole other agenda. Each time I felt myself dosing off, I'd snap myself awake. The IV machine had wheels, which made pacing a hell of a lot easier. What I would have given for a pistol—at least something to make me feel safe—or something I could use against them or me should anything come after us tonight. But there in the chapel, we were safe for the most part. One thing them bloodsuckers couldn't stand was religious stuff.

When the pacing grew tiresome, I tried singing, which faded to humming, any and all hymns I could remember. I had the hymn books right there but couldn't read music worth a damn. After that started wearing thin, I'd slap myself or pull out hairs from my arms or neck. There was no way I was going to sleep tonight. Shit, if Erik wasn't such an asshole, we'd be doing this in shifts. But the way he'd been acting lately, he'd invite the damn vampires in and let them run amuck. And Erik, useful as a sneaker full of soft shit left out in the rain, kept on sleeping and mumbling.

He sure did know a lot about vampires, both from real life experience and book learning. Thinking back on it now, I didn't know a whole lot about Erik—just that he was a researcher and had cash. We never talked about him—always me. I learned a little about vampires from my time with Katherine and more from our stay with the mist men. The way Erik blathered on, it was like he turned into a walking bloodsucker encyclopedia.

I knew about one kind of vampire—the ones from movies. According to Erik's sleep babble, there were all different sorts and not all of them got along too well with each other. With the movies, it's all easy business. They all turn into mist or fog or bats and what have you. They all can fly and have those cool glow-in-the-dark eyes. They grow claws and shape change into these monstrous-looking beasts. Not according to Erik though. If those movie guys knew even a fraction of what Erik did, they'd have to rewrite their scripts and everything else about bloodsuckers.

Finally, I couldn't stand up anymore. I sat down with my back against the podium. Lying on the floor in back of the podium was a small gold cross on a chain, and I clutched it tightly against my chest. I prayed silently, and when the IV bag was empty, the machine chimed a few times. I ripped the needle from my arm. That woke me right the fuck up! I tore at my pajamas and got some cloth on it, not before I felt the soft trickle of blood on my fingers and a few drops hit the floor.

I kicked the IV machine over and listened to it crash. Erik bolted up suddenly and looked around with this crazy glare in his eyes. He finally settled down and fell back asleep, muttering and all. I was able to catch myself almost every time my eyelids started to close. It would be near dawn soon, and once the sunlight came in, I'd be safe. When I could see the sun hanging low in the sky, all would be well again for another day.

If I were back in the trailer park, I'd be up on top of the pizza eatery and looking at the stars, maybe lying in bed, drinking a coke, reading comic books, or sneaking around with Jimmy Riley. I wondered, with all that went on, what happened to him. What stories had circulated around the park about my parents' deaths and my own disappearance? But that didn't matter one bit right now. Each passing second and minute brought my eyes a little closer to being shut. Each time they slipped, something would happen in the room.

I didn't know if it was me, the vampires, or just shit seeping in from dreamland. But I could hear that whispering that had become so familiar to me. I saw the shadows creep forward and then recede back, saw faces, some familiar, hovering outside the chapel's only window—out in the mist, three floors above the street. I heard *scratching* on the walls.

"How you feeling, Elvis?"

I bolted up, my neck was stiff and the cross was stuck to my hand from sweat.

"Where am I?"

"In the hospital."

I listened to his bones *pop* as he stretched. Erik went to the food cart and picked idly at it.

"Want some breakfast?"

I think he could tell something was wrong by the way he looked at me. I have to say, after what I heard him spouting in his sleep, I didn't trust him as much as I used to. Katherine had made me her thrall, her slave, and almost her midnight snack. I didn't want to be there with her—but Erik, he craved that.

"Yeah, some breakfast is good."

"You want to come to the cafeteria?"

"No way, man, I'm staying here."

Erik walked out, pushing the cart. I started to clean up. We'd made quite the mess. At least I did anyway. That patch of cloth was stuck to my arm with dried blood. I pulled it off and tossed it in the trash. I put all the fancy goblets and pitchers away. Hid the lock box back where we found it, but I still pocketed that vial of holy water.

16
Elvis: Pursued

We were on the road for what seemed like months, even though it'd been only a few days. Erik didn't seem to want to talk anymore, unless he was rambling on about some new theory or ancient sect of the bloodsuckers. He hadn't been right since he drank down that blood back in Maine. Shit, Drake had been left to die. I was still carrying that around with me, even though I knew he agreed to the risk of it all. What happened out there and the way Drake was forgotten was wrong. Erik signed the contracts and wavers and all that legal bullshit. He had to sign my life away on account of my age. What I found out, and Erik didn't know, is that the sponsors had confiscated all of Drake's stuff. They owned every last scrap of Drake, from his diaries if he kept any down to his skivvies.

I sighed and looked out of the window of the brand-new RV Erik had picked up with what looked like pocket change. I knew it was a gift from the sponsors. We were headed to Pennsylvania, the next job and like the last four—go in after the fact, do a screen, clean, and haul ass out.

The last four jobs had been mostly on the eastern side of the States. In an old church in Ohio, we picked up remnants from one vamp. We found his coffin, his trinkets, for lack of a better word, and a few bottles of blood. I don't mean, the fucker actually had human blood in bottles. He kept it in a midget refrigerator and microwaved it when he was ready to feed.

We never found the vamp—just what he left behind. Erik said we probably missed the bastard by a matter of hours. After we searched the place and took all we could, I found the mug of blood in the oven. That's how we figured it all out.

In the rearview mirror, which to Erik's dismay, I constantly changed so I could see through it too, was a long line of cars and trucks. Traffic had been pretty light, 'cause we traveled at such odd hours. No way we wanted to get stuck in a site near dusk—whether it was clean or not. Even when it was supposed to be clean, the damn bloodsuckers could come back at any damn second.

In South Carolina, we ended up on an old farm. Nothing at all special there. The barn had burnt down what looked like decades earlier, but the foundation was still there. There was a silo full of rotted wheat, and the house was little more than rubble with broken windows and doors. But we still gave it a thorough once-over and then did it again.

The fields had all gone to weeds, and the equipment sat dead where it had rusted. Inside the house was this old body. It was all dried up and stuff, real nasty business. I took it out into the back and buried it in what was left of the orchard while Erik looked the place over again.

A bloodsucker had killed the guy. It was pretty evident. There was a dried bloodstain on his shirt collar and these bite marks all along the base of his neck. Granted, it might have been mice or insects burrowing through his carcass, but it reeked of vamps.

I was sprinkling the last of the holy water from the hospital over the mound and banging a makeshift cross in the ground when I heard Erik calling. Shit, I didn't even know the guy's name so I could write on the cross—all of two boards lashed together with some ropes. I said a little prayer and headed back to the house and barn where Erik was.

"Listen to this, kid." Erik got weird and quiet on me.

All I could hear was the breeze coming from the trees. The yard was full of weeds and dead leaves that blew around and swayed with the wind.

"There it is again."

I didn't know what the hell he was going on about. Standing there in the burnt-out barn foundation was giving me the damn creeps. Erik wasn't helping any either. Then, I heard it.

"What is that?" I asked.

It sounded like wind, blowing through a tunnel. The only real thing left of the barn were the rotting walls sort of leaning in on themselves and a few empty stalls with old hay and the floor. Erik pulled a can of soda out of his pocket and poured it over the floor. The soda just leaked through the cracks. We heard it dripping. It sounded like it was a long way down.

"It's hollow. Looks like we found our hiding spot." Erik bent down and was about to try and lift up the boards when I pushed him to the side. He was in such an odd position, he damn near fell over.

"Should we do this? I mean, all we know about is the house. We never heard a thing about any underground tunnels. How do we know they ain't down there?"

Erik scoffed at me like he was disappointed and righted himself. "It's light up here, Elvis. If anything is down there, it's not coming out."

"Maybe light up here, but I bet it's dark as sin down there."

"You know, Elvis, you haven't been the same since Maine."

Now that stung me real hard. Erik was supposed to be my guardian, like a foster parent or something. We were a team, and he didn't need to be saying any of that shit to me. I swiped at my eyes and could tell almost instantly that Erik was sorry for saying it.

"Look, kid… "

"No, it's all right. But you know something, Erik? You ain't been the same either." I reached down and pried up one of the boards. It wasn't nailed or anything and came up pretty easily. I got up the next three until the hole was big enough for us to climb down.

Man, I couldn't see shit down there, like all the light had been swallowed up. I watched as some dust caught in the wind got sucked down the hole. One thing was pretty evident though, the boards looked fairly new—new as in after the fire that took the barn. I don't know if Erik had caught that or not. He was always in such a God awful rush that he sometimes missed the little things that could help keep us alive another day.

"I'm going to hit the truck and grab the packs," I called over my shoulder. I ran back thinking all the time that he wasn't going to wait. Inside the RV, I got my pack, checked the rounds in my new gun—another .38 like the one I used to have—and stuffed it under my belt.

I grabbed Erik's pack after checking the batteries in the flashlights and ran back. It was just like I thought. Erik was already down the damn hole. When I flashed the light down there, I saw it was an earthen tunnel with mud walls. Erik was about twenty feet down and looking a little shocked—like he wasn't expecting it to be so deep.

"How the hell do you expect me to get you out of there?"

"You're not. There's a breeze, a strong one. That means another entrance someplace."

I tossed down the packs and was trying to figure out a way down when something grabbed my shirt and pants and threw me in. I landed hard on Erik and we crashed down to the ground. Then, whoever it was that did the throwing, started putting the boards back over the hole.

"Don't do it, you fucker!" I screamed and screamed until the last board was in place.

Then something started raining down on us.

"Holy shit, Erik, it's gasoline! Fucking move it! *NOW!*" I took off down the tunnel, not waiting for Erik or the flashlight.

The fumes were making me dizzy and my clothes were pretty much soaked through. Whoever was up there must have known somehow what we were doing there. The tunnel lit up from behind, and I heard Erik running towards me. The flashlight beam scooted all over the place. He actually ran right past me, slowed for a second, and then kept going. The ground sloped, and from experience I could hear the hiss of what sounded like a road flare being lit up.

The corridor exploded in orange light and there was a roar coming after us. It was the fireball from the gasoline. I started running again. No matter how much my legs and arms and chest burned, I kept running, slipped, and got up on the roll. The tunnel finally leveled out and emptied into a room. We were covered in gas and mud, and the fire was blocking the back way out.

Erik froze. We had found a bloodsucker haven.

It wasn't anything like I had expected or seen in the movies or heard Erik talking about—and man, he went on about them constantly. The only ones I had seen were in the train station in Maine, which wasn't anything more than a few rooms, the cells, and the tunnels that lead into that old library. The place in Georgia was a shithole of a house and so was Katherine's place back home.

But this place was fucked. The tunnel just stopped. Then I remembered the fireball. I dove into Erik—tackled him around the waist—and brought him down hard. I waited for the blanket of fiery death that never came. The gas must have burned itself out in the hallway. I helped up Erik, who was pissed, and finished looking around.

The breeze we felt was coming from an open doorway opposite us. There were a few chairs, nothing fancy or special, a radio, and the floor, which had battery wrappers and boxes all over it. I half expected that goddamn pink rabbit with the drum to pop put and start banging away. The walls and ceiling were just bricks and stones cemented into place and there were a few boards scattered on the walls. I could smell the smoke coming down the passage behind us. It was probably them boards that fell through the hole.

"Erik, this was a set up."

Erik pulled out that tape recorder of his and started talking. I saw him reach down, pluck some batteries from the floor, and replace them in the tape recorder. The only thing I caught him saying was, "and Elvis thinks we were set up."

There was a big carpet strewn across the center of the room. I flipped the chairs off it and pulled up the rug. It was an old trick—put some shit near the edge of a rug, and when you walk on it, you fall into a pit full of stakes or knives or what have you. But under the rug, was a shallow hole maybe three feet deep. In it were four coffins.

Erik damn near pissed himself and turned off the recorder. I reached into my pack and pulled out a stake and a hammer. I felt like Peter Cushing poised over Dracula's grave. Erik took out his pistol and a cross. I held up three fingers and then closed each one. On the last one, I opened the coffin, but it was empty. The smell of death just gushed out from the inside. The others were empty too.

"Shit, Erik, we must have just missed them. Look at this place." I hopped out of the hole and started walking around. "They didn't have any time to clean up, and think about it, all the vamps we've seen—everything was spotless, like a damned museum. These bastards bugged out of here last night."

I looked around some more while Erik scribbled down notes. There were a few wires and stuff coming in from the outside. One led to a phone and the other to a small television inside one of the coffins. I guessed some bloodsuckers liked watching television before they slept. That was new and Erik was all over it.

Then I went over to the walls. Every time I passed one of the boards it had a stink about it, one I had become all too familiar with. After I knocked on it and the thing sounded hollow, I signaled to Erik again. He seemed annoyed at having to stop taking notes. I got out my pistol and fired two shots right through the first board. It fell towards me, breaking into a few pieces. Behind it was a small compartment dug into the wall with a body stuffed into it.

It was a fresh kill too. I saw the look of horror on the poor lady's face. I could only guess she'd lived on the farm on account of how she was dressed. But her skin was all wrinkled and dried up—like she had been fast drained, like the veins and arteries were all sucked dry instantly. She fell out of the niche in the wall and I jumped back.

It was the same in back of the others too. They had been killed at different times. Some bodies were real old. The skin had started to decay and pull back from their bones. That's when we noticed the room had been filling up with smoke. Sometimes it didn't take much to get us off track, but this was different. I headed out of the passage. It went on for some time until it finally dumped us out in back of the house.

Way off in the distance, I could see a trail of dust from a car speeding off down the road. A car had not only been following us, but knew about us and what we did. They'd lured us into this place. Shit, that freaked me out more than the damn bodies. We had been so damn careful, except in Maine and

Georgia, but the sponsor guys were supposed to clean up the messes.

I ran to the RV to check it out. Sure as shit the doors were all open. Someone had been rummaging around inside, though nothing seemed to be missing. What I did find confused the ever-loving shit out of me. It was a Polaroid picture, but it was still developing. The picture slowly formed into the inside of the truck.

Erik finally came running up, choking and wheezing. The damn fool had spent too much time down there and had inhaled a lot of smoke. Erik staggered into the RV, got a portable oxygen tank, and covered his face with a little mask, all the while taking notes—one of the joys of being loaded

I checked out the rest of the truck. The roof was clear, as were the tires and the driver's compartment. I looked under the hood. Daddy had taught me a few things, being under the pickup for so long, but I still didn't know half the shit I was staring at. It all looked okay though. Nothing out of the ordinary—as far as I could tell. Even the underside seemed normal enough.

What was left of the barn was burning. The wind had picked up, blowing the fire to the house and back into the fields. Soon enough if we didn't get the hell out of Dodge, the entire farm would be going up. Erik, as if sensing this, started the engine. I ran around, closed up all the doors, and locked everything down. I slung in packs into the back and hopped in the front seat.

"I saw a car bombing out of here a few minutes ago while you were on the O_2," I said, pointing toward the road.

Erik nodded and took off in pursuit. There'd be no catching up now. It was too late. With any luck, they would roll off the road and end up in fiery wreck someplace close, making it easy for us. But nothing was easy for us. All the way back to the main road, I debated about telling Erik about the photo, but didn't.

From South Carolina we went to Rhode Island, and then to Maryland. Seemed those bastards had us running all over the goddamned place. It didn't matter. It kept Erik happy and preoccupied, and he let me mope and do my own thing. I had taken to reading a lot. Whenever we stopped, I'd get a magazine or some books or whatever. It occurred to me that I hadn't been to school in a damn long time. I almost sort of missed it.

But whenever I got to thinking about school, I'd think of Jimmy Riley, and that would lead to the trailer park and Momma and Daddy. Lord, how I missed them. No matter how bad things were back at the trailer or how drunk Daddy got, Momma could always cheer me up with a song or a joke or make me some cookies. Or to blow off steam, I could go get beat up by Jimmy.

Once I lied to Erik, trying to make him head home. Told him I took a call from the sponsors while he as in the shitter, but the fucker kept his cell phone on him always—even slept with it near his head.

This time, we stopped at a truck stop—a huge parking lot, jammed full of tractor-trailers and cabs and a few cars—even saw a few motorcycles scattered throughout the mammoth trucks. We had the only RV there. Out in front was a small gas station. It was something Daddy called a "choke and puke," meaning if you could choke down the food, you would most likely puke it out later on. A *greasy spoon* was Momma's way of describing them.

I just called it a diner. Didn't want to add any mystery—a damn diner with booths, some stools, a jukebox that only played country tunes, a cloud of cigarette smoke, and B.O. hanging over the place. It was nothing special, full of bikers and truckers who expected nothing more than hot food and cold beer. A few ceiling fans whirled lazily, creating breathable pockets in the smoky haze. It was one giant room. In back of the booths, some boys played pool on a couple stained, faded tables while a biker felt up his woman as she played a pinball machine. The jukebox wailed away with some whiny country tune about a farm burning down. Our waitress's name was Billie Sue. Felt like home to me, but Erik was nervous as shit.

I ordered home fries, steak and eggs, and a pile of grits, which wasn't easy to find in Maryland. Erik just had pancakes with butter and a glass of ice water. We barely talked through breakfast. I kept pumping quarters into the box and every now and again Billie Sue would walk past and smile at me like I was playing her favorite songs.

Erik paid up for the meal and left a shitty tip. I dumped a few more bucks on top. I slipped Billie Sue a note with Erik's cell phone number on it. She blushed, smiled real nice, pinched my cheek, and gave me a kiss. We fueled up the truck and were getting ready to leave when I saw a car that looked familiar.

I stretched across the driver's seat and stomped on the brake. The RV coughed and stalled out. I pointed out of the window towards the car. The driver was a man, maybe thirty, with greasy brown hair pulled back into a ratty-looking tail. He was wearing these dark, dark glasses and had pale skin. Most of the windows were shaded so no one could see in, but the fucker left his window down. The car itself was a shit bucket, an old Plymouth Fury, almost all rust.

"What is it, Elvis?"

"That's the car from the farm in South Carolina. He's the fucker who dumped us in the hole."

The guy knew he had messed up, 'cause he rolled the window shut and peeled out of that rest stop leaving a trail of rubber so long the condom companies would have squealed. Erik started up the RV and was about to chase them when I saw the hose still stuck in the tank. I reached over, tore the keys from the ignition, and dove out after fiddling with the door. I got the hose out. Erik started up the truck again, and we were off—in back of two or three cruisers full of pissed-off pigs who got woken from their naps—but we were going.

That old boy was moving so fast that God himself wouldn't have caught him. And we, in the RV, certainly weren't going to. I told Erik about the picture and showed it to him. He pulled over to the shoulder to look at it some more. When I checked out the side mirror, I could see a few more trailers and cars pulled over—like we were leading a parade. Erik stuffed the photo into the glove box and pulled back onto the highway. I still looked through the mirror. After a ways down the highway, all of them other vehicles started up again after us. I suppose I shouldn't have thought anything about it. Still something nagged at me that it just wasn't right. Erik told me I was being paranoid, but shit, it was like being followed.

I left the cockpit and went into the back of the RV where there was a couch that folded out to a bed. I sat on that and watched out the window. Every time we switched lanes, so did the parade of cars. Each time we slowed or pulled off for gas, they mimicked. I never once did spy the cops with the ugly jerk-off who dumped us in that hole.

I fell asleep, leaning on the couch and looking out the back window. I woke up to the flash of cameras and the *pop* of bulbs.

Wearing overalls, work boots, and a Kurt Cobain shirt, there was some guy out on the back of the truck taking some pictures of me. When he saw me stirring, he all but fell over himself getting back to his car and taking off.

Erik had pulled over at a gas station again. Seemed like he always had to piss. The engine was off and he had the keys. There was a map spread out across the other seat, and Erik had drawn a circle around Boston. I guessed we were going there next—to the land of beans and chowder. Erik had left his coat slung over the seat, and his phone rang. Instinctively. I pulled it out and answered.

"Hello?" I could hear some breathing. Guess whoever it was didn't expect me to pick up. I couldn't believe Erik had forgotten the damn thing. But with a pisser in the camper, why in the hell did he even stop to begin with?

"Is this Elvis?"

I didn't recognize the deep and raspy voice at all. "Yeah, who's this?"

"You can call me..." There was a pause. "You can call me Bill."

"Well, Bill, you can call me Elvis and you're a lying sack of shit." I hung up the phone, stuffed it back in Erik's pocket as he came out of the truck stop.

He was carrying a bag of food, nothing special—just burgers and sodas from the fast food place inside. I ran to the back and flopped on the bed, trying to make it look like I was all innocent and such. Erik plunked the bag down on the table and, first thing, went for the phone. He pressed some buttons, looked over at me, and sat down for grub.

"So you going to tell me who called?" he asked, chewing around a hunk of burger.

"Some guy." I walked over and sat next to him, sliding in back of the table so I could look out the side window. I opened the bag, scraped all the shit off the burger, and started in.

"Did he have a name?"

"Bill." I took a long drink of soda.

It was diet and tasted like shit.

"Why do I think you're lying?"

I choked on the burger and spit it up on the table. "Me? We've been doing this vampire thing for months now and you ain't told me shit! We drive around town to town, and I go in point while you take notes."

"You want out? I can arrange it easy enough."

"I'm not out until every last damn bloodsucker is dead. I got to avenge Momma and Daddy. It was my fault they got killed, and now I have to exact my own revenge on them."

"Elvis, I've been truthful in everything I've told you."

"You haven't told me shit." I could see the anger rising in his eyes.

He put the burger down, carefully wiped his mouth, and went for the door.

"Where you going?"

"For a walk," he said. "I need to get some air."

The sun set in golds and reds, filling up the night sky. I ate my food and wrapped up Erik's. It was going to be cold when he came back—if he came back. He had the keys to the RV so I was sort of stranded. I turned on all of the trailer's lights. I didn't care what it did to the battery. Besides, we were still in the frigging rest area. If the battery died, I'd get some cash from Erik's "secret spot" and buy a new one.

An hour later, his food had congealed into a greasy brick. Two more hours, the sun was gone. So was my patience, appetite, and Erik's dinner. I was bored and started to feel unappreciated, which pissed me off, so I decided it was time to go exploring. Only problem with that is that every time I'd be near a window or near the door, I could hear whispering voices or see shadows moving around the RV.

I checked my pistol and brought along extra rounds just in case. I wasn't expecting any bloodsucker trouble, but you always have to be prepared. I jury-rigged my pack as a makeshift alarm and got it to the door. If anyone came inside, I'd hear it no matter where I was in the rest area. Then I climbed out the hatch on the roof.

The rest stop was full. Big rigs stopped for the night or a hot cup of coffee for the road. The night sky was breathtaking, thousands of little shimmering, sparkling eyes looking down on me. I lay down for a while on the roof and listened to the whispers and footsteps. Couldn't make out any words, but heard the voices—there were a bunch of them.

When I peered over the edge, I saw women and men milling around, doing a piss poor job of trying to look inconspicuous. One was smoking and all but staring into the RV's windows. Thankfully, I closed the blinds and curtains. Some lady kept walking around the front, looking through the windshield. I didn't know why we were being spied on. The questions were why and by whom. I knew right off that it wasn't a bloodsucker. If it was, they could have taken us any damn time they wanted.

I waited until the coast was semi-clear. There was a small ladder going down the back. I slid down it, hopped off, and rolled under the RV. I could see the lights in the parking lot, blotted out by the occasional wheels of passing trucks. I smelled the food cooking in the restaurant and the gas spilled on the pavement. I counted six sets of feet—could have been more, a lot more, but that's all I saw.

I slithered out and then crawled under an eighteen-wheeler, sneaking under the length of it till I hit the cab. Then I made a break for it, weaving through parked cars, RVs, and trucks. There was a safe spot on a white van, and I plunked down on the bumper. The windows were fogged over a bit, and I hoped that I didn't just interrupt some couple in mid-thrust.

In back of Erik's camper was a whole line of vehicles, cars, vans and some other RVs. I guessed they were the ones following us. I did a quick inventory, checking for the car from the farm, but I didn't see it. That fucker was long gone. There must have been close to ten trucks in back of us. The last couple didn't have any lights on or people around them so I figured what the hell, I might as well go and check them out—see what I could see and all that happy horseshit.

Creeping along in back of the trucks kind of made me feel a little like James Bond. The first RV I tried was locked up tighter than a ten-year-old. One of the cab doors may have been open, but I didn't want to risk the noise in trying it that way. The next one was unlocked. I slinked in real quiet-like and eased the door shut, but I didn't close it all the way, leaving it cracked in case I needed to make a fast exit.

Couldn't risk the flashlight so I had to rely on the moon and whatever light came in from the parking lot. It was pretty much the same setup as ours—except there was a laptop on the table, papers and books scattered all over the place and jammed into every free spot available. It looked more like an office than a recreational vehicle.

There were some flyers and photos on the table. I grabbed them and stuffed them into my pack. I also saw one of them little tape recorders like Erik had and grabbed it. Finally the place was awash in maps, with lines drawn on them, so I grabbed a couple of those too. I was reaching for the door when I heard a match spark and saw the glow from a cigarette right outside the windshield.

There are times when adrenaline is a bad thing. I felt like a deer caught in headlights. Either stand there and risk being caught staring or make a break for it and risk being run down. The cigarette hovered outside the window, held by a shadowy hand. The hand tapped it, and glowing bits of ash fell off, fading and blending into the night. A hushed whisper called the hand away, and it was my time.

The door opened slowly without a squeak. It felt like I was looking down at my body from overhead. I could hear the whispers, only louder, like they weren't trying so hard to hide back here. I ignored the words and snuck around back. Then someone went inside. I heard the shocks creak and the door close. Someone started to piss and I walked away—to the last trailer.

It seemed cold—even from the outside—and just a little bit darker inside than the others did. The lights in the lot weren't on around this RV. It looked deliberate. Chunks of shattered glass and plastic littered the lot—like someone had shot the bulbs out. My fingertips brushed the wall. It sent chills all through me. I could feel my skin turning to goose bumps, as if a million little spiders were crawling all over me.

The doorknob turned easily. It was cold. It was one of those times when I should have listened to my insides and turned tail and run back for the trailer, but didn't. I took the steps cautiously, stepping heel to toe so I wouldn't make any noise. There was no light inside, not even from the outside. It was pitch dark. Someone had colored the place black. I risked turning on the flashlight. It was small, but it cut the darkness enough so I could see the hideously scarred and burnt face of that lady vamp from Georgia, staring through the darkness at me.

As she smiled, her scars got all wrinkled and pushed up. They covered the right side of her face, and she made no attempt to cover them. I never realized before how beautiful she was—before the accident anyway. Her teeth grew into wicked points as I watched, and her eyes took on this deep crimson glow that illuminated the inside of the camper. When the claws pushed through the tips of her fingers, tearing her flesh and nails, my bladder emptied. She laughed. I felt the tug of her mind on mine, trying to pull that bloodsucker magic on me. All I could do was stare at the scars.

"Fire doesn't heal quickly." Her voice was seductive.

"I'm sorry?" My voice quavered.

"You killed my daughter."

"It was an accident."

"I'm going to kill you but not yet."

"I'm really pleased about that ma'am." I started backing towards the door.

She matched each step I took.

I tried extending my hand. "My name is Elvis. Why are you following me?"

"Names are not important, and I have to make sure you find your way to the door."

I tripped down the first stair and heard my gun *clatter* to the floor. Her smile widened, and the fire in her eyes began to fade, making it seem like a blood red sunset. I slowly picked up the gun and leveled it at her chest. She watched me, all the while smiling.

"I could shoot you."

"And I could tear your head off."

"I could shoot you and start screaming to high hell."

"And I could make you a vampire, turn you into a slave, and torture you for eternity."

Now that threw me for a damn loop. Me, a bloodsucker? I couldn't help but laugh. Though if I did get turned, it might make this hunting stuff a lot easier, and it sure would piss Erik off to no end. He would finally have to listen to me.

She took another step towards me. I watched her short, brown hair move ever so slightly—what was left of it. I pressed the barrel of the gun to the center of her head. She took my hands, wrapping her fingers around mine. I felt the dead cold of her flesh as it crept into mine. My hand started shaking. Her grip tightened and my little finger broke with a loud *snap*. When I tried to scream, she clamped a hand over my mouth, and I could taste the cold dead flesh.

My ring finger snapped next. The first shot went high, punched through the roof of the trailer, and let in a slight breeze. Pressure grew on my middle finger. I kicked her. The finger broke and she grinned. Outside the windshield, I saw the floating cigarette ash go crashing to the ground.

The second shot blew out the back of her head and coated the back wall in dead brains and dried blood. I got hit by the spray and felt chunks on my face. Her body fell to the floor, smiling all the way down, like she'd wanted me to do this—to see if I could actually shoot someone or not, see if I was up to the task at hand.

The doorknob turned. I heard a round get chambered and knew it was time to haul ass out of there. Jumping over the lady vamp, I shot out the back window and dove through. I bounced off the grill of a truck and hit the parking lot hard. As I rolled, I heard swearing, some screaming and then the lights went on. I started running with two of three broken fingers jammed into the finger guard of my .38.

When the footsteps and shouting finally stopped, I made a bee line for the damn restaurant. Erik was nowhere in sight either. There was no safety in the lot. At least inside there were lights, people, faces, and maybe a payphone or a state cop stopped in for a coffee.

I tried not thinking about the lady vamp I had just aced in the trailer but couldn't help it. Erik had told me, promised me that they both died in the fire, that we wouldn't have a pissed-off bitch vampire hunting us. Turning the tables on us so to speak. I mean, was he lying to me or did he really not know?

I ran in, hearing the *whoosh* of the air conditioners and got slapped in the face by the instant cold. People stared at me. After spying the sign for the shitter, I headed straight for it. I locked the door, got myself in a stall, and barely got my fly down before pissing again. The shakes took me so bad I couldn't do anything except spray the walls and toilet. When the gun finally slipped off my twisted fingers, I screamed.

I could hear people talking near the door, knocking on it, all pensive and such, trying to be concerned but not doing a good job.

"You okay in there?"

"Need some help?"

Stuffing the gun into my pack, I rooted around until I found some tape. With the straightening of each finger came a new shriek of pain.

A key turned in the lock as I got the last finger taped up. Felt like I was going to black out a couple times in there. The door eased open slowly with someone politely knocking, I could only assume the manager. I grabbed a wad of paper, wiped the tears and blood from my face, flushed the hopper, and got poised to bolt.

The fucker went stall by stall, opening each one in turn. People talked nervously from the doorway about the screaming, the smell, and the gun. The stall door next to mine slammed open and I ran. It was like the parting of the Red Sea—every damn person moved to let me through.

I took off from the stall and hit the restaurant, running hard with eyes all over me. I thought a couple times about firing a shot in the air to clear shit out, but I think there was enough attention focused on me already. There was no way out of this one. I was stuck dead. Erik was off somewhere stroking himself. I had just plugged a vamp, and a whole row of trailers following us knew I was on to them now. It was like a mob scene in the parking lot. People clustered all around the trailer where the lady vamp was.

Someone saw me running and screamed, "Stop Him! There he is!"

Wasn't a damn thing that could stop my legs from pumping. I ran so hard, fast, and blind that I knocked Erik over when I collided with him. I was too damn busy looking over my shoulder for the bastards following me. We met eyes for just a second, and I saw all the craziness and weirdness inside his head fade as reality set in.

He grabbed my arm and we ran for the RV. We had a good clip, too. Erik was in the door first and, man, I didn't even see him jump to the driver's seat. He started up the engine with a roar, revved it a few times, and put the bitch in gear. We squealed on out of there, leaving a rubber trail that Mario Andretti would have been hard over.

Erik hit the highway so fast we must have been doing an easy 30 MPH. Yes, that was sarcasm. They may be fun to drive and camp in, but them RV bastards got the pick up of shit. We were a good twenty miles down the road before Erik finally decided to slow down—by then he'd reached the speed limit. I was perched in the back, looking out the window, making sure we weren't being followed, and as far as I could tell, we weren't. I expected to see that long line of vans and campers in pursuit.

Wasn't nothing there though. I went up to the front and took the seat beside Erik.

"You want to tell me what that was all about?" Erik asked, setting the cruise control.

"You remember that house back in Georgia? Our first job with you, me, Frank, and those other three assholes?"

"Yeah."

"Well, one of them lady vamps survived. But she was pissed off and all scarred and burnt up and stuff." I showed Erik my fingers. I had forgotten how much they hurt until that moment. I ran to the back, got some ice out of the mini-fridge, and put them in a bag for my hand.

"You found the other vampire? Tell me all about it."

I spent the next half-hour or so explaining every different way I could.

With each answer, Erik would counter with a new question. "Why didn't you stay in the trailer?" "What happened after you shot her?" "Did she get up after you shot her?" "Did she look sane?" It just went on and on, until finally he just shut up and started thinking. He took out his tape recorder and talked into it.

I went to the back of the trailer again, this time reloading my pistol. I kept thinking and asking myself if I had used my special bullets back there? Had I made a fresh load of them? Would that lady vampire be coming back?

I checked the rounds already in the pistol, three normal rounds and three special. Question was, which ones did I just load? I stuffed the gun under my belt and commenced to peer out the window some more.

"Elvis?"

I turned around to look at Erik. He was staring at me through the rearview. "What is that smell?

I ran to the bathroom and stripped down, jammed the piss-stinking clothes into a trash-bag, washed up, and changed into something clean. Then I remembered the backpack and the stuff I had picked up in that other camper. I dumped it out on the table and sorted through it all, separating my stuff from what I took. I got the map and those pieces of paper and read them. I actually felt all the blood drain from my face and frantically opened the map and started following a line drawn on it. Erik must have sensed something was wrong, 'cause he pulled the truck over and killed the motor.

"There a problem, Elvis?"

"Yeah, man, big fucking problem."

The map had a line drawn on it to each spot we had gone, from Georgia to Carolina and even had the new destination circled, Boston. Erik, however, found this terribly curious. I showed him the papers. There were newsletters, underground newspapers with stories and accounts of what we had done, where we had been, and a running tally of the bloodsuckers we had encountered. Thing is, it was way out of whack. No way in hell had we been on contact with the number they said.

The papers also had some out of focus, badly-copied black and white photos of the different sites we had been at. In a couple of them, I made out our faces. On the very back was a website address to get up-to-the-minute updates on our travels, how to get on the email mailing list, and even how to contact us. A couple more of them newsletters had theories about bloodsuckers, and even some advice on what to do should you ever encounter one. In addition to that, there was information on places and clubs you could go to in bigger cities to get in on the underground movement for the rights and preservation of vampire culture and society.

It had gone way beyond the Goths and people pretending to drink blood. Now, the undead had their own society like Green Peace to protect them. That would explain the lady vamp back at the truck stop. Actually, there must have been two groups of the underground because some of the other newsletters were set up differently and were actually praising me and

Erik for what we had done. But where the hell was the info leak coming from? Sure wasn't me. I knew it wasn't Erik, least I hoped it wasn't, which only meant that both the van was bugged and we'd been followed since the beginning—*or* someone on the inside of the sponsors was spreading this stuff—giving us fame when we sure as shit didn't need any. No use in trying to be discreet, not that we'd been that, but there was no use for secrecy when your faces and names are plastered all over the damn place.

We got to Boston about sunrise. Erik pulled some of those strings he'd become famous for and got us in at the Sheraton—in a suite with adjoining rooms. I didn't know why all of a sudden he needed privacy and his own place, but after spending all that time in the RV, it was welcome. I was asleep before my head hit the pillows and barely got my shoes off. It was safe to sleep during the day 'cause the bloodsuckers didn't come out then. Erik had made damn sure to hang the *do not disturb* signs on the doors.

Excuse the saying, but I slept like the dead. The doors were all locked when I woke up, and Erik was nowhere to be found. There was a note telling me to order up some room service. He'd be back later on. He had some business to attend to, as did I. Digging out Erik's laptop, I plugged into the Internet from the access jack in the suite. I spread out the newsletters on the bed and closed and locked the door so if Erik came back, he wouldn't see me.

There were some sites' addresses written in real tiny print on the back of the newsletters. While waiting for the first page to load, I called up room service and got me some lunch. The graphics were simple, some nice fonts and a plain background, I entered *www.bloodsuckersnow.com.* It asked me for a password and user ID, and after entering a bunch of different words from the newsletter, it let me in. The shit was simple—a request to be put on an email list or a hard copy mailing list. There was the latest in articles and news about how to kill vamps and new theories about them. Told us that new types of the critters were popping up all over the country and no one could understand why. Seemed like all this stuff could have been in like a *Guns and Ammo*-type magazine. There were links to other pages around the web, but I had to be pretty quick so the charge in the hotel bill wouldn't be too big—make it look like it was just Erik online doing his thing. He'd flip if he knew I was digging behind his back like this.

Then of all the strangest stuff, there was an icon—a small-digitized picture of my face. I clicked on it and went into a new area. It had all of Erik's travels and mine and a map of where we had been and how we were in Boston now. It had details of all the other missions, but nothing came up under Boston. They knew who and where we were.

I don't think they knew we got shacked up in the Sheraton though so we still had a little edge over it all. The other website *www.kill-them-all.net* looked like it had been put up by a bunch of vampire-fearing KKK neo-Nazis. Nothing at all to do about us, except a note telling about the good we were bringing back to the world of the living. I never knew there were so many people who believed in this stuff and I'd bet everything I owned not one of them bastards had ever seen a real bloodsucker face up before either.

The last page was *www.save-the-blood.com*. Looked like one of those *save the rainforest* places. Went into great detail about the habitats of certain types of vamps—what they liked, how they lived, ate, and slept. From what I read, it sounded like the "mist men" me and Erik found out about in Maine—the kind that only lived off animals and only fed off people in desperation—the ones who wanted to preserve the secret get left alone and survive.

That was the most interesting of the three sites. There was more information there than I knew about, and hanging around with Erik, I considered myself to be pretty hip on the subject of vampires. Nonetheless, there was shit there I'd never even dreamt of. I made a subdirectory on the hard drive and downloaded all the info to it in simple text files—then renamed them so if Erik got curious, he'd pass them on by. I logged off, unplugged and got the laptop wrapped up and put back into Erik's bags as he came back in. He asked me what I was doing, and I said looking for money for a tip for the room service guy when he showed up.

Erik had dumped the camper and picked up a gray conversion van in its wake. Inside the van were leather seats that folded out into small beds. There was a surround sound system, a small television, and a VCR/DVD too. It didn't have a fridge or an oven, so we'd be getting an ice chest and eating sandwiches for a few days no doubt.

The club, our destination, was down a dark side street, lined on either side with apartments, the kind they stuff three or four college students into. After all, Boston was a college town—four big ones that I know of. At the end of the main drag where we turned off, there were Irish pubs, coffee bars, and more rock clubs. Nothing at all like what we were in for though.

The street was jammed with cars on both sides. We were in the middle of one of them four-way crossroads type of things. There was a parking deck somewhere, but you could only take left-hand turns to get there—if you could find them. We pulled into the deck, took a ticket, and got ready to go.

"The rest of the team is meeting us here, right?"

Erik busied himself with ignoring me and gathering up what he needed.

"We're meeting them outside the club, right? The rest of our team?"

Erik closed and locked up the van and pressed the alarm. The lights flashed and horn went off twice. "There is no rest of the team, Elvis. We had to move too soon. We're it. No others."

"But this is a live site, right?"

He nodded and checked the film in his camera, making sure it was all loaded.

"We're going to get slaughtered, just the two of us."

"We'll be fine. It's a popular, crowded bar, Elvis. Nothing is going to happen in public. They don't want any undue attention brought on themselves."

"It's a Goth bar full of freaks and would-be vampires, Erik. No one in there is going to give a shit what happens to us. To them, we're just part of the stage show. We could get captured, have the whammy laid on us, get sucked dry, and get applauded for it."

"Just be cool, Elvis. Everything is under control."

I took a deep breath of the cool night air—felt eyes and headlights on us. Took a peek over my shoulder every few seconds, just to be sure. If nothing else, hunting vampires makes you pretty damn paranoid, especially when there's one after you.

"What's your plan then, Erik?"

"Wait in line, go up to the bouncer, slip him a fifty, and get in."

"Man, your head is full of shit if you think that numb-nuts plan is going to work."

There was a line of leather, rubber, and vinyl-clad people waiting to get inside. Died hair, painted faces, thigh high fuck-me boots, and leather hoods greeted our passing glances. The brick wall in front had been painted black, and a huge red neon, back-lit sign with the words *Electric Raven* hung above the door. Three Guido-looking guys dressed in black checked IDs and let people in after stamping their hands with something.

I led Erik back to the parking deck and sat on the curb. We needed a plan—any damn plan. Erik paced up and down the sidewalk, looking at the sky, his watch, then the nightlife. I drummed my fingers and tried to think. He started rambling some shit about posing as caterers, making a delivery, and forcing our way in. Problem was, no truck and nothing to deliver.

"Give me the keys to the van, Erik. I have a plan."

We stood in line outside the club, getting all sorts of fucked-up looks from the tattooed, pierced freaks waiting to get in and heard talking in back of us, even a few giggles.

"I can let you into the club, mister. I shouldn't, but I will. But not the kid." The guy was maybe 24 or so, short dark hair in a Mohawk with tattoos on both sides of his head. He had sparkly teeth, spider web tattoos going the length of both arms, combat boots, ripped shorts, and fishnet stockings. Dude had more silver and chrome on him than the van did.

"Please, mister," I said, putting on my best frown and blinking tears into my eyes. "We're looking for my sister, Amanda. She ran away like four months ago." I wiped my eyes and nose on my sleeve, sniffled a few times for good effect, then handed the guy an instant photo from my pack. "That's from when we saw her last."

He took the picture and looked at it real close. Recognition came to his eyes. He passed it to the other bouncers and they whispered hurriedly.

"She's a regular here."

Some voices in the line started to rise and the others went over to calm them. The lead guy talked into a hand held radio and then listened to the static filled response. "Go on in."

Beyond the doorway was a hallway of mirrors, floor to ceiling, with spider web paint on it. Behind some of the panels of one-way mirrors, lights flashed, and shadowy figures danced to music that sounded like a whisper. Red laser lights criss-crossed our path, reflecting off the mirrors.

From the end of the corridor, strobe lights blinked furiously, and we felt the pounding music before actually hearing it. The mirrors stopped at a steel cage hanging six inches from the floor. Inside it was a white-faced woman with exaggerated lips. She was dressed in rubber and collecting the cover charge. She nodded and let us through.

Trying to make our little show convincing, we passed around the photo of "Amanda." She was a regular. Everyone in the place seemed to know her, but no one had seen her yet. The place was packed full of bodies, swaying, dancing, and sweating to the music. It totally reeked of sweat and cigarette smoke. Ceiling fans fought bravely to keep the air circulating, but were in the process of losing.

Forcing his way though the crowds, Erik was quiet, not asking any questions. I could tell he was curious by his darting eyes. Walking through the club, we saw a lot of pale skinned, crushed velvet, fake-fang-wearing vampire wannabe's, but thankfully none of the real thing. Some of the dancers looked strangely at Erik and me like they knew us. They went quickly back to their trade with an excitement barely hidden in their eyes.

We wandered around for the better part of an hour trying to get a grip on things, and man, that music was starting to hurt my head. I thought we'd found a dead-end. Erik must have had similar thoughts too, when all of a sudden this girl came running out of the dancers and grabbed me.

"It's you!" she squealed "I mean, it's really *you*." She had a shaved head, chain mail bikini top, and clear plastic skirt revealing black lace panties and a great set of legs. She got hold of my hand and started leading me through the club, pushing past the dancers and anyone else getting in the way.

I grabbed Erik by the shirt so the damn fool wouldn't get left behind—not to mention the fact that I didn't want to be alone in this place.

She led us in back of the bar into a small storage room full of cases of beer, crates of liquor bottles, and barrels full of empties. Then we tripped down a small flight of wooden stairs, through a dimly lit corridor that was damp and reeked of mildew. I thought I heard the squeaking of rats but didn't see any of them scurrying around. Erik was in a daze—just following blindly. I still had a fistful of his shirt.

The hallway stopped at a room filled with grayish light, two or three chairs, a card table covered with fried chicken takeout boxes, a copying machine, computer desk with computer, and computer geek typing away at it. Off in the far corner was a bare mattress and a few lumps that resembled pillows. The computer guy stank. His greasy brown hair was pulled back into a loose tail. He wore stained pants, a shirt that was once white before accumulating dried sweat circles, black glasses with thick lenses, and a scraggly beard with fried chicken batter in it.

"Holy fuck!" he yelled out. "They're here."

Erik and me were ushered into the good chairs, and he took up a wooden folding chair across from us. His name was George, and Emily the skinhead girl, offered us fruit, wine, and soda. George got up, started circling around us waving his arms, creating this ill wind blowing out from his armpits.

"Jesus, man, it's like meeting a movie star or something, like catching the winning home run at the World Series, like finding a winning lottery ticket. Man, I want to be like you two."

"Cut the horseshit, George. What's this all about?"

My question froze him in his tracks. The computer screen was a web page that I recognized instantly. It looked like he was updating it or something. Scattered across the floor were newsletters and pamphlets, written and published in this room. To the side of the desk was a bundle, tied loosely with string, and looking like it was about to be mailed out. There were endless shelves of vampire books fiction and fact, and books on the occult and astrology. The walls, where there were free spots, were plastered with tabloid headlines.

Dracula's Tomb found on the moon. Space Vampires prepare to invade. Half Man, Half Bat terrorizes village.

"You're the real deal, Elvis. We're your fan club."

"You guys are the ones following us?"

George smiled, pushed up his glasses.

Emily plunked down on the floor in front of Erik and smiled. There was something similar in her brown eyes to Erik's.

"Yeah, man, we assigned someone to stick with you," George said.

"Who's leaking the information to you?"

"I can't tell you, man." George was flailing his arms like crazy. Thought for sure the dude's heart or brain was going to burst. Wasn't sure which one was going to blow first though. He was sweating so much, he left a trail of drops from his face while he paced. He had to keep pushing up his glasses 'cause they were sliding down from the sweat on his nose.

"You have to tell us, George," I repeated.

"All I can say, man, is that the leak isn't like malignant or anything."

On the floor, Emily inched up closer to Erik who was still strangely quiet. His eyes were darting all over the room, like he was looking for an exit—least I hoped he was anyway.

"Why us?"

Emily giggled at my question.

"Why?" George asked, stopping dead in his tracks. "Because, man, you are like a God or something."

I choked on my spit as the last of the moisture in my mouth went away. My eyes teared up. Emily blushed and Erik looked vacantly around.

"You," he said, grabbing my shoulders and shaking me, "have seen the dead—talked with it, ate with it, slept with it, fought and killed it."

Erik stood, stepped over Emily, who seemed to be making a bee line for his crotch, and started reading the articles taped and tacked to the walls.

"I wrote all those," George announced proudly. "Made up every damn word too. Got the pictures from the Internet and used a graphics program to edit them together. The half man-bat took me the longest."

I had to get up. This was way too much to deal with. I didn't know what this dude was trying to sell, but I had an idea.

"What about that wagon train following us?"

"That was an accident," George said, hanging his head and pushing up his glasses. "The newsletters got out early one month. Some of the subscribers found out about you and your mission."

"What the fuck do they want?"

"Same thing as you, man. A glimpse of the vampires. These people are fanatics. They live, sleep, eat, breathe, shit vampires. They go to Goth clubs, drink real blood, sometimes animal, sometimes not. They play with rats and snakes and sleep in coffins."

"I never wanted any of that!" I yelled out. "All I wanted was to kill them. I never wanted any fame or fans or anything. I just want them all dead. Real fucking dead!"

Now it was time for the rest of the room to go silent. Everyone, even me, was shocked by my outburst. I didn't give a shit though.

After I had quieted up the damn room, Erik came back over. "One of them, the ones in the caravan, was yours, right?"

George nodded, almost smiled. "We needed to keep tabs on you. Keep track of where you went. Make sure you were okay."

I reached into my pack, pulled out some of the pamphlets and tossed them at George.

"You weren't supposed to find out about us, Elvis. It was pure luck Emily saw you in the club. Pure luck you got the lead to come here. I still don't know how you got the clue for that. If she didn't see you, you would have never known."

"Let's blow this place, Erik."

He got up to leave and gave the place the once-over.

"You know," Emily added, breaking her silence. She kneaded her hands nervously, like she was trying to rub something off. "We were at all your sites except Georgia. And in Maine, we were there for just for a couple hours before getting called back."

"Yeah?" All I wanted to do was pull out my gun—put a bullet between her eyes and George's, make them think. Or at least threaten them for a while—make them sweat and cry and beg. They needed to realize that they didn't want *that* lifestyle. "Did you know that you had a fucking vampire in that RV caravan of yours? Did you know that? With all your computers and cameras and following us that you had one right under your nose?"

I thought for sure Emily was going to puke from the *mewling* emanating from her lips. She sounded like a hurt kitten.

A second later, I heard a small *hiss* as all the air left George's chest. He paled a little and licked his lips. "We didn't know. When we went to investigate the shooting, the truck was already gone—just some broken glass and a couple confused sons of bitches."

Even down here in the dank darkness of their little worlds, I felt the club. I couldn't hear the music, but the base *thump* was like a second heartbeat.

"Think about it…" Emily squeaked.

George spun on his heels like he knew what was coming, like he was going to snap, but instead dropped down into one of the chairs, all defeated.

"With all the false alarms, the empty sites, abandoned buildings, old rotted farms, everything, you've been on the trail of one group of vampires," she said. "Getting there each time just after they've left. Someone's playing you two like a record."

"No fucking way," I said, turning in my tracks.

Emily nodded sadly, forcing a smile. George sweated some more, while Erik continued doing not too much of anything.

"Think about it, Elvis," Erik said, speaking for what seemed like the first time since we entered the club. "Think about all the false alarms, all the cold sites, the steaming cups of tea, radios left on, smoldering ashes in fireplaces, and candle-wicks still smoking. Far as we know, they could have been there at the site watching us, depending on the vampire."

"For fuck's sake, Erik, why?"

Erik shrugged, almost on cue, Emily and George did too. It didn't make any damned sense. But in a way, I'd guess it did too. Erik started pacing around the room—like he was trying to put two and two together, find a logical conclusion to what was happening. It was funny in a way though. Here we were, the investigators, and our "followers" were the ones making the connections.

"Let's get out of here, Erik." I left him behind, headed towards the tunnel before he did. I shook George's hand, gave Emily a quick kiss on the cheek, and walked away. I made my way through the dancers, smoke machines, spilled beer, and felt the eyes on my back as I walked out. I stepped outside and felt the cooling night air wash over me.

The line had gone down considerably, and the bouncers just looked sadly at me—like they pitied me. I plunked down on the curb, put my head between my knees, and just breathed deep, oblivious to the slowing cars and passing pedestrians. I felt a hand on my shoulder and Erik sat down next to me.

"I know how you feel, Elvis."

The bouncers, assuming we were discussing my *sister,* Amanda, came over to us.

"Sorry you didn't find her, kid. But she's a wild one—has a new *friend* every night she's here. Hell, half the club has slept with her, men and women alike."

I stood up, wiping at my eyes and shot Erik a look. He leaned back, knowing full well what was about to happen.

After handing Guido the photo, it started to come out. "You stupid fuck. Take a good look at that photo. The image is smudged a little. It's your thumbprint. It was still damp when I handed it to you, like it was taken tonight. Want to know why you didn't see her tonight?"

He nodded and let go of the photo. It drifted silently to the street, got caught up in some runoff water, and washed down into a storm drain.

"I took her damn picture two blocks from here, paid her off not to come, and then we came here. A few tears and you dick-heads bought the whole damn story. We found out your secrets."

I guessed that I had finally discovered Frank's *red line*.

"You ought to be in fucking Hollywood, kid."

Erik saw and heard me getting ready to cross over that line and dragged me off by the shirt. It just seemed all so damn futile, like those fuckers that sponsored Erik were using us. Here I was, all along thinking we were doing some good, striking out against the bloodsuckers, even taking out a few along the way. Now it was all corrupted or something.

We got back to the van and pulled out. Erik paid the guy at the garage gate in change and headed off down the street towards the main drag. The lights of the city were beautiful. Funny how I never really stopped to look at them before.

"Pull over, Erik."

"Why?"

"Just do it."

He steered off the road, underneath the bridge to the highway. The parking lot was pitted and full of holes. It felt more like off-road driving than coming to a stop. He kept going, letting the van slow itself, and then came to a complete stop at this chunk of sidewalk leading to an old building. Of all the fucked up spaces and our shit luck, we were parked outside a building due to be demolished.

"When was the last time you got some sleep, Elvis?"

"Why?"

"You're bitchy, pissy, cranky, and moody."

"Couple days maybe. Too much thinking."

Erik's phone rang. He killed the engine and stepped into the back of the van to dig it out. He took a pencil and note pad out of his pocket and answered it. "Hello?"

I didn't know what came over me. I grabbed my pack and hopped out of the van. Erik was looking out the window after me. I took out my flashlight. It was time to investigate, to get away for a few minutes, find a quiet dark place, not too dark, plunk down on a brick, and think. I heard Erik talking on the phone, his words getting softer with each step I took.

Yellow warning tape crisscrossed the door. It had once been revolving, but the gears were rusted tight. Someone had knocked out all the glass making it easier to get in. Right near the entrance was a brick with *1906* inscribed in it. I crawled through the shattered panes, listening to each step *scrape* and *crack* on broken glass.

Inside were the shattered remnants of what must have been one hell of a hotel. Now, it was little more than a squatters' paradise, littered with junk, shit, and old wine bottles. Funny part is, the place looked like a war zone. There were piles of debris all over the place. The wallpaper was ripped and tearing, exposing giant holes blown in the walls where you could see right through the jagged slats and cracked plaster.

Looking closer through all the junk on the floor, I found some spent shells, some fresh rounds—well, I don't know how fresh they were—and a grenade pin. There were little blotches running down the walls too, like someone had been firing paint guns. Someone had been training for something big in here. My flashlight started to dim, and I banged it against the floor a couple times till it came back to full strength. I was getting a bad feeling and there wasn't any way I was going to stop and change the batteries right now.

I started backing slowly for the door, listening to the *echo* of my footsteps fill the hollowed-out room. On the balcony, something skittered by, sending up clouds of dust and dropping chunks of plaster and strips of wallpaper down. I heard the *screeching* of metal against metal and caught the edges of the elevator doors opening in my light. A slow damp mist started to creep out.

The sound of a shrill child's laughter filled the lobby. I stepped on some round casings and ended up on my back staring up at the ceiling. I got up and made a lunge for the door. Then I caught the movement out of the corner of my eye. It was something small and round. I got my light on it, a small red ball bounced across the floor. Tiny, quick footsteps charged at me. I dove into the mist, trying to hide, looking for some shelter, but I felt the hands around my neck before I could move.

I was dragged towards the elevator shaft, scraping and scratching at the floor, tearing up my fingers and arms on the broken glass and boards. I shifted around, got out my pistol, and fired wildly. The shots punched through the wall, sending up showers of plaster and boards. The hands let go, and the footsteps went running through the lobby, followed by an insane *cackling*.

My feet dangled over the edge of the shaft, I could feel the mist creeping up the duct, crawling over me.

I started inching away. The fog glowed in a spot and I found my light. I shone it all over the place. Written high up on the ceiling in a spot I didn't see earlier was a giant red cross, faded with age, and big jagged letters that read ***Jesus Saves***.

"Elvis?"

"In here, Erik! We have a live one!"

The words weren't out of my mouth more than a second when I felt those small, cold hands wrapping around my neck again, dragging me towards the elevator.

"You have more than just *one* live one."

The words were whispered in my ear, and then my legs dangled from the knees down into the shaft. The voice was high, childlike, pre-pubescent, a girl's, the hands, small, cold but soft. "Crawl away, little piggy."

I started off again on hands and knees, moving fast as I could. I put my hand down on a nail, screaming as it pierced my palm. I heard Erik call for me, but the mist was everywhere. With nowhere to go and no way to see, I kept crawling blind.

She jumped on my back. Like this was some big fucking game, grabbed my hair, and started riding me like a horse. Her fingernails dug into my scalp. Blood trickled down my face. When I reached out again, my hand touched nothing—just empty air. She jumped on my back again and knocked me to the ground—the air blew out of my lungs.

"Bad piggy," she scolded and put her hands on my shoulders and edged me forward.

The floor dropped out and she pushed.

I kicked, screamed, fought and she pushed.

My shoe came off, fell I don't know how far, and she pushed some more.

I hung from the floorboards by my belt, my legs totally over the edge of the shaft now. I heard the material in my pants start to tear. The hands left my shoulders, I scrambled for something—anything to grab hold of—something to pull myself off. A deep, dark growling came from inside of the shaft far below me. I felt hot breath on my face and warm hands around my arms.

"I got you, kid." It was Erik. He freed me up and pulled me out.

I got to my feet. The growling coming up after us grew louder. I tripped over something in the darkness and went face down again, feeling glass dig into my cheeks. I searched the floor until I found what it was. It had been my gun, only the barrel was bent and the cylinder ripped out. It was nothing more than a souvenir now.

I got up, heard the girl's laughter again, took out a stake, and jabbed blindly—I connected with something. I heard someone cough and choke and then go down hard. I searched around till I grabbed a handful of hair and dragged it towards the door.

I saw Erik outside, taking up aim on the doorway and screamed for him not to shoot yet. Whatever I had weighed a ton and was starting to struggle. I got to the door.

Erik's mouth dropped wide open and he nearly shit himself. He fired two shots into my prize, pissing off the adult male vampire even more.

The stake had hit home, right through the eye. Erik had pumped two slugs into his chest and the holes started to burn and smoke. He'd used my special rounds this time. The bloodsucker fought furiously to get the stake from his head. He grabbed hold of the end and snapped it off, tossing the extra chunk to the side. He clutched at his eye and howled. Fog oozed from the building.

The vampire stood up, towering over both Erik and me—behind him, the girl giggled again. She looked to be maybe five-years-old, curly blonde hair, and dimples. She was dressed up like a baby doll and held a red ball.

I grabbed another stake and lunged for her but the big one just batted me aside. I saw the stake go skittering off into a hole. Erik emptied his clip into him, and he fell real hard. Bits of dead flesh, scored on the sides, littered the ground where he dropped. The girl just looked at him, shaking her head. Her teeth grew in, small, but still vicious. Her eyes took on a reddish glow and she slowly started for us.

I hit her in the head with a couple of quick jets from the squirt gun. Her hair and skin erupted in flame and smoke. She screamed and ran at me. I heard Erik fumbling with his gun, trying to get a fresh clip in. I sprayed her across the eyes, one down her chest and once across the throat. She screamed again as blood foamed and frothed from her neck.

Then she was on me, clawing at my face, trying to get her damn teeth in my throat. I just sprayed and sprayed blindly. She grabbed my hand, crushed the squirt gun, and wailed as the water burnt her hand. While she clutched her hand, I fumbled around, found the stake I'd dropped, and sank it halfway through her chest. She collapsed.

Erik had loaded a fresh clip and emptied that into the male. He was out of it now. Half his face was blown off, and the bullets had burned holes all through him—a few of them still smoked. The guy was almost seven feet tall, with long black hair in a braid, pale skin, and dressed like a biker. Off at the edge of the lot I saw three pairs of headlights coming fast.

"Let's do this, Erik."

"No, wait for the fan club."

"Please." The big guy whispered. He tried to move and his cheek slid off, exposing his skull to the night. I ran in back of the van, opened her up, and got out a gasoline can. I shook it to make sure it had something in it.

When I got back, Erik was turned towards the headlights, talking on the phone, and the big male stood, poised in back of him.

"Erik!" I yelled.

Erik spun, dropped his phone, and the vampire lunged. I saw the male rip across Erik's chest, cutting him wide open. Erik collapsed against the van and then sagged to the ground. The vamp made a move on him. I grabbed my last stake, used the girl for a springboard, and jumped on his back. I sank that stake in real deep. He fell on his side and lay there twitching.

Erik wasn't as bad off as I thought. There was a shitload of blood, but most of it wasn't his. The vamp had scratched him from shoulder to belly, but just made it through the skin.

"Now we're even, Erik. Let's do this and get out of here." I started pouring the gas on the two vamps before the headlights got too close, in case the headlights weren't those of our followers. I looked at the girl. She seemed innocent, like a child should. A bloody tear slipped down her cheek as I wondered just how old she really was—how old when she was turned. The gas splashed across them, soaking through their clothes. There was no tug of the mind, no brain games. Was this another new kind of vampire? Or a couple who had just given up? A couple of strays.

Erik picked up his phone, started up the van, and left the dirty work to me, which was fine I guess. I reached into my pack and pulled out a road flare. Part of me hesitated for a moment. Then I heard the first car horn. I lit the torch, watched the red glare, and the strange creeping shadows. I dropped it on the male and ran.

They caught instantly, but the *roaring* of the van's engine cut the sound of their flesh burning as we bailed. I went to the back, got a first aid kit, and did some quick work on Erik, then got him a clean shirt. I changed too, put some bandages over my cheek and pulled crushed glass from the palms of my hands. I ripped out the nail still stuck in the meat of my palm.

"Elvis, hospital first, then we're out of New England."

"Drive faster and stop talking, Erik."

"By the way, kid, thanks."

"Like I said, we're even this time."

"Still think I'm in with the vampires?" he asked, looking down at the bandages on his chest.

"No, I was just mad."

We got onto the bridge, took the first exit off, and headed back into town. I saw the headlights in the parking lot. Three campers watched the burning bodies of the vamps and the people now assembled around them.

Hospitals are the same no matter where you go. They made us fill out all sorts of paperwork, proof of insurance, and everything else. They numbed up my hand and gave me stitches from where I pulled the nail out, checked on the fingers that had been broken, broke them again and set them straight, and put them in a cast. I took eight stitches in my cheek and blamed the entire thing on skateboarding in an abandoned building, which the doctors seemed to believe right off.

"Just another stupid kid," I heard him say as he walked out to check on Erik.

Erik had it pretty much the same. They stitched him up, nothing too serious. They wanted him to get the stitches pulled out in a week and, if the bleeding continued, to get back to an emergency room—*pronto*. We got antibiotics, a stern warning to watch out where I skateboarded, and to be careful. Back in the van, I waited while Erik made a quick call. I pulled my gun from my pack, looked at what was left of it, and dropped it in the parking lot.

"Gather up your stuff, Elvis. We're going."

"We're in the van, Erik."

"Not anymore we're not." He gathered all his stuff—clothes, notes, laptop—and went outside.

I got my pack, the pamphlets, and emptied what was left in the cooler into a paper bag. Erik took the plates off the van. Then he went around the side, pulled out the registration, and burned it.

"What's up?"

"They want us off the ground. Too many people know about us now. It's not a secret anymore. They're trying to avoid the fan club following us."

"Fair enough."

We got out of the parking lot, and Erik hailed a cab. "Logan Airport. There's an extra hundred in it if you can get us there in fifteen minutes."

Didn't have to tell that driver twice. Scariest ride I ever had in my life. I didn't know whether to laugh, cry, or piss. But we got there. Erik dropped two Ben Franklins on the driver and told him he never saw us—that his fare stiffed him, and ran away.

We paid for the tickets in cash, using aliases. I don't know how Erik got the guns on the plane, and I didn't ask. When we put our bags through the X-ray, the operator turned away. I didn't know if Erik bribed him or knew him. The flight was bound for New York, the plane, nothing more than a fancy puddle jumper or a turbo prop. It lasted less than an hour. We took off, ascended to twenty thousand feet, stayed like that for forty minutes, and then landed in the Big Apple.

"What's the mission this time?" I asked, waiting outside the terminal for a cab.

"Another cold site until things calm down a bit. Then a simple screening—go in, collect some evidence, and bug out."

"No one knows?"

"That's what the sponsors tell me, kid."

"How long we in the city for?"

"No more than a few days max. We go in, we get out. After this assignment, we're laying low for a while."

"How long? And what will we do?"

"I'll go back to the sponsors, or wherever they put me, and do R&D, I guess. I don't know about you. You're welcome to come with me if you want."

"Got no place else to go 'less I want to go back to the trailer park. Ain't much left behind for that though."

"Worry about it when the time comes, Elvis."

The cabby was a smelly fat guy who chewed on the nub of a cigar. Erik handed him a piece of paper, and he just looked at us through the mirror.

"This will cost you."

Erik held up a wad of twenties, and the guy was all business getting us to our destination. Next thing I knew, we were at the place, plain and simple. I had passed out on Erik's shoulder, and he'd fallen asleep too. It must have been in the 'burbs. I didn't know where the fuck we were, but it wasn't New York City. That was for damn sure. Erik handed the cabby a nice package of bills, and the guy left us there. Bastard didn't even ask us if we wanted him to wait.

We were on a street corner. There were homes, shops, everything, and it was pleasant, rural. The people looked friendly and not mad. Sitting across the street from us was a green Ford Taurus. Erik reached under the rear wheel, pulled out a magnetic key-holder, and climbed in the front. He looked expectantly at me through the window, and to tell the truth, I was still a bit drowsy from the flight. I *did* notice that the sun was going down.

"We're finding a hotel, right? Then we're going in?"

"We're already there."

The car was parked outside this old movie theater, boasting five screens, five big movies at all times. There was a small lot out back, but ours was the only car parked in it. The rear door, the emergency exit, was boarded up, as was the entrance to the main lobby. All the doors to the outside had planks nailed over them, and being a movie theater, the main windows looking into the lobby had been painted over. A large *FOR LEASE* sign was planted in the grass outside the sidewalk.

There were still some faded movie posters hanging in clear cases outside the main doors. Water had gotten in and the only name I could make out was *Aliens*. There were two sets of double glass doors leading in with chains running through the bars. Where some of the paint had cracked and fallen off the windows, you could make out a hallway leading to the ticket counter. In back of it, was a giant cardboard movie ad for *The Crow* that someone had taken a knife to. Behind that we couldn't see much of anything.

"How are we going to get in?"

People walked up and down the street in back of us, smiled and waved nervously.

"Jesus, Erik, where are we?"

"White's Corner."

"Where's that?"

"In New York," he beamed. He pulled out some lock pick tools and went to work on the chains.

Sometimes when you think you know someone, you realize you don't. He had the locks off in less than a minute. I stood guard and kept an eye on things. So far he had been right—no sign of the fanatics following us. Hopefully, we ditched them all in Boston.

He carefully got the chains off. Then he started on the doors. Erik had those open quickly too. He looped the chains loosely over the bars so if anyone came along things would look normal at first glance.

"Erik," I whispered "I don't have a gun, any stakes, or special bullets."

He reached into his coat and handed me a pistol with three spare clips. "Best the sponsors could do with short notice."

I popped the clip, took out a bullet, and saw there was a little cross etched in the front. I guess Erik had told them about my idea. I didn't know if they had been dunked in holy water or not, but I was out of that, too. We stood in the hallway, and I got ready to get my light out when Erik grabbed my wrist.

"There are people on the streets, Elvis. We have to be careful and quiet on this one. No shooting. Nothing."

"But the site is cold, right?"

He nodded. I put the gun under my belt and the three clips in my coat pocket. Erik pulled the low light goggles out of his bag and slid them on over his head. I grabbed hold of his belt, and he started leading us through the hallway. I felt real nervous and uncomfortable being there in the darkness.

Every time a car went by or I heard people talking on the streets, I'd snap my head over towards the noise to see nothing but blackness. We walked slowly. I listened to Erik breathing. He wasn't talking at all. We walked on carpet, I could tell that much. When we got to the ticket counter, he stopped and put a flashlight in my hand.

"Use it, but keep your hand over the lens."

I did it, and my hand glowed. It didn't cut the darkness, but it helped ease my mind a little. I heard another car go by outside, then a cop car and sirens. The lobby was filled with cardboard displays of movies, most of which had fallen over or gotten warped with time and age. The floor was littered with popcorn tubs and soda cups. Around the perimeter of the theater were some benches and along one wall were video games. Five double doors led to the cinemas.

The floor, what I saw of it, was carpeted in green with this annoying pattern in it. There was a set of stairs leading up to the projection rooms and a snack counter with a glass display case. Inside were candy wrappers and empty boxes of Snowcaps, Goobers, M&M's, and Licorice Bites. The soda machine had cups upturned on the spickets so they couldn't be used. The popcorn machine was empty, and the little freezer that used to hold ice cream had defrosted. I chambered a round and took off the safety.

"What is it, Elvis?"

"I heard something." It's then I noticed that the exit signs still glowed red. I heard another car, muffled screams, and shots. I dropped to the floor and took aim on one of the doors. I felt Erik on the floor next to me taking up aim, too.

"What the fuck, Erik? We're dead! We're screwed in here. It's a live site, isn't it?"

"I don't know, Elvis. Let's look around a little bit."

"You look around! We're defenseless in here."

I kept Erik covered and got my back to a column in the center of the lobby. I took my hand off the light and let it spill out. Erik stood his on end like a torch and then did the same with three other lights so we could at least see when we would die. He opened the first door and leveled his gun—then he waved me over.

The cinema was empty, I could tell that, but there was a movie playing. Mel Gibson and Danny Glover ran across the screen, chasing cars in traffic and shooting guns. Erik closed the first set of doors. He pointed and motioned to the second and then opened them up—same story, only this time *The Crow* was playing. The next theater had *Interview with the Vampire.* We had come to expect the madness of the place but the last room had people in it watching *Aliens.*

Erik slammed the door and I jammed one of the flashlights between the handles. We ran for the exit. We didn't get far enough though. The doors burst open. Knocked off the hinges, they crashed on the lobby floor. We were in the stretch of the hallway when we got caught and dragged back to the lobby.

The lights flickered on and the place just filled up with vampires and their minions. It was like a goddamned bloodsucker convention. Two sets of hands, human hands, warm and full of life, held us. At last, their leader came out, draped in robes, walking with silver tipped cane. He smiled wickedly, rolled my face in his cold dead hand. I spit on him and he laughed. The hands holding me tightened, and he pressed his thumbnail into my cheek, breaking the skin. He licked it clean.

"My name," he announced, walking back and forth in front of us, "is Jonathan Kane. How wonderful to meet you both at last."

17
Elvis: Thrall—The Sequel

I don't know how long they held us in the lobby while a crowd of them hustled in and out of that last set of doors, carrying everything from tables to fancy goblets. When they finally led us in, the fifth theater had been transformed into a dining hall. All the theater chairs had been ripped out and wood floors had been put in. Gigantic brass chandeliers hung from the ceiling. The speakers that once filled the room with gunshots, screams, and soundtracks now piped in classical music.

Thick red curtains were draped across the walls, covering almost every inch. At the bottom, near where the screen used to be, was an oak table set up like the Pope was visiting. We were seated in these heavy wooden chairs, polished so we could see ourselves. On the table next to linen napkins were silver place settings. Candles stood in gold holders between the settings where plates of fruit, cheese, and bread were spread out before us. The thralls and minions appeared from the folds of the curtains. Each one took their place at the table—humans on one side, bloodsuckers on the other. Kane emerged from behind the curtains, taking his seat at the head of the table, smiling all the while. A thrall walked among us, lighting the candles. A few of the dead winced at the flame, but showed no other emotion aside from a hunger burning in their eyes.

Our plates were filled with roasted vegetables, hot meat, warm rolls, and fresh, softened butter. Water was poured into goblets, and the humans ate while Erik and I watched them.

The dead drank from their goblets as well, but it wasn't water or wine.

"Eat, won't you?" Kane smiled. "My children have worked so hard on this meal."

"Fuck yourself," I spat.

Kane still smiled at me, delicately dabbed at his lips with a napkin, came over to me, and crushed the cast on my hand, exposing my still-healing fingers. I took a bite of the meat and he walked away, humming classical music.

"What do you want from us?"

"I want you to eat, drink, listen to some music, maybe read some literature. And if you're really good, I'll teach you how to play chess."

"Then what?" I asked.

Kane's eyes glowed for a second. "Then, we'll welcome you to the family."

Our plates were cleared, the table was cleaned off, and fresh plates of cakes and chocolates were set out. Erik and me each chose a few pieces before it was taken away. The table was stripped, all the silver and gold removed so business could be done. Crystal chalices were put in front of us and filled with a red, thick, steaming liquid. Kane dipped his finger in mine and then licked it clean.

"Drink," he commanded.

I looked at the cup and knew right away what it was. The other vampires sat across from us, their thralls standing obediently in back of them, silent, staring, each waiting for our move, waiting to pounce if necessary. It smelled coppery, and I almost puked. I knocked the cup away. It shattered on the floor, staining it red. Erik looked at his pensively and, for the second time that I knew of, drank blood.

Kane smiled at Erik, knowing that he had him. Me, however, he didn't smile at. In fact, for the first time since we saw him, his smile faltered. Three pale-skinned men came out from behind him, slapped me from my chair, and dragged me off.

I awoke in a cell. There was a cot, a washbasin, and a canteen on the floor. Next to it was some fruit and candy. The door, of course, was locked. I didn't bother trying to scream or yell or kick at the door. I knew it wouldn't do me any good. The light switch was near the door and a bucket was in the corner. There were some books, magazines, and even crossword puzzles stacked neatly on the floor near the cot. I kind of wondered what happened to Erik. This was, after all, what he wanted. He was in with them, and I being the fool, actually believed the fucker, thinking he had come around.

The door opened and three men came in, the same three that had bitch-slapped me earlier. They led me into the lobby where whole slews of them were gathered. Kane was up on the balcony overseeing the entire operation. Erik was on one side of him, and on the other, the burnt vampire lady. Her eyes exploded with hatred when she saw me, but Kane had her under his thumb—like he had Erik.

I was hustled into a room, stripped to my skivvies, and put into a new set of black clothes. Four others joined me back in the lobby and soon we were on the streets. Not one of them was talking, just looking all around. The people who were still out didn't seem to notice them—like they had become accustomed to bands of black-clothed thugs roaming the city. They climbed into a car, pulled me in, and drove off.

We traveled for about an hour until we came to this small town. It was totally dark, aside from a few streetlights and house lights on behind shades and curtains. Dogs barked as the car rolled down the street.

"You all know your parts." The driver turned, looking me in the eyes. "You stick with me, kid. Do what I say or I'll gut you."

We piled out. Three of them went one way, and I was with the driver walking casually down the street. A few minutes later, we were on a street corner with a little yellow house in back of us. The front door opened and the other three came out, dragging an old woman in back of them. She was struggling, but they had taped her hands and feet together and gagged her. The driver ran lookout as they dragged her back to the car. The others stuffed her into the trunk. Then we were headed back. No one knew, no one saw.

"What if we were seen?"

"Shut up, kid. No one saw us."

"Someone will miss her."

"No one will miss her."

"She saw our faces."

The dude backhanded me and split my lip wide open. I dove for him, grabbed the wheel, and tried to steer us off the road. Least maybe that way I could make a break for it, run to the cops before Kane had a chance to clear out. But the others dragged me over the seat and sat on me until we got back.

They got the old lady in first—me second. One of the exits hadn't been boarded over. We didn't notice that last night, or whatever night that was. I saw a room full of chaise lounges, each one with someone seated in it. Erik was putting tubes in their arms, bleeding them out. The blood was put into bags and then brought into a second room where I couldn't see what was going on. In the last chair, I saw the old lady in her powder blue nightgown, hair still in curlers, frightened and bleeding.

"This is what we do, Elvis. Come in."

Kane's voice was seductive, but I still hated the fucker. I walked past each chair, saw the fear in each person's eyes and wished I could do something to help. But anything I did would be painful for me and probably fatal for them.

"This is better than killing them, and they have no recollection of what happens. They're returned to their homes and have a good night's sleep."

"Why do you force these people to do this?" I turned to Kane.

"Everyone here is of their own free will, Elvis, except for you. I knew you'd be coming—just not this soon."

"So I can go whenever I want?"

"No, you would expose us. You've killed us." His voice rose and I heard the anger in it. He calmed quickly, fixing his cool façade and replacing his smile. "You will have a special place among us."

Erik looked back at me. His eyes were apologetic. Kane motioned and the burnt lady came out of the shadows where she was hiding. She had done the same thing back in Georgia, her and her friend. I rubbed my hand. Kane noticed and smiled.

"Those fingers will never heal right."

"They were healing right till you broke the cast."

"I have doctors within my flock. We'll just set them again. This is Lauren," he said, ushering the lady vamp towards me. "She will be your new master."

And with that, she bit down into my neck, drank some of my blood but not much. A bunch of the others, even Erik, held me down as she bit open her wrists and held it to my lips, forcing me to drink.

"Just let it happen, Elvis," Erik whispered. "If you fight, it will be painful."

I gave up—surrendered. There was no way out. But I asked myself if being her slave was better than being dead. Would I be able to have conscious thought after this night? I grabbed her hand, pressed the gash to my mouth and drank deeply of her blood now mixed with mine.

"That's it, Elvis. Just let it happen," Erik said to me.

Lauren pulled her arm away and I was dragged back to my room. Once inside, I jammed a finger down my throat and threw up as much of that blood as would come up. I don't know if anyone heard or saw me, but the door was locked again. I washed my mouth out with water from the canteen, pissed into the bucket, then lay down and slept with the light on.

That night I was in Bloodsucker College. They started training me on the proper way to present myself to my master—how to stand behind her far enough not to be seen but close enough to do her bidding—how to offer my neck and wrist to her when she hungered for blood. It was all glorified bullshit, but I went along with it.

Lauren fed off me every other night, and every other night I'd go back to my room and stick a finger down my throat. I knew there was still some in me, but the main portion of it was being flushed. After a week, they stopped locking my door, figuring that I had been fed off of and forced to feed from Lauren enough. She would pull that vampire mind control stuff on me, and I would go to her. When I was near her or the others, I played the mindless slave, trying hard as I could to serve and please the mistress.

In return, they fed me, got me some new clothes, and kept me in a warm bed. I saw Erik only once in the hallways. The rest of the time they kept us isolated from each other, just in case. Far as I knew, he was still in contact with the sponsors. I didn't know if he was communicating our plight, though.

They wouldn't let me out of the theater alone yet for hunting. When we went out, it was always in groups of four or more, and I had to wait until the time was right to make a break for it. I tried not to think about it too much so the bloodsuckers wouldn't read anything in my head. I'm sure that escape wasn't one of their objectives.

My second week into it, they started teaching me more about the different vampires factions, how Kane was trying to unite everyone, but there were still some who didn't want to abide by his laws. They didn't want to expose themselves to the mortals, but also didn't want any type of political system.

Sometimes, the factions would intermix and create a new line. Jonathan had parts of most of the sects in him except one. Kane was still allergic to sunlight. He could turn to mist and all that, do the animals forms, change shape, and use the mind control and magic type powers. He was by far the most powerful bloodsucker in the States. But even among the thralls, the rumors existed how he thought the could never be whole until he could walk in the sun. There were only a handful of them in the States, and he had tabs on all of them.

Apparently, there was also great risk in, for lack of a better term, cross-breeding the factions. Seven out of ten times it didn't work, and the vampire would die from crossing the different bloodlines. But those other three times, you had some kick ass vampires. In another political struggle though, the crossbreeds weren't especially accepted by either end of the spectrum and usually stuck it out for themselves. They didn't have the support or resources of the factions.

Three weeks into my stay, they let me see Erik again. By this point he was so far gone he might as well have been one of them. He had scars on his neck and wrists and the pale skin, all the telltale signs of a thrall. Puking my guts up night after night still kept a healthy pink sheen to my skin, and the scars eventually would heal. They all thought it was good that I adapted so easily to my new lifestyle. I just prayed all the time and hoped that no one discovered my nocturnal retching.

That one time I saw Erik, he didn't say much. We stopped in the hallway of the theater and talked briefly. He said how Kane was pleased to have him as one of his own, and that there was talk of bringing him across. Luckily, Lauren had said nothing of the sort to me. I don't know what I'd do in that case.

The first night of my fourth week in the theater, it was time to hunt—this time for Lauren and by myself. I knew that

I'd have a shadow on me so it had to be a damn good show. I dressed up in the black clothes and took a knife and a few other supplies. I was going to hunt in White's Corner. They didn't trust me enough to let me out of the city yet. Besides, still being a kid, I couldn't drive legally. A kid speeding along the streets in a car would bring attention to the group.

I got out on the streets, looking like any other kid in any other town. The locals nodded and smiled to me. They sent me just at sunset so I could get a head start and not feel like I had a tail. I scouted out some locations, some possibilities, and even escape routes. I just hoped I was far enough away from Lauren's influence for her to pick up my thinking.

I found two main ways out of town, both of them leading to state highways—though there were some other back roads leading up into the mountains. I'd have to see if I could remember how to hotwire a car. Daddy once showed me when he lost the keys to the truck in a bar and needed me to drive back to the trailer 'cause he was too drunk.

I'd not had a thought about my folks since I-don't-know-when. I sat on the curb, broke down, and started crying. I had a picture of them in my wallet, wherever it was. I actually missed the park, Momma and Daddy fighting, the old truck, Jimmy and everyone else. I felt a tender touch on my shoulder. It was an older lady with a nice smile. I wiped at my eyes and forced a smile back.

"Is everything all right, son?" She had lipstick on her teeth and too much on her lips. Her face was wrinkled, and I saw the corner of a tissue sticking out of her bra strap, which kept sliding down under the shoulder of her dress.

"Yes, ma'am."

"What's the matter then? Goodness, you look a fright."

"Just lonely, I guess." I looked all around for my shadow, but didn't see anyone or anything. "My name is Elvis."

"I'm Edith. Why don't you come for a walk with me, son. We'll get you some cookies and milk."

We walked the few blocks to her house and I got her life story along the way. She was widowed, almost ten years, husband named Sam had been killed in a car crash. She had four kids who lived all over the county and eighteen grandchildren.

She lived alone with six cats in a two-story brownstone with a small driveway, back porch, and flower garden. Sitting in the driveway was a shit brown 85 Mercury Marquis. There were three cats waiting on the stairs for Edith to come home so they could get fed.

"Nice car," I said, giving it the once-over. Tires were a little worn, but no body rot. An old inspection sticker shone on the windshield.

"That junky thing? That was my Sam's. I never had the heart to sell it. It hasn't worked for years. I just thank the Maker that I live in walking distance of the market."

Inside the house, it was like stepping into a 70's retro scene. But all in all it was cool. I took a seat at the table, and before I could say bloodsucker, there was a big glass of milk and a plate of sugar cookies in front of me. Edith went about her business, feeding the cats and tidying up. I ate cookies and we chatted.

I told her both my parents were killed by a tornado last year and that I was staying with my uncle. She invited us both back for homemade beef stew the next night. Didn't know how I was going to pull that one off. Finally it was time to go. She gave me a hug and bag of cookies for the road. Outside, I leaned up against the bumper of the car and waited.

Soon enough it happened. The house and porch lights went out. A cat went trotting across the street, and the shadows started shifting and moving—until one of the vampires appeared in front of me.

"You failed."

"No, actually you did. I knew you were coming."

"You didn't bring back any blood."

"I couldn't do it, okay? I'm going to need some more time. Nabbing old ladies out of their homes maybe isn't my bag."

"You weren't sent out to make friends, Elvis."

I shrugged, ate a cookie, and offered him a bite. He slapped it out of my hand.

"Head back to the theater."

I walked down the driveway until "fang face" had vanished back into the shadows. I waited by the side of the road for the better part of an hour. When nothing moved, I retraced my steps.

The driver's side door on Edith's car was open. I slid in and checked around for the key. It was hidden neatly under the seat in a yellow envelope. The key fit. It turned and nothing happened, not even a click. When I opened the door, there was no light. Inside the glove box was the hood lock. I popped it and snuck around front. After checking the streets again, I lifted the hood and looked around. The battery cables were disconnected. Far as I could tell, that was all that was wrong. I hooked the wires back up and prayed that the battery still had a charge.

The car started right up. I popped it in neutral, rolled out of the driveway, keeping the lights off until I hit the street—then it was all or nothing. I changed gears and floored it, leaving rubber in back of me. I went bombing down the street as fast as the car could take me. There weren't any cruisers out. In fact, the police station looked closed. I took the first route out of town headed for the highway.

It was weird driving without the lights on, but my eyes adapted to it pretty quick. Besides, I had gotten used to being out at night. When I saw the first car, it was time to flick on the lights. What a damn mistake that was.

It came up fast on my ass, smashing into the back, shattering the taillights, fucking up the bumper, and rocking the shit out of the car. I lost control, weaved all over the place, and did a few lane switches before getting righted again. Next hit came from the passenger's side. It broke the window, almost pushed me into the median. But I jerked the wheel hard, forced it back into them, and they skidded off to another lane. There were three cars in all, full of pasty faced thralls dressed in black.

They waved at me and pointed to the side of the road, but I still tried to outrun them. I was doing okay, gaining some ground, until something in the engine blew. The car coughed, sputtered, and wheezed. Smoke started to billow out from under the hood, and hot oil splattered the windshield. When the power steering went, I thought I was dead. The car veered towards the median, and it took all I had not to crash.

It finally started to slow and then stopped dead in the third lane. They dragged me out of the window, after breaking it, and stuffed me in the trunk of one of the lead cars. I heard a gunshot, then an explosion, and could smell the smoke and hear the fire. The trunk filled with the stink of burning rubber smoke, and I puked all over myself.

When they let me out back in the theater parking lot, Kane, Erik, and Lauren were all outside waiting for me. They presented me to Kane and hit me in the back of the knees with a rifle butt to make me kneel. I coughed a few times and then looked up at Lauren. I couldn't tell if she was furious or embarrassed. Kane was pissed too. Erik looked—well—like Erik.

"All we went through, Elvis, keeping you alive. This is how you pay us back?" Kane's voice was strangely calm, never wavering, deep, melodic, and perfect. "We feed you, clothe you, and give you a warm bed."

With each of his words, I could feel the tugging at my mind. I knew it wasn't Lauren and it felt different from when Katherine did it to me.

"Erik begged me not to kill you—to keep you as a thrall so you would adapt and turn to our ways."

My mind snapped and bladder loosened. I felt the hot wetness spread across me but was powerless to do anything. Erik lowered his head to the ground, looking ashamed that he had somehow betrayed Kane.

"I was going to give you to Lauren as a snack. Let her play with you—for what you have done to her and our kind, for all the senseless murders. Yes, Elvis, I know of your travels with Erik."

Erik took a step forward, turned to face Kane and then quickly took his place standing in back of him like the good little thrall that he was. His life's research into the vampire world was about to become complete with his turning. But me, I still had more vamps to kill. Kane lifted me from the ground and the urine dripped down my shoe, spattering on the pavement. He tossed me to a group of the thralls.

"He said keep you alive, not to kill you." Kane walked over to Erik and tore off his shirt.

I saw the scars and fresh wounds all over his neck and abdomen.

"You could live with the scars." He forced Erik to his knees. "Now live with this."

The thralls held me tight. At one point someone stuck a knife under my chin. The more I fought, the more blood trickled down my neck.

Kane bit into Erik. Erik didn't scream, though he did wince. I saw a tear slip down his cheek. There was a spray of blood that coated Lauren's face. She ran a gloved finger through it and licked it clean. Kane sucked on Erik till he was near death and let him fall to the pavement. Erik squirmed on the ground like a worm left without moisture. His body started to shake, going into death throes.

"Commit your loyalty to me or he dies in pain." I looked at Erik. I had never seen anyone in so much pain before. His body twisted and convulsed. Foamy spit oozed out of the corner of his mouth. What choice did I have now? Let Erik die? He wanted the afterlife more than I did. Maybe this way they would kill me. Somehow that seemed better.

"Okay," I yelled.

Kane bit open his wrist. The blood flowed from his wound into Erik's mouth. Erik drank greedily until Kane pulled his arm away.

"Do what you have to, just keep Erik alive."

Erik continued to shake and spasm on the ground. They made me watch and eventually pulled the knife away. I was still bleeding but didn't care. They should have finished the job and slit my throat. Nothing was worth this.

Finally, Erik's heart stopped. Kane smiled, looked at his watch and rocked back and forth on his feet triumphantly. They dragged me back to Lauren and dumped me on the ground in back of her. She fed, then fed me too.

"Watch now, Elvis. This is the most amazing part."

Erik's eyes snapped open with an unearthly glow. He had fangs—long jagged ones. As if he couldn't yet control his new found powers, he turned to mist and turned back. Then claws grew out of his fingers as he melded with the shadows surrounding Kane. It was then I realized that the shadows around Kane were his vampire bodyguards.

"That's right, Elvis."

The shadows coalesced and turned into human form, four men, two women, and Erik.

"He's one of us now. Everything he was is ours. Everything he has and owns is ours. Soon, my boy, you will be too." Kane turned around, draping an arm across Erik's shoulders. Erik looked at me hungrily and apologetically—like he knew my fate—only now I too had an idea.

Lauren dragged me back to the room, threw me inside, and locked the door. I leaned over the bucket and puked, then stripped, washed off from the basin, and got dressed in some fresh clothes. Unlike every other night, there was no plate of fresh food waiting for me. There was water from the canteen. I used it to wash myself so I didn't even have water.

The next night, they started my training all over again. Some of the thralls there felt sorry for me. Others were a little excited at all the commotion. Rumors abounded wherever I went. There was talk of bringing me over—of a public execution. Didn't matter though. They had broken me. What they did to Erik just wasn't right, and it was all my fault.

Aside from waiting hand and toe on Lauren, they also assigned me to Kane and Erik. Kane was taking special care of him, making him the best vampire he could be. Until he got his sea legs in the undead world, Kane let Erik feed off him. Lauren continued feeding off me, until I collapsed one night. They had to force feed me. I stopped eating, but that didn't last too long. My blood was too thin for Lauren to properly sustain herself so she borrowed from other thralls, waiting for me to get better.

One night, I found Edith strapped down in a lounge chair, tube in her arm, and Erik hovering over her greedily, waiting for the process to finish. I offered him my wrist, trying to spare her, but it was no use.

Erik was too far-gone, and Kane too powerful. Lauren had me all but taped to her side. I walked with her, bathed her, brushed her hair—whatever was necessary at the time. When I wasn't with Lauren, I slept. They stopped sending me out to hunt with the others and stopped my thrall training. I was a servant, nothing more. I would have to learn my place on my own or be killed doing otherwise. Either way kept Kane happy and smiling.

I was awake in the room one night when the door lock *clicked*. In proper fashion, I handed out the dirty plate, empty canteen, bucket, and washbasin. A few minutes later they were replaced. The door closed and was locked again. I ate some fruit, lay on the bed, and thought. I needed a plan to get out.

From under the bed I pulled out the puzzle book and went to the word searches. I started humming old Elvis songs in my head, filling my thoughts so if anyone was peeking in, all they would get is Blue Grass and Rock and Roll. I circled only specific words that I needed, trying to create a plan from the puzzles. Then I wrote the page numbers and word orders on the inside cover. It took me all damn night.

I didn't sleep. No one came to check on me and no one let me out. In my little mind that meant only one thing—my time had come. They were trying to fatten me up for my last night as a human. No matter how many times I went over it, the plan was no good. Everything relied on me getting alone with Kane. I could do that. I was sure of it. But from there on, it was all gray. I had no gun, no stakes, no holy water—nothing.

The lock turned and I rolled over in bed. I reached for my cross, but it was gone too. I saw it across the room, sitting in the corner under a magazine where I kept it hidden. I lunged for it and jammed it in my pocket. The door opened and I was led out into the hallway by four of Kane's finest.

I could hear the movies playing as we walked past them. Kane had a good selection and kept them rotating, even bringing in new ones—whatever it took to keep the thralls happy when not serving him or the others. If I lived through the experience, I was going to come back and watch *Braveheart*.

They left me in Kane's personal chamber. I sat in a chair and looked around. There were two doors, the one we came in and the one that led to the dining hall. The room was elegantly furnished in leather with a coffin on a pedestal surrounded by a thick black velvet curtain.

Kane came in through the door. I half expected him to pop out of the coffin in typical bloodsucker fashion, but this was real life, not the movies. He sat across from me and waited to speak until Erik and Lauren joined us as well. They sat on either side of me.

"We've made our choice, Elvis."

I gripped the arms of the chair and gritted my teeth. Lauren lay her hand on my shoulder and squeezed.

"You're to become one of us—join our ranks." Kane smiled broadly, stood, and opened his arms to embrace me.

Then Lauren and Erik followed. Erik had never hugged me before. It was weird—like he didn't know how or something.

Lauren and Erik left the room. The shadows whirled, formed into men, and flowed from the room like water. Kane again sat across from me.

"Make your decision, Elvis. Few vampires get this choice, but you're special. Choose who will make you. Whomever you decide upon, you will be indebted to as if he or she was your parent."

"*You*. You do it," I said.

He seemed pleased at my choice, like there was any other logical choice. "Why me?"

"I don't think Erik has the heart to do it. It'd be like trying to put your puppy down or something. Regardless of how things turn out, Lauren will always hate me. I might have a chance with you."

Kane sat on the couch next to me and pulled me to him. I could smell his expensive cologne.

"You saw what happened to Erik. Turning isn't a pleasant thing, but the afterlife is truly glorious. I will teach you everything as if you were my real son."

"You have any kids?" I asked. "I mean before you got changed?"

"Three, I watched them all grow up, bear children of their own, grow old, and die."

"Must have been rough."

"More than you can ever imagine." He went for my neck.

"Kind of like watching your parents get butchered."

Kane stopped. I slipped my hand into my pocket.

"That was a terrible mistake. Katherine wasn't one of mine. She was a free spirit, always on her own." He pulled me close.

"And what happened in Maine. Man, I bet you had some damn good explaining to do on that one. Shit, Drake and me must have taken out a couple dozen of you guys. Imagine that spot though, risk the fire or face the sunlight."

"You'll repay that tragedy as well."

I felt his cold breath on my neck. The press of his fangs as they rested on my skin. I got out the cross, jumped back, felt my skin tear, and jammed the cross against Kane's face. It started to burn the second there was contact. He screamed and tore at the cross, but couldn't touch it. It was like the thing was burning a hole in his head.

I saw the anger and intent in his eyes as the pain overwhelmed him. I kicked over a chair, jumped on the legs, breaking off two of them. I jammed one square into Kane's chest, grabbed my cross, and ran for the door. By the time I was in the hallway running for the exit, the alarm had gone off. They swarmed from every shadow, every corner. I was about to dive through a window when a hand pulled me in back of the ticket counter. I stared up into Erik's dead eyes.

"I always knew you had it in you, Elvis." He slipped a pack over my shoulder and took the other chair leg from my hand. "I was weak, always wanted this. Needed a way to finish my research. This was the only way."

"What are you going to do?"

"Create a diversion."

"How?"

"To keep them off your back for a few hours, I'm going to try and start a fight between Kane and Lauren. I hope the ruse works. Now get out."

I dove through the window and watched as Erik jumped on the chair leg, driving it into his gut. He fell to the ground and writhed until the others began to hover about him.

I ran for the street with no one following me. I hadn't done much damage to Kane, but they would be after me—that was for sure. Nothing in the damn world could keep them from me. I dove under the porch at Edith's house and checked through the pack. Inside were plane tickets, credit cards, money, passports, a cell phone, my wallet, and a business card with just a phone number on it. In the front pocket were a set of car keys and a folded piece of paper.

Elvis—

If you're reading this then it's too late for me. It's all for the better. Be well, and take care of yourself. Call the number on the card when you get far enough away. They'll help you. There's a car waiting on the corner of Main and North Street, take it and drive, don't stop.

Erik

Sure as hell there it was—a little Ford Escort, white, two doors and hatchback. I hopped in, started her up and sped off. I found some tissues in the glove box and put pressure on my neck. It was just a rip, nothing deep, no veins hit. There was a map and a route drawn on the thing for Connecticut. Erik had been looking out for me all along and I felt bad because I doubted him. I missed the fool already. But now I was on my own in the world.

Halfway through Connecticut, somewhere on I-95, the car started to jerk. I had run the bitch straight out of gas. Lucky for me, though, rest stops were everywhere. I pulled off the road into one, filled the tank and my gut, paid in cash, and took off again. I didn't stop until the sun came up.

Practically on the Massachusetts border, I pulled off again and stopped. I dug out Erik's cell phone, the card, and called the number. It rang a few times before someone finally picked up. Guess I had woken up the bastards.

"Erik?" The voice on the other end was scratchy and sounded groggy.

"Close."

"Elvis..." The dude was starting to wake a lot sooner than expected. "How can I help you?"

I re-arranged the mirrors to get a good view in back of me. Even if the bloodsuckers couldn't come out in the day, the thralls might. An eighteen-wheeler went passed, spitting up diesel fumes and was soon out of sight.

"Erik is gone. I need help. They're on my tail. I don't know how much time I have." I crawled over the front seat into the back and got on the floor. "I attacked the king vampire and hightailed it out of Dodge. Erik helped me, though. He's one of them."

There was silence on the other side of the phone.

"Are you listening to me?" I asked, "He's a mother-humping vampire now."

"Yes, Elvis, I'm still here. I need you to go into the trunk of the car and look for a package."

"Hang on." I left the phone open on the seat, reached for the keys, and crept from the car. I snuck around back and opened the hatch. Lying under a pile of stuff in the trunk was a brown paper-wrapped package with an address scribbled on it and postage paid label in the corner. I tossed it onto the back seat, closed the hatch, and returned to the front..

"There's a box here for you, least I assume it's for you, Bill."

"Drop it in a box—first chance you get. It's imperative."

"Look, it's nice you have your box, but what about me? I'm screwed. The longer I sit here, the more they catch up to me. I need a place to hide out. Let me come there."

"No."

"Why the fuck not? I can just get to the address on the box." I said that before seeing the address was a P.O. Box in New York City. No fucking way I'm ever going back to New York City or State.

"Just do what we say." The dude rambled on for the better part of ten minutes, giving me instructions and directions. I gassed up the car again and headed for New Hampshire. They didn't want to risk me in New York and didn't want me back in Boston after the incident at the old hotel.

I was bound for Manchester, New Hampshire and the airport. Took me the better part of the morning to get there too, and let me tell you, fatigue was setting in pretty damn good. As instructed, I left the car in the long-term parking, took off the plates, and lit the registration on fire. I dropped the package into a Fed Ex pickup box, got a locker for the car plates, and flushed the key. There was a ticket waiting at the counter for me—a non-stop flight to the West Coast. I had finally hit the big time—nothing but first class for me. Even Erik never got me in the good seats.

I was going to Hollywood.

18
Elvis: Leaving on a jet plane

The flight was actually pretty decent—what I remember of it. The attendant, can't call them stewardesses any more, wore this little skirt and a white shirt and black bra. Ask me how I know that. Wearing just enough lipstick, she liked to lean over people, getting her business in their faces. I kept making excuses for her to come back to me. I needed a blanket or to have my pillow fluffed. In first class they do that shit.

I pretty much crashed soon as I settled in. Only had my backpack and a small case so I carried it all on the plane and jammed it in the overhead. The dude next to me, a three-piece-suit business guy stayed on his laptop all through the trip. I know because I heard his damn fingers *clicking* away every time I woke up.

My story for flying alone was simple and to the point. I had an aunt out in Hollywood with terminal cancer. Not only did I get pity and a choice seat, but that attendant gave me a sympathy hug. The idea crossed my mind to play the heartbroken, grief-stricken kid, but I was just too damn tired. When I was in California, first thing I would do off the plane was call the sponsors.

The airport sucked. We landed early and had to taxi all around the frigging place, waiting for a terminal to open to disembark. I had half a mind to yank open the emergency exit and slide down the inflatable ramps when they popped up. One thing was certain. I woke up damn cranky.

Everywhere, all the damn phones were in use. About eight bald guys tried to hand me some religious pamphlets. I took one just to be sure it wasn't about me. I kept an eye out in case anyone decided to follow, but I couldn't see how.

On the road there were no tails, as far as I could tell. I was clean in the airport back in New Hampshire, too. The terminals though, I just didn't know, too many freaks and even more fucking weird people. I hung around the magazine stand waiting until a phone freed up. Damn near got into a fight making a flat out run for it. While digging for spare change, Erik's cell phone started ringing. Let me tell you how much a damn fool I felt like. After blushing, I made my way away from the payphones, found a fairly quiet spot in a gift shop, and picked up.

"I'm here."

There was a slight delay, I half expected, half wanted to hear Erik on the other side. Regardless, I'd miss the bastard.

"We're here."

"Very good, smart ass. Want to tell me where I'm going?" I rubbed my eyes and realized how tired I really was. I was six hours and Lord knows how many time zones from the East Coast. I think I arrived four or five hours before I left or something.

"Go to the exit in front of the American Airlines Shuttle and look for a limousine. There will be a driver holding a placard with your name. Inside will be more instructions."

"Want to stop this *Mission: Impossible* bullshit and give me the facts?"

The line went dead. Too many people in the gift shop to throw a hissy fit so I picked out a T-shirt I liked, paid for it, got a couple magazines, and headed for the exit.

The driver was there as instructed, some scruffy-looking overpaid surfer dude with a bad dye job and too much tan. We walked to the car. He didn't open the door or anything—just went straight to his side and crawled in. The back was crowded with junk, clothes, a suitcase, some books, magazines, newsletters, comic books, and a box of video tapes, all with my name on them.

After digging through the rubble for about five minutes, the driver lowered the divider between me and the front seat, handed me an envelope, and raised it again. Inside was a business card with a different phone number on it, an ad torn from a newspaper, and more money. The car started rolling. I had no clue where we were going, but we were going.

I called the number on the card. An automated message answered. I jotted down the details on my arm. Didn't know what all the cloak and dagger routine was about. There was some food in the back, nothing special, a sandwich, couple cans of Coke and a bag of chips. The sandwich had turkey, ham, and cheese. I dropped it out the window, no more cold meat. Even the thought of biting into it brought up some Eagle Snack-tasting bile into my throat. I let the warm air drift in through the window, looked at the scenery, cars and motorcycles.

I ate the chips really fast and downed the Cokes. Guess the stewardess lady hadn't woken me for my airplane dinner, and in first class, you know it wasn't the garbage they serve to everyone else. I sat back and tried enjoying the rest of the ride. It ended soon enough as "Buff" pulled into the hotel. Found out though it wasn't a hotel, but a condo complex. He unloaded the car while I watched and then followed him up. The place was made up of four, four-story brick buildings, with a swimming pool, tennis court, and playground for kids dead center of the buildings.

They set me up on the top floor so if I ever decided to jump, they'd be sure of me dying. No way to make a quick escape either. I could try to drop down a floor, praying I hit a balcony and not the pavement. No way to fling myself into the pool. I was in the farthest corner of the second building.

Inside, we took the elevator up. Buff didn't talk. Neither did I. He handed me a key and I unlocked the door. He literally dumped all the stuff on the floor and left, closing the door in back of him. The place was nothing special—six rooms, two bedrooms, bath, living room, kitchenette, and a walk-in closet. Living in all them fancy places with Erik had spoiled me. I went to the can and washed all the writing off my arms.

The condo was furnished already. Looked like it was a place the sponsors used to hold people up on a regular basis. I wasn't in Hollywood proper. In fact, I didn't have a clue where I was. The fridge was full, the sheets clean, and the cable paid for. I got a soda, and a can of peanuts. Then I watched some television. I should have called the sponsors, but I was still feeling a little sore about being led around like I was.

I sorted through all the boxes and bags on the floor, found the envelope the driver had given me, some folders full of paperwork, and sat down to read. The envelope had a spare key—to what I don't know. It was small enough for a safety deposit box, but could also have been a post office box, which made more sense. We passed a wall full of mailboxes on the way up here.

The ripped-out ad was a casting call for a movie looking for walk-ons. Open auditions—pretty much all you had to do was show up. I stuck that under a magnet on the fridge. I ripped up the old business card Erik gave me, took the money out of the two envelopes, and counted damn near six hundred dollars. I found a safe spot for that too, kept a hundred on me, just in case, and stuffed the rest in a Zip lock bag in the water hopper of the toilet. The spare time stuff they gave me—the comics, magazines, books, videos, everything—was all about vampires.

The clothes were cool and they fit. It looked like they had tried to make a new image of me. Might be why they uprooted me and stuck me out here. Every other kid my age on his or her own in California was probably a street kid. Maybe I'd find some and let them stay in the condo to get off the streets for a while.

I grabbed the extra key, ran down the stairs yelling and stomping feet, listening to the echoes coming off the walls—anything to let off some damn steam. I was sure that in just a few hours I'd be bored as hell—soon as the jetlag wore off.

The key fit into the last box I tried—box number twenty-four. Should have guessed that since that was the apartment number too. The box was stuffed so full it all kind of poured out onto the floor when it opened. And let me tell you, there was another box full of stuff on the floor too. I guessed no one had been in that condo for a good couple of months. But they had just come in to clean up before my arrival. I toted all that stuff into the elevator and back upstairs. Pretty much figured I'd be doing this all night.

About five minutes into it, I got the urge to swim. I changed into my new bathing suit, grabbed a towel, checked it out of habit to make sure it wasn't crunchy, and headed for the pool with an extra shirt and some cool shades. The pool was pretty crowded, full of some of the hottest women I ever saw outside of a magazine. Of course each of them was with someone who looked like The Incredible fucking Hulk. There were a few kids my age, but they didn't even acknowledge me. I got a few looks, didn't know how to interpret them though. Back home we had only two or three looks—friendly, unfriendly, and I'm going to kick your ass. None of these were like one of those.

I took off my shirt after spreading the towel out on a lounge. I heard a lady next to me gasp when I exposed all the scars and stuff on my chest and stomach. I suddenly got self-conscious.

"Poor dear, you shouldn't be here. This pool is for the people who live here."

It's then I understood the look—how presumptuous and pompous. Granted, I didn't look like the people who lived there, but I didn't deserve being talked to like that.

"I do live here, you pretentious bitch," I said.

I jumped in the pool and did a cannonball, like Daddy had showed me once—tucked up tight, got real high and loosened up on impact, made one hell of a splash. Soaked that snatch good. Showed her a thing or two. Also got a bunch of other people pissed off at me, and the lifeguard asked me to leave. I got the job done though. I cooled off and went back to the condo—after mooning that lady.

The mail was mostly garbage, a stack of local papers, a month's worth of *The Weekly World News*, some of the pamphlets and newsletters from Boston, a shit-load of junk mail, an open invitation to a Goth club up in Hollywood, and coupons for some free pizza. I whipped out a big ole black trash bag, filled that bad boy up, and dropped it down the garbage chute.

When I got back, the phone was ringing. It was the landlord yelling at me about the pool incident. Didn't take the bitch too long to call that in. I apologized, blamed it on the jetlag, and got off with a warning. I called for the pizza, waited five minutes, and called the sponsors.

"Yeah, it's me. I'm in the condo." I didn't recognize the voice on the other side, but it was a guy. That's all I knew.

"You're late checking in." The voice chuckled.

"Been busy."

"Tomorrow morning, go to the studio for the walk-in call."

"Want to tell me what it's all about?"

"Tomorrow."

"No, right now. You've been dicking me along for the past couple days. Now that Erik is gone, I'm on my own and not too fucking happy about it so give me some damn answers."

"What do you want to know?" I heard the resignation in the guy's voice. Like he was used to giving up.

"Every damn thing."

He rambled on for the better part of a half-hour. I even put the phone down, answered the door, paid for the pizza, got a plate, glass of water, and when I came back, he still hadn't stopped talking. The pizza was warm, thank goodness. It was only cheese. If there was any meat on it, it'd be sliding down the garbage chute. After all his talking, it all came down to them wanting me to do a job.

Go to this movie studio and pose as a walk on. After the shoot, hang out for a little bit—look around until the pass expires—simple screen and clean. If there's any sign of the "unlife" then check in and call for a team. Guess this was my big break into the business.

Soon as the call ended, I phoned the operator and got the name and address of the dude who just called me. It was too late to start a manhunt—not too mention the sun was going down. Hollywood or not, no way I was going on the streets tonight. I locked the door, closed the windows, locked the sliding door to the balcony, put in the bar, and cranked up the air conditioning.

I got out a couple stakes, put them in key locations throughout the place. Loaded a pistol with a fresh clip and left it on the kitchen table. I hung my cross over the sliding door, put the extra gun under the pillow, and lay down for a long night's sleep. The bed was comfy, worn in and had a slight give to it on the right side like a chubby guy had slept there for a long time. I rolled into it, covered myself with sheets, blankets, and gripping a stake tightly in my hand, let the sleep wash over me.

The phone rang just before seven. I woke up, flung the stake at the door, and leveled the pistol at the window. By the time it had rung a third time, I had a bead on the phone and was about ready to blow it away when common sense came back. I rubbed sleep from eyes, coughed up a big wad of phlegm, had to chew and swallow it, and reached for the receiver.

"What?"

"Just giving you a wake up call, sport. Don't want you being late your first day going solo."

"Who is this?"

The line went dead before I got another peep. I slipped it back into the cradle, stretched, and got up.

That water from the shower felt great and, man, it was still cold as hell in the place. I killed the AC after some shrinkage from it being so high and coming out of the damn shower soaked.

Breakfast was quick and simple—the way I liked it. Every now and again you get the craving for something big, but going out to do a job, I wanted as little as possible in my gut to risk any chance of puking. I hated dealing with the dead, and man, they could reek sometimes. I reread the casting call about a thousand times over my orange juice and toast. Each time I shook my head, and I still couldn't believe the BS assignment.

Just easy business—go on set, hang in the studio, walk around on "the street," and then go home after some discreet sneaking. One thing I can say though is that without Erik around, I could be more careful and not worry about him tripping up the works. I wondered for a moment just what the hell he was doing. Sleeping in his coffin, or in a mausoleum someplace next to that Kane bastard. I'd taken a shot, maybe not my best, but I got away. Sometimes it seemed too easy—like they let me out. But if they had, I'd be dead already, or worse, a damn vampire.

I called a cab and waited out front after stuffing an extra cross, gun, and stake in my backpack. I still had two road flares left, but I was running low on everything else. I needed more ammo, more holy water, more of them Jesus crackers, and more importantly, crosses. Needed those everywhere. The two I had left were nice and all, but too damn small.

The driver was Spanish or Indian or something. I couldn't tell. He spoke too fast, and his accent, so damn thick I only picked out about half the words. He dropped me off in front of the studio gates. A fat guy in a polyester uniform was taking names and comparing them to a list on a clipboard. I skirted over to the sidewalk and was about to walk through when he stopped me and asked for my ID—my name and business on the set. I showed him the ad for the walk on parts, and he waved me through.

What a *clusterfuck* Hollywood is. The studios, or what they called them, looked like giant airplane hangers. People were zooming all around on golf carts, talking on cell phones, and shouting. People pushed racks of clothes on wheels. The parking lots were all filled, and there were some pretty pissed-off people looking for spots. And right in front of it all was this giant office building, maybe seven or eight stories high, crammed full of chrome and windows. Executives in suits marched back and forth in front of them, waving their arms while talking on speakerphones.

A couple of guys in costumes walked past me, and I decided to follow. Man, I'd have no problem looking around the place from the looks of things. But being discreet wasn't going to happen. If I were quiet or polite, I'd look out of place. It was time to put on my asshole shoes and get to stepping.

I found my way onto the lot of Studio A. There was this line, maybe two hundred people long waiting in front of one guy and a girl sitting in back of a table, taking names and asking more questions. A lot of the people waiting were like me, straight off the street. They were looking for their big break into the business, and I was looking for bloodsuckers. A good chunk of them were talking on phones, or drinking bottled water, or reading lines from scripts and then reciting them.

An hour and a whole lot of bitching and cussing later, I made it to the table. I gave them my name, my real name. They gave me a pass, a bottle of water 'cause I looked so pale and dehydrated, and a questionnaire to fill out. I sat on the curb for a minute or two, filled out the papers. Then turned around and handed them back. The girl directed me over to a smaller hut with people streaming in and out of it. I walked over, took out the cell phone trying to look more important, and strolled in.

It was totally crammed with people—people getting into costumes, other people plastering makeup across more people, and two little guys shouting directions, motivations, and instructions through bullhorns. I got ushered into a chair.

A chunky guy put some thin base on me and a little blush on my cheeks. He looked at my neck when my shirt slipped down a little and yelled out, "Done!"

Next, another man hustled me over to the costumes, took off my pack, and all but tore my shirt off. He put me into this white shirt with all sorts of ruffles and frills on it. Looked like a girl's blouse, but I wasn't about to argue. Shit, I barely had time to breathe. From costuming and makeup, they rushed a van full of us to a whole different part of the studio. Way off in the far back corner of the lot was a small hut, but it was still damn big.

They dropped us off and before I realized what the fuck was happening, I figured out I was in a van full of vampire clones. Just like that Goth club back in Boston, all of us dressed for the part.

We walked through this tunnel of planks, wires, and lights to a set. There were fake columns and raised platforms all over the place, and a stone-looking staircase in the very back leading up to the catwalks. When you looked real close at it, you could see it was fake, but the stairs weren't the focus of the cameras. The director, at least I think he was, sat in a chair watching everybody file onto the stage. He pointed out locations in corners, sitting on the stairs, or just standing, leaning against the walls. Red lights flooded down from the ceiling as a light mist started to creep across the floor. A wind machine blew in low, just enough to keep the fog circulating. The director guy looked up at the ceiling and some guys dressed in black adjusted the lights and mixed in some different colors.

"Okay, people listen up. No one speaks. When I call action, you all shut up. What's going to happen is an actor dressed as a vampire will come down those stairs. The stage will overflow with fog, and the lights will dim. From the center of the set, a woman will rise from the floor. The vampire will go over, bite her, and let her drop. Then all of you rush over and bite her too. But not really, there will be no close ups. The actress is rigged with bladders and hoses so blood will spurt up from her as you all chew. She'll scream and die. That's the end of it."

I was perched on the bottom step of the staircase in my frilly shirt, listening to the guy ramble, when the damn phone started ringing. Man, a whole lot of people got suddenly pissed-off at me. I reached into my pocket and turned off the ringer and waited for things to settle back down.

More fog rolled in, the lights dimmed, and the director guy stood, waved his hand, and yelled out, "Action."

Everything went like clockwork. The actor came down the stairs, walked right past me, and raised his arms, his robes flowing in the artificial breeze of the wind machine. The mist gently licked at his fingertips and swirled with each motion of his arms. The woman was dressed in a fluid-like white gown with plunging neckline. She had red hair below her shoulders and brilliant blue eyes.

The actor approached her, ran his hands across her breast, and her head reared back in delight. He teased his tongue across her neck and untied the shoulder straps of the gown letting it fall into the fog to expose her intensely beautiful body. We all looked at her greedily for one reason or another. He stood in back of her, reached around, and bit her on the neck. The blood flowed over shoulders, across her breasts, and she fell into the fog.

The rest of us converged and circled her on the stage as the wind blew away the fog. We pretended to chew on her flesh and the blood spurted from everywhere. She screamed as more fake blood pumped into the fog-filled air, circling all around us.

She breathed her last breath, the blood stopped, and the director called out, "Cut. That was fantastic people." The director came out from the shadows and wrapped a robe around the fallen actress and everyone applauded when she got up. "One take—that's all it took. The van is waiting outside. Go back to makeup and costumes and get your old stuff. You're free. If you want, you can wait around for a little bit, watch us film some more, or wait for a studio tour. You all should have gotten a free pass for one in your packets."

The van ride back was all full of chatter how beautiful the actress was and how great it was being in the presence of the great Goth film director, Shane Douglas. I didn't know what all the damn fuss was about, though I had read of Douglas in one of the pamphlets I took from that camper. When we got dropped off, I changed, got my pack back, checked my packet, and aside from the tour pass, found a lunch ticket, press photos of the actors, some propaganda for the movie, and some promotional stuff, key ring, baseball cap, and T-shirt. I stuffed it all into my pack, took out the tour pass, and headed for the gates.

What better way to look around the place than on a tour, out in the open, looking like a tourist? I'd hang out on the bus, sit next to a couple, making it look like I was with them so no questions would get raised. I saw a couple of the walk-ons looking at me, heard them talking, and realized that they knew me from the newsletters. Not two days in California and already I was having attention drawn to me.

I ducked out of the crowd of actors and snuck out. The tour bus was a double decker, never moving more than ten miles an hour. The bus driver a bored, balding man, spoke into a microphone as he drove, pointing out stars and studios where some future blockbusters were being shot. I sat next to a couple from New York, judging by their accents, who seemed to take a picture every few seconds or so, hoping for a glimpse of a superstar.

I looked all around, but didn't see any empty buildings. Nothing was boarded up. Everything was in use and had people buzzing around, which meant I had to get into the studios proper or see if there was anything in the offices. That seemed just a little bit more public than the studios so I crossed out that idea. I hopped off the bus as it stopped, waiting for a man to walk a pack of yippee dogs across the lot, pulled my ball cap down low over my face, leaned up against the side of a studio, and when no one was looking, slipped in.

Most of the lights were out, and I didn't want to risk using a road flare for light. I had forgotten my damn flashlight back at the condo and was shit out of luck. The exit signs were lit up, burning globes of red over the two or three doors that I could see. I heard talking, footsteps, and more talking. I went down a hallway made of flimsy plywood with a lumpy gray carpet thrown on the floor covering up cables and such. When it ended, I was on the set of another movie, least it looked so anyway. There was a circle of people and equipment huddled around a set that looked like a bedroom. I couldn't see much, but what I did see was two women, naked as day one, kissing and stuff on the bed.

No matter how much I wanted to stay, there would be time for this one later on. I found the bus, climbed back on, and got brought again to the front parking lot. I walked back to the set of the vampire movie, produced my lunch ticket, and ate off the catering truck. Everyone seemed to be at lunch. Some of the actors were picking at the buffet table. Others were talking to the press or with the walk-on actors. I found a spot on a milk crate and started eating.

Sometimes there were more eyes on me than the stars. Felt kind of spooky with all those neo-Goth people looking at me from the corners of their eyes and wondering if they should approach me or not. But if they knew who I was, then they knew why I was there, too, which meant I had to be extra careful and make sure no one followed me anyplace. Didn't need any accidents on my first mission alone. Besides, the sponsors were trusting me with this one, and if I was right with my hunches, I'd be getting a whole load of information after this was over.

Lunch ended and everyone got herded out of the set and onto a bus. I ducked in back of the studio and hid in some boxes while the bus filled and left. Then the director came back, looked around, and went into his office. He came right out a second later with the script tucked under his arm, headed for the men's room. When it was clear, I called the sponsors, and told them I hadn't found anything yet and planned to look around some more. A couple of the actors walked into their trailers. Then a bunch of workers came and started dismantling the set while others began building a new one.

They told me to stay as long as I could and snoop around. What else was I going to do? My ride had left without me. Things got quiet and I came out from the boxes. I walked around the hanger to the back, eased open the fire door, and went in. The place was practically empty, save for a couple of sets under construction and movie equipment. I walked all around, climbed up to the catwalks, saw all the lights and fog machines strung up, but nothing else.

I was running out of clues and ideas, didn't know where else to look. I mean, if I were a vamp that wanted to blend, I'd be here on the set. But where could I hang without being seen and only coming out at night? I wanted to call Erik. He would know. He knew everything about vampires. Of course, now he *was* one.

I heard someone else up on the catwalks with me. Heels clinking against the metal walkways. The ramp started to vibrate. Whoever it was got closer. I found the ladder and started down, when I saw a pair of eyes looking down at me. Someone started to yell and shout about me sneaking in. Then that fellow started down after me. He was big and strong-looking, like he carried the lights up or hoisted them or something. He took his feet off the rungs and slid down the rest of the way. Thought the fucker was going to hit me so I let go and fell through the roof of the set onto a couch.

I rolled off, heard more footsteps coming up fast, and bolted for the doors. I was almost there when the door opened. The sunlight blinded me for a second, but I got up a good run and dove, slid on something through the guy's legs in the doorway, hit the pavement, and started running. I ran around the side and dove back into those boxes again and waited. About a hundred people ran by—or so it seemed. I stayed buried in the boxes and waited and waited and waited.

I crawled out, shook off some of the bits that had stuck to my shirt, and made my way for the front gate. New plan—stand on the corner, call for a cab, and hang until it shows. Then I'd go home for dinner and maybe a swim.

I was out in front of the studio, inching my way along with my back pressed against the wall so no one could sneak up on me. I kept looking in each direction. I wanted to take out the gun and walk out bold, but that wasn't going to happen. It went slow, too slow, but at last I reached the corner. The catering truck was closed up, the buffet table gone. Douglas was headed into the hanger followed by a whole flock of people.

I hesitated, looked over my shoulder, and made my move. I ran to the truck, hid in back of it, looked under it, looked to the sides. I waved to the driver through the mirror and watched while he pulled out a butt and sparked up. The gates opened to let in another tour bus. I could trot along side of it until cleared of the set and then run out to the street. But that didn't happen, nothing even close.

I felt a crack to my head as something slammed into it. The truck pulled away with tires squealing. I looked up from where I lay on the lot, waiting for my blurry vision to clear, and felt blood flowing down my face. Standing over me was the vampire's stunt double. His fists were clenched. Blood dripped off the knuckles of his right hand.

He had dyed blonde hair and eyes that glowed with the daylight. Then I saw it was more than the sunlight making them glow. He picked me up with one hand. My feet left the ground. I landed two or three good kicks to his crotch, chest, and ribs, but it didn't phase him. He slapped me down, split open my lips, picked me up from the back by my shirt and dangled me inches above the pavement. I could feel his cold, dead breath on my neck. He knew why I was here.

He lifted me higher and threw me into the side of the building. I slid down in a heap, reached into the pack, pulled out the gun, and chambered a round. When he came in for the kill, I raised the gun, pointed it dead between his eyes, and pulled the trigger. *Click.*

"Safety is on shithead."

I threw the gun at him. He knocked it away,

I heard it hit the lot and skitter out of sight. "I don't suppose you want to discuss this, do you?"

He shook his head.

"How come you're out in the sunlight?"

He looked at me crooked, like I had an asshole growing out of my forehead.

"Oh, shit."

He raised his fist, looked like he was getting ready to punch me through my chest and rip out my heart. I let the pack slide to the ground from my shoulders.

He looked at the blood on my face and licked his lips. "How does it feel knowing that you're going to be my lunch?"

I rubbed my fingers through my blood, held them up in front of him. "You want some of this?" I licked my fingers, wincing at the coppery taste.

"All of it."

I did it again, this time getting enough so that the blood dripped off my fingertips. I could see smoke starting to rise off the guy. Like he couldn't take the sun all of a sudden. He lunged at me and I sidestepped him. His hand erupted in flame and he howled. While he clutched his hand, I got the stake from my pack. His arm ignited and he started shrieking like a banshee. I ran up to him, felt the flames on my face and hands, and drove that stake home, right through his chest. He clutched at it and fell helpless to the lot as the sun claimed him in a fireball. When I looked around, there was Shane standing in the doorway, giving me the eyeball.

When I stood back to look, the last of the bloodsucker was burning up. I ran over, got a fire extinguisher and put out the fire. Shane just stood there, jaw hanging down to his knees. I dropped the canister at my feet, then found some boxes, got what was left of the bloodsucker into it, and headed for the dumpster.

"You got a choice," I said dumping the ashes and bones into the dumpster. "Keep your pie-hole shut or I plant a cap in your skull." I got my gun and leveled it at him to make my point.

Shane nodded

"Can I get into a trailer or office to clean up and make a call?"

Shane pointed over at a little side door with the word *Director* written across it. I hadn't noticed it before. Stuffing the gun into my pack, I went for the door.

It was a cramped little office with a smaller washroom attached, and it was crammed full of junk—old scripts, posters, mounds of paperwork, a desk, chair, phone, and filing cabinet. After locking the door to the head, I washed my face and got all the blood off. I took a long look in the mirror, which was smudged and needed to be washed. I had to wonder how much longer I was going to let this go on. What would be in store for me afterwards? More importantly, would the sponsors let me go with everything I'd seen and done?

I heard the outer door open and took my gun out. Shane was sitting behind his desk scribbling furiously on some paper when I returned. He looked up, nodded acknowledgement and that was it. I was near the door when he called out to me.

"Hey, kid."

"Yeah?" I stopped with hand poised over the knob.

"What's your name?"

"Elvis. Elvis Taggard." I heard him going through a stack of papers.

"So it is. Got your questionnaire here. All you did was write down the title to all the Elvis Presley songs."

"Not all of them—just the ones I remembered."

"Want to tell me what that was all about out there?"

"No."

The ringing of the cell phone saved me.

"Excuse me," I said and stepped back into the bathroom.

"Is the job done?" asked the unidentified voice on the line.

"And hello to you too."

"Is it done?"

"Yeah," I replied. "Anything else?"

"No. When you get back to the condo call and check in."

I hung up and left the phone on the sink. If I ever had a chance to get out, this was it. No going back. I'd only have one chance to get my things and the money I stashed away at the condo, then I could be on the road and, with any luck, never be found. I could live a long life where no one knew my name. Shane knocked on the door after not hearing anything.

"Everything okay in there, kid?"

"Yeah." I came out of the bathroom, looking worse than when I went in.

"So, kid, you ever give any thought to being in the movies?"

The next few months were just a giant damn whirlwind. Shane stopped production of the movie and started rewriting the script. While all this was going on, he got me an agent, an older fellow with big belly and stress lines on his face—a guy named Ralph Roussa. Ralph's face was perpetually red, like there was too much blood in his head and had a tendency to chain-smoke, but only when on the phone. I went to his office once to sign some forms, and then every other time I dealt with him, it was at a fancy ass restaurant where he picked up the bill.

I had made it back to the condo, just once, and never even tried to go back again. I got all my stuff, the money, my clothes—just the old ones, not the ones that the sponsors bought me—and left. I kept all my vamp hunting stuff in case they ever tried to enact some sort of revenge on me. But I had a good feeling that Erik, wherever he was, wouldn't let that happen.

The studio people had me packed up and moved into a trailer within two days. The first night I spent in a hotel under an alias, and Shane said that maybe I should think about changing my name, just in case. He didn't know a damn thing about my background, and I didn't know how much if any to divulge.

They blamed the movie production stoppage to a change in script and one of the big shareholders pulling out, though that was all a crock of shit. First thing they did with me is send me to a tanning place to try and cover up some of the scars and bites and stuff. Then all the hoopla started. In order to do what he wanted, Shane needed to get my name out on the market and fast. I, of course, opted not to change it, which may have been a very stupid thing, but it was my name and I was proud of it.

It started with a cereal commercial for Frosted Flakes—great stuff. The shoot lasted an hour. They called me a natural, but shit, it was eating—anyone could do that. Then I had to do some stuff for the big money holders in the movie, a thirty second television spot for Pepsi, then an ad for Winnebago and Reebok. Shane had me doing small interviews about the movie, and I didn't even know my damn part in all of it yet. But Shane had been pumping me for info, and I gave just what he needed and nothing more. It was going from a Gothic romance—type film and an action movie, and no one in the movie seemed to object. Apparently the market had been flooded with whiny bloodsucker movies with no action. This was going to change it all. They even switched the name of the film to *The Darkest Thirst.* I didn't think sounded like an action flick, but Shane had made up his mind.

I did some radio interviews and all of a sudden I was on television in a short-lived prime time sitcom. It of course had all been a ploy of Ralph's. He had found a series that he knew wouldn't succeed, paid out a lot of money for a prime time slot during the week, and bang, I was all over it.

Next came the photo shoots, posters, postcards, and some shots for those teeny bopper magazines. They kept trying to get me to take off my shirt, but I wouldn't.

Shane finally came around and showed me the first draft of the script and let me read through it, which was a very good thing. I liked it, but they had to go back and reshoot a lot of the other scenes. While that was going on, I had to learn my part. This was of course going to bring the movie seriously over budget. But the guys paying the bills didn't seem to mind. I knew I was getting paid. I signed the damn contracts, but none of it made a lick of sense so I just let Ralph handle everything.

All the time this was going on, I had an eye out, making sure I wasn't being tailed. I didn't know how the sponsors were going to deal with this. Shit, I had never called them back and hadn't heard from them since. I knew they were around, but I had no clue who or where. The only hint I had to their real existence was that fellow's name and address from the phone trace.

The movie started shooting again two months later. With all the stuff they had me doing, I felt so damn tired I didn't want to do much of anything. My role was small but important to the movie. I am supposed to be the long lost son of the lead actress, Juliana Morgan. The male lead, Rory Johnson, is a vampire who has fallen in love with Juliana—only she's mortal and has no intention of being with him despite how she feels for him. Sounds like a damn soap opera already. So, in order to get to her, I am kidnapped and held prisoner as an exchange—my life for hers. She had me before her first husband died and then sent me to an orphanage, a secret that has pained her all her adult life. And now, suddenly re-acquainted with me, she doesn't want to lose or give me up again.

While in the custody of the lead vampire, Shaun, Lenore played by Juliana, has to come and get me and break into the vampire's lair to free me without getting caught. Then we would run away together, forever, right? Nope, she gets discovered and has to fight her way in and out. Only at the last moment, she is captured using me as bait. Then Shaun takes her to a cabin way out in the mountains and forces her to make a decision. That's where I come in again. Somehow I've managed to escape the lair and follow them. When Lenore can't kill Shaun, it's my job to follow through and kill the lead bad-guy.

19
Elvis: Here in the Now

So that's how it all happened, how I came to Hollywood from the trailer park and got famous. Shane keeps me on a pretty short leash, seeing that I don't have a legal guardian at the moment, and keeps DSS out of the picture.

That opening scene I was telling you about so long ago? That was the last of the film. Luckily all my scenes had been shot already. I didn't have anything to do but sit around and watch. Now the film goes to sound, editing, special effects, and all of that. I'm not sure what happens to me next. That seems to be my life story of late though.

I headed back to my trailer to settle in, had a feeling it was going to be one of my last nights on the set unless they needed some scene reshot. As expected, the line of paparazzi was still there. I didn't even look at them. I thought my days as a star were numbered.

When I got back into the trailer there was a new stack of paperwork waiting for me, which really pissed me off. That meant someone else besides me had a key unless I left the door open, which I never did. I heard the toilet flush, reached under my shirt for a gun, and saw the grip of it sticking out from under a pillow on the couch. Rachel came out and damn near died when she saw me.

"Sorry, Elvis, I had to pee and didn't have a cart."

"How'd you get in?"

She blushed and showed me a bent bobby-pin and her credit card.

"Pretty smart."

"Have to be extra ingenious when you're a woman in Hollywood and have to pee."

I laughed and sat down, patting the cushion next to me after sliding the gun under the pillow some more. Rachel sat next to me.

"They just finished the shoot. Movie is over, save for the final editing stuff."

"Really? I thought we had at least another week."

"Nope. Apparently Shane was happy with that final scene, and it's all up to the other people."

"What's next for you, Elvis?"

"I don't know, Rach. If there's not another job in that stack of paperwork there, I'm out of work and a home."

She shuffled through and handed me a folder.

"Another movie, huh? Only I get the lead in this?"

"You bet, kid. And if you wouldn't mind, I'd like to stay on as your assistant."

"Hey, that'd be great."

She had such a nice smile when she wasn't worried about every damn thing.

"Should I take it?"

"Read it through, but I would. Also, Ralph wants to speak to you and there's a press conference in a week for the movie. When we need to reach you, where will it be?"

"I don't know," I said shrugging. "You have room on the couch?" I smiled nervously and she jotted down some notes on the back of the folder.

"That's the address and phone number of my apartment. It's not big, but you'll fit on the sofa." She handed me a spare key and gave me a peck on the cheek. "I'll call you here later on, Elvis, and drive you over."

"Thanks, Rach."

She got up to leave and I couldn't help but give her a big hug. If she had a social life outside work, which I assume she did, I'd be a major thorn in the side of it. But with any luck, I'd be able to find another place to live, maybe even in the same building if anything was open.

I woke up the next morning to a note on my door to meet Rachel and Shane in the studio for a quick photo shoot in full costume and makeup. Wardrobe was in the other building and since no one was beating down my damn door, I did my own—a little bit anyway. Just added some color to my cheeks and neck, hiding some of the marks. I think that's what attracted them to me in the first place. The makeup guy didn't have to add any scars. I came with my own.

It was back to the original set, where I was an extra. Nothing had been torn down yet. Juliana, Rory, and a few of the others were already there waiting for me. I stripped out of my shorts and Nike shirt into some ridiculous outfit that Shane had wardrobe pull together for me. We spent an hour on the set with some Spanish photographer taking pictures—solo, posing, in action poses, on the stairs, sitting on a coffin. Whatever the guy felt like doing, we pretty much did.

"Shane, how much longer is this thing going to last?" Rory asked, checking his watch.

"Another half an hour max."

"All right, I have an audition."

The photographer took some more stills, packed up his gear. Then he and the assistant left, flanked by Shane.

"God, I hate doing these things." Juliana moaned.

"I don't know," I said, sitting on the stairs. "Aside from the guy staring at my ass for the past ninety minutes, it was kind of fun."

Juliana rolled her eyes, wobbled in her high heels, and strutted back to wardrobe. I did the same thing later, stripped down, and got back into my *kid* clothes—while Rory went in back of the stairs to change.

"How many photo shoots have you done, Elvis?" Rory called from in back of the stairs.

"For the movie, just this one. But I've done some commercials and stuff. I've only been doing this Hollywood stuff for a few months now."

"With all the publicity you've been getting, it seems like you've been doing it forever. You'll be getting lead billing pretty soon." Rory came out dressed in jeans and a sweatshirt. "It was fun working with you while I did. Shane must have seen something special in you for that last rewrite."

We shook hands and he walked out. I was expecting Juliana to come out and do the same, but I never actually saw her leave the studio.

Back at the trailer, a yellow plastic bag waited for me, hanging from the knob with some more paperwork stuffed in it. Inside was an invitation for lunch at the corporate offices with Ralph and another script. This script was for something weird though, a press conference. I had two days to learn my part. Apparently they were going to make a grand spectacle of this thing, using me, Rory, and Juliana.

I went inside, dropping all the stuff on the trailer table. I called Ralph real quick. He wanted to make sure I was going to show up for lunch. Ralph said he had another stack of scripts for me. I started reading the one I had. It was some sappy, angst-laden teen romance film about a redneck kid from the sticks and a rich girl. I didn't read through it, but called Rachel on the cell phone and told her I'd take it and that I was going to talk to Ralph and see if she could manage me from now on.

Ralph and me ate dinner in the office cafeteria. It was obvious Ralph wasn't going to wine and dine me over this one. We talked about the movie and other upcoming projects. I told him that I wanted to take the new movie offer, which he was very pleased about. His newest little meal ticket wasn't a one-time thing. I didn't ask him about switching management, though. He seemed to have something else weighing heavy on his mind.

"What's got you so flustered today, Ralph?"

He kneaded his napkin in his meaty hands, took a swig of ice tea, and a mouthful of potato chips.

"This press conference thing. We can work Arnie into it for you if you want."

"No, it should be simple, right? Just a lot of running around and screaming. Shit, any kid could do that with enough sugar and caffeine." I emptied my glass of root beer while Ralph continued his kneading.

"They're planning a lot of special effects, Elvis. Pyro and such."

"What's that mean?"

"Explosions and fire, Elvis. The entire place is going to be rigged."

They extended my time in the trailer, which was a damn good thing. Rachel had to fly to Florida on a family emergency. I had to get carted around in a van everywhere I went too. I read over the newest stack of scripts. The only one that really appealed to me was the sappy one on account of all the smooching involved. I hadn't had any time for a girlfriend and was missing some of the finer things. This was a chance to get a little action, even if it was all acting.

I got to the press conference an hour early just like everyone else did. Shane was there, Juliana, Rory. I was the last to arrive. They hustled me around, getting me into the costume from the movie. Then the makeup guy did his magic. The thing was being held inside a ballroom of a plush hotel. We'd gone through all the footsteps and rehearsals. The special effects wizards had been there for hours setting things up.

The buffet table was loaded with food. Posters were hung all over the damn place. The one they chose was me, holding a stake and standing back to back against Juliana. Juliana was holding a cross and a pistol. The entire background was Rory's face in full bloodsucker embellishment. It looked really cool, and I was pleased. I didn't get top billing like Rory had said, but it was cool seeing my name on the poster.

The plan was for Shane, the Pepsi guy, some of the other sponsors, and the producer, who I had never met personally but had seen on the set, to start talking to the press and media people. Then Juliana would come out in full regalia. She would talk. I had a little preaching to do, give some answers—nothing too personal, future projects, etc. Then Rory, supported on wires, would drop down from the ceiling and attack Juliana. There would be a brief pyrotechnic as the ceiling broke away. Rory, or should I say Shaun, gets to Juliana, Lenore, and then I tackle and stake him. But not really. We had rehearsed this forever. I was being given a real stake with a collapsing tip filled with fake blood, so when I stuck him, the blood would squirt out.

The press pit was filling up. Guess some of the vultures decided to come early for free eats. I waited outside the room and looked in through one of the side doors. The press people from the studio were the first ones to enter. Then came the head of the production company. Shane made his entrance with the producer. They did a brief announcement, each under the glare of camera and lights and whir of tape recorders.

They fielded questions and introduced Juliana. There was a strobe effect from all the flashes going off. She strolled onto the stage in all her regal elegance, wearing a Victorian gown and with her blonde hair piled high. They had paled her skin and given her a dimple above her lip. Special contacts added an ice blue gleam to her eyes. She took a seat next to Shane and read a little speech of her own. I could feel the butterflies in my stomach starting to stir.

Now it was my turn, I spun and puked into a flowerpot. The press thought that was cute, and I could imagine the headlines from this. I washed my mouth out with some bottled water, took a deep breath, and strolled in.

"And now, the newest teen superstar, Elvis Taggard!" Shane shouted.

The room got quiet as I walked in. I smiled and took a quick seat. I hadn't prepared a statement so I poured a glass of water and waved. Then like a deep breath had been released, sound came back to the room—the *pop* of flashes, the *clicks* of cameras. Shane shook my hand, pointed, and posed for some photo-ops with me. Juliana looked disgusted by the entire ordeal, pissed off that I was getting more attention than she was.

"Now, Elvis will field some questions." I didn't move on the podium. Felt like my damn shoes were full of rocks and my legs were all rubbery. Shane moved the microphone down in front of me. A bunch of arms shot up into the air. Shane pointed, and a woman wearing a dress stood up.

"Elvis, what are your plans for the future?"

Shane looked and nodded at me.

"I just accepted a role in a new movie. They're still casting it. I don't know who else is in it."

Shane pointed to another raised hand. A guy with a beard, ponytail, and notepad stood up, scribbling away.

"What would you say is the source of your recent rise to the top?"

"It's all that man," I said, pointing to Shane.

Another hand and another question.

"Do you prefer doing series television or movies and how do you feel about the downfall of the television series you were in?"

"That's not fair," I joked. "Two questions."

A bunch of the people laughed. A bunch of them started to look bored with me.

"I liked doing both. The series was fun, but the shooting schedule was grueling. The movie has longer days sometimes, but it's not as long a shooting schedule as a series. You get some time off between projects."

Another round of questions went by and it seemed like it was never going to end. I told them I was from a trailer park in Kentucky. Told them I was an orphan. They asked about education, and I said that after this project I'd like to push my schooling up a notch and finish it early. I hadn't made any choices about college. I didn't want to think of it yet.

Shane nodded his head and the lights dimmed. Red lights filled the room, a fog machine pumped in tendrils of cold mist. Sound effects of a thunderstorm helped set the mood. As a giant thunderbolt boomed out making the lights flash, the ceiling exploded over the emergency exit, and Rory came dropping down in his flying rig. In full vampire gear—robes, fangs, and red eyes, he swooped down and landed on the table in front of Shane.

Rory reared back and kicked Shane upside the head. I heard his nose break and was sprayed with blood. He reached over to Juliana, kissed her, and chewed off her bottom lip. Something was fucked! The crowd was loving this, thinking it was all an act. I grabbed the fake stake, not realizing it was fake, and brought it down into Rory's chest. The tip slid, the fake blood spurted out

He stopped smiling, went into his death throes, and fell "undead" at my feet. He winked at me and then spit Juliana's lip into my open mouth. I coughed it up, nearly puked again, but when the lights went on, nothing had changed. Juliana was still crying, clutching her face, blood seeping out between her fingers. Shane still lay unconscious, slumped against the wall and nose pressed flat.

The table evacuated instantly. The pressroom doors all slammed shut. The special effects men came falling from the roof, tied in cables, necks snapped, blood seeping from puncture marks.

"This time it's for real, Elvis." Rory smiled at me. His eyes glowed. He threw me over the table. I landed in the press pit, knocking down four or five of the reporters. Rory jumped up on the table. The press pit erupted. Five of the reporters sprouted fangs, and eyes started to glow. Man, that fucked-up Rory. He didn't seem to know what to say or do. Neither did I. I didn't have any of my damn weapons with me. And I didn't want to do anything that might risk the innocents.

Then I saw that none of them were innocents. Somehow, this entire thing was a damn set up. I ran to the corner of the room and watched all of the reporters take their true form. Rory smiled and stood facing them, trying to take control. On stage, the others didn't know what to do. They just kind of huddled around their fallen comrades. There was no way I could take all of these guys, either. I was fucked.

"There's no escape, Elvis."

"Let the others go. You only want me," I shouted.

"Whether you live or die, they're dead. The movie will never come out." The guy with the beard and ponytail took the lead, pushing Rory aside. He shot Rory down with a look, and Rory visibly resigned to a position in back of him.

"There sure are a lot of you fucking bloodsuckers around," I said.

"We've been working overtime. You've taken out too many of us."

"Can we make a deal?"

"No deals. You die."

I could tell by his tone that he was serious.

"We've separated you from your friends and weapons. You can't defend yourself. It'll be a pleasure to bring you over Elvis, to be my thrall for eternity."

I started looking around for an escape, but I was cornered. No doors, no windows, nothing.

"How're you going to do it?" I was trying to stall.

He knew it. Over his shoulder, my coworkers started to stir, looking at the fire escape. But the other vampires had encircled them, penning them in like herded animals. That's all we were to these bloodsucking bastards.

"I'm going to beat you down, break you, and then drain your blood. Enough with the talk, Elvis. Come to me."

"You know, Mr. Vampire? You're an asshole."

I saw Rory's harness up in the roof panel. I jumped for all I was worth, grabbed hold of it, and pulled myself up into the ceiling tiles. Below the tiles, they began to tear up the ceiling looking for me. I climbed up farther, weaseled my way into the ducts, and started crawling. They were going crazy, ripping up the room back there. I hated running from the fight, but there was nothing at all I could do except stay and get killed.

I saw a light source up ahead and headed for it. The shaft started filling with mist and the sounds of claws *scraping* across metal—some *growling* and *whispering*. That old familiar tug of vampire magic started to fill my head. I kicked out the panel where the light was and dropped out into the lobby.

There were a whole lot of startled people at my sudden appearance. I caught the eye of the desk clerk. He snarled and I saw the hint of fangs under his calm exterior. I beat feet and made an escape into the protective caress of the sunlight.

On the street, I hopped into a waiting cab. Inside the building, the bloodsuckers emerged from the vent, but they started to combust when they hit the sunlight. Bastards must have been waiting in the hotel all night. Pretty damned convenient, too, since there weren't any windows in the conference room. Made me wonder how long they had Rory. First stop was a department store, where I bought up a mess of squirt guns and a canteen.

The driver wouldn't sit and wait so I told him to keep the meter running. Money was no object. I flashed him my wad of cash to make the point. Next stop was the first Catholic church. I ran inside, dropped a fifty on the priest to make a bucket load of holy water and proceeded to fill the canteen and squirt guns. He looked at me pretty queerly—not like gay queer, but weird queer. I smiled and didn't give any details. Besides, how does one explain to a priest about going into battle against the forces of evil?

I also picked up some Jesus crackers, rosary beads, and a couple small crosses. No way I was going into this damn thing unarmed and not ready. If they wanted me, it was going to be a bitchin fight. When I got back outside, the sun was starting to set. I didn't realize how long I'd been in the church, preparing and praying. The cab was still there, and the meter was racked with zeroes.

One final stop, then the studio. That was where I was going to make my final stand against the vamps. Be honest and all, I was getting sick of all the shit. I wanted to be free of all of it. Only way that was going to happen was either die in the attempt or take out as many vampires as possible and put the fear of Elvis into them.

I got into a gun store, one that Erik had told me about a long time ago in case we made it to the West Coast. The stores were everywhere, but finding one that sold to a minor without a gun license was another. Erik kept a list of stores all over the States where you could get ammo, no guns, but ammo. In the store, I got six boxes of 9mm rounds, a box of .38 shells, some speed loaders, and spare clips. I looked at the shotguns, but the guy behind the desk scowled at me when I asked to hold it. I paid in cash and left without saying anything. Went back in the cab and to the studio. I paid the guy in cash, gave him a twenty-dollar tip, and told him he never saw me.

I ran to my trailer just as the sun peeked below the horizon. I was alone, and the entire mother-fucking vampire nation was on my tail. I dumped the bullets on the table, etched a small cross into the tip of each one, used the squirt gun to coat them in holy water and filled the clips and speed loaders. I got some stakes and a mallet, put the crosses around my neck, the rosaries in my pockets, and the squirt guns under my belt. I ate a handful of the crackers, washed them down with holy water, said a prayer, got my pack, loaded up, and took off into the night.

It was only logical that I came back here. This is where most of the madness began—here on the set. No way I had the time to rig some traps. It was too late for that. Thank God the only people I saw on the set were a few security guards who knew me. Everyone else was headed for the gates. I didn't know what time the bloodsuckers would be coming for me—just that they would.

I stayed away from the movie set. That'd be a little too obvious. The trailer was totally out of the question. I could hide out at Rachel's until morning, but then I'd be putting her jeopardy if anyone found out.

I had been running in back of a set when all the damn lights over all the parking lots snapped on. Only thing to do was wait, and it didn't take too long. They started coming out of the shadows and the shadows were everywhere. It all got liquid as the vamps emerged from the darkness—every corner, every damn rooftop, seemed every free inch of space had a bloodsucker on it.

There wasn't enough time to get into a building. Weren't any cars nearby either. I could see and hear them coming from all directions. Scouting around, I saw my only source for sanctuary and dove into a dumpster. After burrowing down some into the garbage and covering myself, I got out business—the 9mm, and the .38 and one squirt gun. I kind of laid them out in front of me within easy reach, just in case.

All around me, I could hear them tearing up the place, breaking windows, overturning crates, and smashing the shit out of anything in their way. Even a passing fire truck and ambulance couldn't drown out the mass destruction going on. I didn't think my hiding spot would last long with all the vamps' carnage. Just had to wait in here until a break showed up or my cover was blown.

Every now and again, they would all just stop for a few seconds, and then take up the search again. By now the studio must have been in ruins. Everything would come to a crashing halt, and boy was Shane going to be pissed-off at that. One of them started snooping around the dumpster. I felt the vibrations as it scratched at the metal with claws, probably still slick with blood from popping through its dead flesh.

I eased back the hammer on the .38, held it flush against my chest, took a deep breath and waited until I felt pressure on the trash and opened fire. First two shots caught him square in the gut. He fell back screaming as the bullets started burning and eating through him. When he hit the pavement, I saw he was just a kid, like me, maybe one or two years on me—in appearance anyway.

"Sorry," I said as I ran past him, shaking off the trash. I put another cap in his head hoping it would end his pain, at least for a while anyway. I ran.

The call was out, my hiding spot was gone, and I was in the open. The shrill screams from the plugged bloodsucker drew them all in closer. Only one place to go now—back to hell.

20
Elvis: The Twins

I took off like a madman firing blindly in back of me. I used up the cylinder in the revolver, dumped out the casings, and pumped the first quick-load into it. I didn't do any real damage, but slowed a couple of them up anyway. They'd seen what happened to the other one. I found a cart, jumped in, and peeled out.

I was right. The vampire movie set was crawling with them. I killed the lights on the cart—not that it mattered much anymore. I hopped out, leaving the thing running, watched it run over a couple of them, didn't even make them break stride though. I pumped off three more rounds and took one down.

I got into the lot while that vamp hissed and screamed on the tarmac. Things slowed down. They stopped chasing me, formed a line stretching from one end of the lot to the next—men, women, and children. Fuckers were fencing me in for the final kill. The lot was ringed with these giant spotlights. When they went on, night turned to day. I was blinded temporarily from the sudden flash. The vamps never missed a pace.

My back hit the door of the set. There was a thick chain wrapped around the handles, doors were unlocked though, just to taunt me. They gave a bit—opened not quite enough for me to squeeze through. The line continued to advance.

I had nowhere to go. After emptying the .38 into the nearest bloodsucker, I dropped the revolver and took out the 9mm. I chambered a round, took off the safety, pulled the hammer back, wrapped my hand around the trigger, and stuck the barrel in my mouth. This may have been a sin to Jesus, but there was no way I was becoming one of them. I closed my eyes tight and took one last deep breath. It tasted like metal and oil. When I pulled the trigger, someone slapped my hand away. The shot went off and punched through the wall in back of me. The gun dropped from my hand.

When I unlocked my eyes, thinking I was in heaven, I saw I was still in hell. Another kid stood in front of me. I recognized him from the movie set. We had bumped into each other a few times. Had lunch once. His name was Dorian, he played an extra in a few scenes. He was smiling—like none of this was happening.

"What the fuck did you do that for?" I cried out. The first of the tears started to come. "We're going to die here tonight, you ignorant fucker!"

Dorian reached down and picked up the gun. The line of bloodsuckers hesitated. He ejected the round into his hand, his flesh burning from the contact.

"Oh my God, you're one of them."

"Not really." Dorian pointed the gun into the crowd and fired all remaining eight shots, dropping two of the bloodsuckers. Mist started creeping out from under the door, clouds and clouds of it. Shapes began to form and come together. The phantoms appeared and took up their spot behind Dorian—like he was the damn leader.

"What the hell is going on?"

"Tell me, Elvis. What do you really know of hell?" Dorian's eyes flared red for a moment before regaining his composure. "What do you know of it? What do you know of war?"

I watched the lot. The other vampires had stopped, like they were confused, waiting for more orders from someplace else.

"Now, Elvis, if you know what's good for you, you'll be off."

"No way, man. Them bloodsuckers are going to kill me."

"Elvis," Dorian's voice flared. His eyes pulsed the color of the sunset. "Be off."

I felt the familiar tingling inside my brain, shook it off, and smiled at Dorian. "Not until you tell me what's going down."

From the tones surrounding us, I could tell things were uneasy—that something awful was brewing.

"I left Ireland to get away from this. Protestants against the Catholics, faction fighting faction. Now the trouble has followed me to the States. There's a force at work neither one of us can comprehend—trying to take over the underworld. And once that force gains control, you surface dwellers are doomed to be felled by it most certainly."

"It's a damn vampire civil war, isn't it?"

"In a manner of speaking, yes. In a not so positive light, Elvis, you've helped to spur it on. We'll talk about it later." Dorian spread his arms and the winds carried him up high.

The other vampires seemed to shrink back. I took a step away myself. I was in awe at what this *kid* could do. His voice boomed out over the lot as if through a megaphone.

"Brothers, the time for war is over. Let us be done with the madness. Hasn't there been enough bloodshed already? We are all kin. Let us not fight for this. This is petty and futile. We must not be controlled by another. It would be the plague of what our race has stood for and survived for the past thousands of years. We walked before Christ and will continue to, long after."

The lot filled with stirrings and mumbling. The forces to me looked even. I didn't know what each side had for bloodsucker magic, but one thing was for sure—I was with Dorian. I don't know if that gave him an edge or not, but it did leave me a place to fall back to.

Dorian landed gracefully, like a bird. None of the others opposite us moved. They stood confused, waiting. They were lemmings, willing to follow whomever made the first move, be it flee, stay and talk, or leap off the damn cliff. Dorian did seem to have some type of power over them. The vamps across the lot almost seemed dumbstruck or something.

"What happens next?" I asked Dorian.

"We wait, see what comes to pass. We'll either walk away or be dragged away."

"I ain't afraid to die, Dorian."

"You should be."

We stood motionless—like zombies, staring and waiting for the first stone to be cast. Nothing transpired. While *I* was edgy, both sides were eternally patient. It was the world's biggest and deadliest stare down. No telling if there would be a winner or not. Truth be told, I was afraid to die, and right now, afraid to live. I think some of the vamps thought that, too, but were too proud to say—or too afraid.

"Enough of this," Dorian shouted. "Give me your answer."

One of them stepped forward. Looked like a young man in his twenties—blonde hair, sharp features, as though chiseled from stone, cold, pale skin, and colder brown eyes. Dorian's eyes reflected the harsh artificial lights and the gentle glow of the moon.

"We've no choice, Dorian, but to fight. We have mass, you are few. There will always be more of us." That was it. He turned his back on Dorian, daring him. Then he took his place back in the ranks.

Without a whisper, claws sprouted through skin, fangs extended from teeth and gums, eyes took on the deep shade of red. Both sides were poised, prepared to strike. They'd only get one chance. So would I. Someone handed me my gun. I slapped a fresh clip into it and pulled out a squirt-gun, being careful not to splash any of the "good guys."

"I'm ready to fight with you, Dorian."

"Are you ready to die, Elvis?"

"No, I ain't."

"Then you're at least ready to fight."

I took out my rosaries, wrapped them around my wrists, slipped my cross out from under my shirt, and let it hang openly in view. I pointed the squirt gun, took the safety off the pistol, and chambered a round.

"I wish you would put that cross away, Elvis."

"Wish all you want, Dorian. I respect you. Hell, if we live, I might even like you—but this thing is staying out."

"You've got spunk for a human. I was like you once."

"When?"

"Over a century ago."

Across the lot, the others poised for the attack.

The moon reflected off Dorian's polished teeth. "Let it begin."

Dorian leapt into the air, screaming like an animal. The others were speedy to follow, putting themselves between the enemy and me. I made a quick attempt to memorize some faces, to avoid any accidents, but it was war and to be expected. I saw the gleam of light from Dorian's claws as he raked the throat of an enemy. No going back now.

I took aim with the pistol, eased back on the trigger and let off two shots. One hit home, the other didn't—like the fuckers could see them coming. It only caught the woman in the chest. It burned, she howled, and then looked right at me. I took two more shots, but my damn hands were shaking so bad I missed both times. She waded through the good and bad guys. I had chosen the wrong target. She had long red hair, green eyes, and looked just like…

"Deirdre!" I heard Dorian cry. "No, Elvis, don't touch her."

She reached out, grabbed my neck, and tossed me aside. I slammed into some trash cans, and the pistol jumped out of my hand. She grinned wickedly and charged back into the fray, leaping over the bad guys and slicing up the ones not with her.

My breath wouldn't come. I could still feel her vice grip on my neck. I struggled for air, for lungful after greedy lungful. The carnage went on about me, but something kept them away.

I saw Dorian eyeing Deirdre. With every movement they took, they avoided each other. But where Dorian went to wound, she went to kill. Dorian would cripple and she would crush. The resemblance was uncanny, unnatural. The *snapping* of bones and the *squeals* of the undead brought me back.

One got right on me. I hadn't seen him sneak up. Wasn't one of ours. I reached for the pistol when he pulled me up. My feet dangled inches above the lot. My cross glistened in the moonlight. He shaded his eyes. It was that fuck who had started this madness. I pumped off a few shots with the squirt gun, watched holy water streak and burn dead flesh. He howled while his face fizzed and dripped off in pink, fleshy blobs.

I dodged a few of his swings looking for an opening, but he cradled his face and shrieked. The stink of burnt skin was making me sick. He dropped his hand. His left eye had burst and now bubbled down his cheek. The right one glowed fiercely. I stuck the barrel of the .38 into the good eye and fired one shot, blowing out the back of his skull. Fucker went down hard, and when it was time, I drove a stake through his chest.

I was no match for any of these bastards, regardless what I thought. Self-confidence began to wane. The other bloodsuckers knew it. Dorian got between the opposing forces and me. There were a half dozen of them sneaking up, circling around me. Of the six, one was a security guard from the movie, the other I recognized as one of the paparazzi. The other four looked as if they had been plucked from their houses after a hard day's work.

Dorian crashed into the center of them. The fighting began, but only Dorian got up. Limbs hung by ligaments, bones stuck through skin, flesh, peeled in strips, lay strewn like streamers on the asphalt. When he stood, his clothes were torn, his left ear dangled from a flap of flesh. I turned, puked, and when I looked back, he had healed it. The others were trying, but it looked like Dr. Frankenstein's lab more than a movie set. I wondered how long until the cops showed up.

I began to fire at random, hoping to miss Dorian's people, but I was pretty sure I hit a few. Deliberately, I didn't aim at his sister, no matter how many times she glowered and sneered at me. The pistol was empty soon enough and throwing bullets was useless. Another two or three crippled by him and four more dead by her. It was chaos, plain and simple. I knew nothing about war, especially not like this. Using the squirt guns like grenades I launched them into the crowd, heard them *explode* on the pavement, the *hiss* of burning skin, and the *screams* of the inhuman.

When the smoke finally cleared, and it cleared quickly, there weren't anymore than a dozen standing and well over eight dozen lying scattered over the lot. Deirdre stood in front of six, Dorian before three.

"The odds are against you, dear brother."

"Why have you succumbed to this madness?"

"While you were off making a name for yourself among the mortals, I was doing the same—only with our people. You're not one of them, Dorian. Not one of us, either—anymore."

"Deirdre, don't let it end like this, please."

One of her followers burst into flames, howled then exploded, showering us with his remains. Deirdre screeched and looked up into the first rays of the sun. From their pockets, both Dorian and his sister pulled out thick dark glasses to cover their eyes. The others began to run for cover, shielding themselves from the sun with arms and clothes. But they fell to its heartless power. Dorian and Deirdre stood toe to toe, defiant of each other and the sun.

Those injured by Dorian soon went up in flames, while the bodies of the already critically wounded burned. Their cries drowned out the normal sounds of the morning.

With a shrill laugh, Deirdre reached into the dead, pulled up a body leaking blood, and drank deeply from it. "Cold and stale, Dorian. Join me?" She tossed the body aside and dissipated into a cloud of mist. The mist slowly filtered into the cracks of the rain gutters and storm drains. Then it was gone. Dorian found a similar body not on fire, and drained it.

"If you want to live, Elvis, come with me," he said, wiping his bloodied lips on his sleeve.

21
Elvis: Q & A

We walked for what seemed like hours, spending as little time as possible in the sun. Dorian was more than impressive—an incredible foe and an even a more powerful ally. About an hour into the trek, Dorian went into the subways. We mixed in with the early morning crowds going to work. No one looked or talked to us. To them we looked like street kids, with torn and dirty clothes. If they only knew. I had an urge to call the sponsors, tell them what went down. But it was their damn fault I got into this mess.

We took one train after another, stood on platforms, waited for them to empty, followed the tracks on foot—took tunnels that human eyes and feet hadn't seen in centuries. There was a whole different world down there. It looked like a burial crypt. Brick walls with alcoves held the bones of the long dead. We were so close to the damn subway, and this had never been discovered.

"Where are we going, Dorian?"

"To haven."

I had to follow the sounds of his steps. It was so dark I couldn't see. I didn't have a light and didn't want to spark up my only road flare. Shit lot of good it would do me anyway. "It's not much farther, Elvis."

"I know you can walk in the sun, Dorian. I figured that much out."

"You know that much, do you?"

"Yeah I do. How'd you know about the movie set tonight?" I asked, trying to keep up with him.

"I didn't, Elvis. One my friends was on the set and saw you in the trailer. Figured something was up and he called me."

"Can I ask you some questions? Some vampire questions, I mean?"

Dorian stopped. I heard him take a quick breath. Guess he needed to run something past his vocal chords. "Ask away, Elvis."

"Can you do all that vampire magic stuff, like turning into a bat or mist?"

Dorian chuckled, stopped walking for a moment. "I can shift between wolf and mist, but not to a bat. I can only do things of similar body mass and size. Bats take more practice and I've not had the time."

"What about the mist? You said size and body mass."

"When you transform into mist, you start off a cloud approximately your own size, then you expand, move about, and what have you."

"When you were bit, did you want to be brought over?"

"No." He fell silent and resumed walking again. His footsteps got softer and I realized he was moving faster. I had to run to catch up. My eyes, were almost adjusted to the darkness. Dorian was a vague gray outline ahead of me moving with intimate knowledge of the path. I lost track of the time we spent down there. He could have changed to mist or a wolf and left me stranded. No way I would have gotten out. But Dorian was somehow different from the others. He actually gave a shit about us people.

We came out of the darkness into the headlights of a subway car, speeding right for us. The horn blared and brakes squealed. Sparks from the tracks lit up like fireflies. Dorian threw me to the ground and pressed flat against the tunnel wall as the train raced past. The train rumbled inches above my foot. If I lifted it, it would have been sheared clean off. When the train cleared, Dorian started again. The light from the platform hurt my eyes. Dorian seemed to have no trouble negotiating in light or darkness.

We'd been walking for a few hours. We stopped at a small station, nothing more than some turnstiles, a booth for the person selling tokens, some benches and a large rail map on the wall. Dorian avoided the sunlight streaming in from the street entrance. There were a few people milling about, fewer than I expected. They all looked startled when we strolled in from the tunnels. We took a bench and waited patiently for the train to come.

The passengers unloaded and Dorian looked hungrily at them. He'd been silent for a while as I had, wondering what was next, where to go. His problem was his sister. Mine was I had no place to go next. The set wasn't safe, even if the damn movie was completed. Everything I had left in the world was in the lot trailer—and the key to Rachel's place.

"Oh shit, Dorian," I waited for the doors on the train to close and took a seat next to him.

He looked pale—paler than usual. Something was wrong.

"Rachel, a friend, gave me the keys to her place. I forgot them on the lot."

"Then your Rachel is dead, or wishes she was."

"We have to go there."

"We can't, Elvis. I'm too weak."

"We have to!" I screamed, attracting a few pairs of eyes to us. Even though the other people on the train watched, they kept their gazes hidden carefully in back of newspapers and paperback novels.

"We can't, Elvis. Not now."

The train emptied at the next stop. I had no clue where we were, but some quick glances from the departing passengers made it clear to those boarding to move on to the next car, no matter how crowded it was.

"What's wrong with you, Dorian?"

"Even though I can walk in the sun, it takes its toll on me. I need fresh blood. Vampires aren't supposed to be so active during the daylight hours of mortals."

I knew I'd regret it later on, but I offered my wrist to Dorian. He took my hand, rolled up my sleeve, hissed. With fangs sprouting, he turned away squeezing my arm so hard I thought the bone would break. I saw the rosary still wrapped firmly around the pink flesh of my hand. I took it off quickly, threw the bracelet across the train, saw the beads scatter and roll under the seats.

"Sorry." Closing my eyes, I turned away, tried to block out the pain as he bit into me. No matter how many times it'd happened before, it always hurt. I never figured out what was worse, the pain or the noise.

Dorian took little, enough to keep his composure to fight what he called *the raging animal within.* "Thank you, Elvis."

"What's with those glasses?"

"You never do tire of asking questions, do you?"

I shook my head and cradled my hurt wrist. Blood oozed out slowly from between my fingers. Dorian wrapped a torn piece from his shirt around it, tying it tight.

"Although in my faction of vampires we can walk in the sun, it can still easily destroy us."

I raised my hand to ask another question.

Dorian shrugged it off with a glance. "As long as the blood is fresh and the glasses are in place, we do it. You see Elvis, the eyes are the source of real power. They control others and work our *vampire magic.* If the sunlight gets into our eyes, we're dead. If the blood is stale and cold, then the flesh burns—it depends on how fresh."

The car slowed to a stop. Dorian stood and stepped out with me in tow. We pushed through the crowds in the station, waited for the train to leave, hopped to the tracks, and followed. This time there were lights, green and red, no doubt to tell the drivers if it was okay to go into the station or not. The lights cast eerie glows on the walls, making colored psychedelic shadows—glowing ghosts that seemed to mock us somehow.

"How many factions are there, Dorian?"

"I don't know Elvis. New breeds seem to pop up every decade—crossovers from different factions, unifications like me that shouldn't exist."

"Then why do…?

"Elvis, would you please shut up for a moment? I need to think," Dorian took a side passage jutting out from the main tunnel.

Cobwebs tickled my forehead and cheeks while I walked. I swatted at invisible long dead spiders as my mind played games, putting phantom arachnid legs all over my body.

Dorian stopped suddenly. I walked into his back. I took out the road flare and sparked it up. Ahead of us was a solid wall. Dorian seemed somehow comforted by the pulsating red glow from the flare. He traced the wall with his fingers. Near the base of the wall lay a dead rat, worm ridden and practically stripped of meat. Dorian pressed down on a stone. There was a mechanical grinding, stone against stone, and a door in the wall opened. Dorian slid through. As I followed, he took the flare from my hand and threw it to the tunnel floor.

"You cannot bring that flare in here. This is *our* haven. I can keep you safe in here. I don't know for how long, though. Your reputation as a slayer of our kind betrays you. After what went down at the movie set, we'll both most likely be killed."

"Then why did we come?"

He turned, and for the first time, I saw the humanity in his eyes. "Rather die like a man than run like a coward for all eternity."

I nodded and we shook hands like men—then we advanced into haven.

22
Deaths

"Stand and be recognized." The voice was powerful, deep, and commanding.

Already defeated, Dorian trudged into the room. It was a long empty building, the windows painted black. At one time it must have been a Sears or a K-Mart. Under dust, cobwebs and animal droppings, *For Rent or Lease* signs littered the floors. The aisles that once housed dolls, baby furniture, and clothes now stood barren, with broken and rusted shelves emptied by looters. Ceiling tiles clung precariously to their frames while water dripped down through exposed pipes from useless air conditioning units. The lights were on and everybody was home.

"It's me, Dorian." His voice was flat and beaten.

I stepped out into the light, but Dorian waved me back. The voice was familiar. Something inside my head went off like a siren, but there wasn't a damn thing I could do about it.

A girl's voice was next. "And look, he brings the mortal with him—our slayer!" It was Deirdre, her voice in hysterics.

Along the previously deserted aisles, vampires now appeared, a whole department store full of them, waiting. Some of them I recognized from the lot—broken, burned, and scarred from the fight. Dorian's head dropped. I stepped out from the shadows. The room came alive, shadows swirled, and the darkness seemed to dance.

A small cubicle had been constructed inside. Among his thralls sat Kane. My breath caught in my throat. I know I should have anticipated this day would come. I didn't think so soon. Behind him, Erik stood obediently. I could see the remorse in his once crazy eyes, like I was dead already. Next to him hovered the vampire lady from Georgia, Lauren. She grinned wickedly and licked her fangs. A drop of blood leaked out from her tongue, spattering against her lip.

"You see, Elvis, you can never escape," Kane said, almost glowing.

Dorian looked from me to Kane and back again, not knowing what was happening. He stared at me like I had set him up. That southern bell bitch of a vamp slithered out from behind Kane, put her hands on my shoulders, forcing me to my knees. Erik tensed up. Deirdre took her place.

"What am I to do with the hunter turned movie star and the vampire turned model?" Kane asked. "You could both mysteriously disappear. The talk would go on, the hype would build, but it would end. And what of this new-found alliance between mortal and the dead?"

"Please, Jonathan, he just got caught up in all this. Set him free," Dorian said, eyes still cast away.

Kane jumped up, his eyes afire. Dorian backed away as if he feared his wrath.

"He has slain dozens of us, some with your help. You are *my* creation, Dorian. Never forget that. If I hadn't saved you, you would have died building those damn roads."

Kane waved his hand, and I was dragged off by the scruff of my neck by Lauren. Her nails dug into my skin, drew blood, and she chuckled silently. My feet left trails in the dust. I didn't struggle. There was no use in it. Kane approached Dorian—then the darkness set in.

I awoke on the cold floor of an abandoned restroom stall. The doors had been torn off and lay twisted on the floor outside. The air was stale, fetid—smelled like backed up sewage. My neck was itchy. When I went to scratch, my fingers became covered in dried blood. My head felt like someone had danced all over it. I stood groggily, fell back down, cracked my head on the toilet's edge, and started bleeding all over the place. I wadded up some soaked-through toilet paper, applied pressure to the gash on my head, and started to cry.

This was how it was going to end. Dying frightened me. Fighting did too. But those few moments of freedom were worth all the pain and hurt. The lock to the door *clicked*. Erik came in holding some towels, squatted down, and handed me one.

"Why did you let it go this far, Elvis?"

"How can you ask me that?" I wiped the tears away, blew my nose on the towel, and threw it at him.

My legs were shaky, even wobbled a little. Erik helped me stand, but I shrugged away from him.

"You turned your back on me," I said.

"You know this is what I wanted from the beginning, Elvis."

I wanted to throw up my hand, expose my neck, jam a stake in his heart, and run away again. But where to? I still had to get to Rachel's and warn her. "So what was I then?"

He hung his head and the other towels slipped from his grip. The light overhead flickered.

"Never mind, don't answer."

"I have some information if you want it."

"Might as well, Erik. It won't do me any good. I'm going to die here."

Erik opened his mouth and looked around to make sure no one was in with us. He stared at a pool of shadows for a moment. His eyes flared.

"What about the sponsors?" I blurted out. "Maybe they can get me, *us*, out of here."

Erik shook his head. "It was all Kane. He *was* the sponsor. He did everything."

My jaw dropped and a tear cascaded down my cheek.

"All of our work, fighting—everything was for Kane. I realize now that I may have been wrong. It's too late." He handed me a key, which slid through my fingers. "It's Rachel's key. If you get out, go there. It's the only chance you'll have."

I slipped it into my sneaker. "Why, Erik?"

"Kane is mad. He wants to rule the vampires. He's been going crazy over the past few months, making an army of vampires—trying to take control of his world and yours."" I got up again, put down the seat on the toilet seat, and sat down. Brown, murky water stirred inside of it. I'd tried to flush it, but the lever was limp.

"He paid us—funded everything we did—exploited us. Emily, from that club in Boston, was right. Kane played us like a record. Our whole purpose wasn't for research like I had been tricked into believing, but to eliminate the factions that wouldn't follow Kane."

"What about our first job in Georgia? She's still alive and now aligned herself with Kane."

"It was a mistake. After our little incident, she decided it was safer to be with Kane. He planted her in the trailers following us."

"What about the underground, the newsletters, and all that?"

"I had those contacts long before I went in with the sponsors. I fed them information as I found it. Until Kane started funding me, it wasn't much. After a while it became habit. Kane never thought it was doing any harm so he let them continue. After all, they were making him famous. The movie set was all planned. You were sent to investigate. Your killing that first vampire was icing on the cake so to speak. You were supposed to die so many times I can't count. I begged Kane to let you live, Elvis, but you knew too much and killed too many. I even asked him if I could bring you across."

"No fucking way that's happening."

"That's what I told him you would say."

"Tell me about Dorian," I said.

Erik stood up and stretched like he used to.

"Do you sleep in a coffin, Erik?"

"No, in a bed."

"What about having to sleep on a bed of the ground you were buried in?"

"I was never buried. Besides, it's just old superstitions made up by Hollywood. That first one, Katherine, believed all the myths."

"Is my movie going to come out?"

"Oddly enough, yes. Shane and a few others from the press conference lived. Juliana is in for plastic surgery, and Rory—well, he's one of us now. They're going to use his stunt double and pass him off for the premier. In a few months, Rory will be involved in a terrible accident. He'll be reported dead and the body never found."

I had to pause a second to take in everything Erik was telling me. My head started bleeding again, and Erik pressed a towel to it—the way a father would.

"About Dorian—he's Irish if you couldn't tell from the accent. Kane brought him and his twin sister Deirdre over to the undead more than a century ago. They're hybrids."

"Hy-whats?"

"Hybrids—cross breeds, whatever you want to say. They have the blood and powers of all the different factions within them. They're supposedly the only two of their kind. But I know I have records of more of them someplace. They have powers that even Kane doesn't have—and deep down, he fears them for it. He's been working on Deirdre, taking her blood on a regular basis to get her daytime abilities. But it always fails. He burns each time."

"Why is he here? Why are *you* here?"

"He's been keeping track of Dorian, following him since he left New York. Kane lost track of him though. Couldn't find him until he turned up in Hollywood very close to you. You were supposed to find *him*, not the other one you killed. Kane packed up the operations. Moved them all to LA. What we did, most of the time, was follow Dorian from city to city trying to find him. It's the only way Kane could keep his eye on us and actively search for Dorian as well."

"I don't know what to say, Erik. Why are you helping me?"

"I don't want you to die—not like this. Vampires have been hidden for centuries, and Kane feels that time is over. But there are still several groups that disagree and want to remain hidden. The battles will continue above and below ground. I'm going to help you, Elvis, and do what it takes." Erik stood up, walked out of the stall and bathroom, and locked the door.

Not having much of anything else to do, I stayed put and tried to plot. Nothing came to mind. I didn't have anything left to fight with or for. If I had the means in the bathroom, I could have ended it all before I wound up a slave to Kane. The key to Rachel's dug into my heel, driving those thoughts away. I sat and waited and waited in the flickering lights and dripping water. I hoped that Dorian was still alive. He had become a fellow warrior, maybe even a friend.

Time passed. My head spun and eventually stopped bleeding. I ripped one of the towels to shreds and made some makeshift bandages that looked more like a stained bandana, but it did the trick. When the time came, it was Erik who showed up for me—with Lauren on his heels.

Erik started to talk, and she cast a glare at him, stopping him in his tracks. I walked between them, Erik in the lead and Lauren with a firm grip on my neck. Erik looked back occasionally. We went through the employee lounge, passed the management offices, skirted by the fitting rooms, and ended our trek at Kane's cubicle. Dorian was lying unconscious at the foot of his empty chair, being tended to by Kane's thralls.

They had rubber hoses tied around his arms, neck, and wrists. Clear tubes slowly leaked out what was left inside of him. They were bleeding him out, forcing out the animal within, but who was the target of his rage? The puddle beneath him expanded and grew. The lights shifted, changed, and Kane materialized from the shadows, taking his seat. Lauren and Erik joined him—then Deirdre, after a fleeting look of concern for her twin.

Erik wouldn't face me—just looked down at his feet. Lauren, however, kept her gaze locked on me. I heard her voice in my head as she whispered suggestions. I ignored her. Something happened when I was with Katherine all that time ago that made me able to fight it. Lauren was talking crazy notions though—fight against Kane, rebel, take the chair, and lead the damned into victory over the humans. She was fucked.

"Elvis, you almost had me once, and for that you are a formidable enemy," Kane said. "However, you are a vampire hunter, the slayer of our race."

"I only killed the ones you paid us to."

Erik nodded at the floor.

Kane raised an eyebrow. "I see we have an information problem."

Dorian groaned from where he was slumped. The other vampires winced at his condition. Deirdre seemed oblivious. I wished I could somehow reverse that mind stuff and send some suggestions back at Lauren—to maybe bitch-slap Deirdre, set Dorian free, or even maybe cleave off one of Kane's nuts, whether the nuts functioned or not.

"In New York, you could have killed me. Instead you chose to flee. Why?"

"'Cause you had more people than me."

"Yet you come here to my haven and make a bold stand in front of me?"

"What else am I going to do? Run for the rest of my life? Hide from you bastards until you finally track me down? I won't be a slave, thrall, or a bloodsucker. You're an asshole, Kane."

There was some chuckling in the room. Kane raised his hand, then eased it back into place on the chair. Erik moved behind him. Dorian reached towards his thigh, took out one of the hoses and pulled the tube from his leg. He tried to sit up, but fell backwards instead.

"He still fights," Kane whispered. Then he stood.

He advanced on Dorian's prone form. I kept checking his chest, looking for the rise and fall of breaths. Deirdre looked worried, fearing what might happen to her brother regardless of which side of the political ladder they climbed.

"Leave him, Jonathan, *please*." Deirdre's tone was quiet, reserved, but you felt the power in her words. She had a special place in Kane's kingdom and was using a favor to save Dorian's life. "You brought him across—brought me over as well. There's no doubt or question of it. We are the only two strong enough to survive the transformation. Let him feed."

Kane approached Deirdre and stared her down.

Her strength seemed to wilt.

"He is a traitor. He'd have me dead."

"He is still my brother."

"Perhaps you're right." Kane lashed out, grabbed Erik by the throat, holding him fast.

Erik tried to struggle, but didn't have Kane's will or strength.

"If you care for the humans so much and tell them our secrets, then you should be helping them and their sympathizers." Kane tightened his grip.

Erik grimaced, fought out, striking Kane about the face and neck. Kane smiled and lifted Erik from the floor. His feet kicked out wildly, looking to connect with anything. Erik's neck snapped with a sickening *crunch.*

Anger started to well in me. If nothing else, I wanted to see Kane die before I did. There was nothing so important in my life than seeing that fuck die.

Erik's eyes rolled up and body went limp. Kane threw him to the floor in front of Dorian. The hunger in Erik's eyes burned and he seemed to struggle so hard to fight it. He squirmed on the floor and his eyes darted around the room looking for help.

"Haven't you done enough, Kane?" I took a step towards him, and his thralls moved protectively in front of him, offering themselves to my rage. "Let me kill him and put him out of this."

Kane looked amused, almost laughed, hiding his mouth with a gloved hand. He waved at me, like dismissing a servant. I walked over to Erik and saw him lying there on the ground. His fingers twitched. Erik had started the healing process, but being a vampire for such a short time, hadn't mastered it yet. I winked at him, then carefully dragged his prone form over to Dorian.

Dorian struggled to raise himself onto his elbow and prop himself up. *"Be prepared Elvis."*

I heard him in my mind. The others began to circle around us, hungry, curiously waiting for the show.

"Dorian," I thought back at him. *We only have one shot. You have to bite Erik, don't drain him though, just enough to heal."*

It took most of Dorian's strength to nod at me. Kane looked to us suspiciously.

"All Erik ever wanted was to be a bloodsucker. He told me so. He got bit by *that bitch,*" I said pointing up at Kane. "Born a vampire, he dies by one." I untied the hoses around Dorian's arms and leg, pulled out the tubes that leaked his blood across the floor, and dropped him on Erik.

Dorian bit in. With each mouthful of Erik's blood, the color returned to Dorian's flesh. His strength surged back as he now bent over Erik to get every drop of blood he could. Dorian was losing control of the feeding. I rushed over and shoved him off. He eyed me animalistically for interrupting his meal. Composure was not coming back to him, and the others began to egg him on, chanting his name. Dorian approached me like a predator, waiting to deliver the killing blow. In his chair, Kane inched closer and then it started.

Dorian lunged at Kane, and in a quick motion, ripped out his throat. Kane fell back, clutching the torn flesh with a surprised look on his face. Blood spurted out from between his fingers as he tried to cover the damage. His minions moved to circle us, but stayed out of the fight. This was Kane's. Seeing their master fallen, his slaves rushed to him, bit open wrists, bled into his mouth. The blood flowed over his mouth and clutching fingers. The healing happened almost immediately with the flux of fresh blood. Kane sat up and wiped it from his face.

Erik crawled to the stairs, weakened but alive. "Just you and me, Kane. Just you and me."

Kane pushed through the hesitant onlookers.

Dorian stood eye to eye with him.

"You'll die, Dorian. By all rites, your death should be mine. No others will deny me that." Kane slapped Dorian so hard and fast his jaw broke. His head whipped around facing me, a mask of pain.

Be ready yourself, Elvis, Dorian said, his voice filling my head.

I helped Erik stand. When I did, he stuffed something into my shirt. I braced him up against the wall. Deirdre and Lauren joined the fight. Lauren stood near Deirdre and me and in front of Erik. Erik shook off the remaining cobwebs in his head. Recognition came back while blood dripped from his fingertips and claws punctured the skin. His teeth enlarged to jagged, harsh daggers. Lauren's eyes flared, mist collecting at her feet. The shadows pulled together and swirled about her. Deirdre stood idly, seemingly unimpressed by Erik's new skills. Then she spread her arms and took flight.

Lauren vanished before me in a cloud of swirling vapors. The first blow came unexpectedly. She jumped from the shadows, raking my chest and drawing blood from the base of my throat. She laughed and dove back into the darkness that birthed her.

Erik futilely charged at Deirdre. She rose to the ceiling, plucked out an air conditioning unit and dropped it on his chest. He crumpled beneath it. Even some of the bloodsuckers winced from the action. Erik pushed it off, holding his ribs, and fought to stand. Dorian had taken too much from him.

Kane charged Dorian, this time picking him up—taking flight as he did. They flew across the room. Kane let go of Dorian. Dorian fell through a glass display case, shattering the panes and lacerating his flesh. The jagged shards stuck in his face and arms. Kane, Deirdre, and Lauren formed a line in front of Erik and me. Dorian pulled his way free from the glass and joined us.

"You took your best shot, bitches. Now it's our fucking turn," I said, looking to both Erik and Dorian, seeking the agreement in their eyes. We stood back to back in a triangle. Erik rushed Deirdre, who faded into the darkness just as his hands closed on her throat. She looked around confused, searching for her opponent. This time, Erik dropped down on her from the ceiling, driving a water pipe through the top of her skull. She wailed, grasped the pipe, and fell to the floor, trying to pull it free. Dorian turned away, trying not to look at the pain his sister was in. He took a step towards her, but I held him back. Kane snarled with hate in his eyes.

Dorian sat on the floor, closed his eyes, and lay back, refusing to fight. I, however, chose a different route. I pulled the wooden stake out of my shirt from where Erik had stuffed it, wincing as the point pulled out of the flesh in my waist. I felt the warm trickle of blood but ignored it. Lauren screamed as I leapt on her, but like earlier, she faded into the shadows. Her laugh echoed throughout the store. Not fully whole, she emerged from a pool of blackness. I jumped on her, jamming the stake into her chest as she materialized. She didn't scream, didn't flail—just fell to the floor and stopped moving.

Deirdre freed the pipe from her skull and blew into the end, forcing out a chunk of brain and skull. Her red hair was matted down, thick with brackish blood. She jumped on Erik, sank her teeth into his neck, and drank. Despite his struggling and fighting, it was over quickly. Erik slumped to the floor in a heap, truly dead. His eyes pasted over and his body soon just faded into the shadows that had spawned him earlier in the fight. Deirdre clutched the pipe and gripped it tightly, holding it like it was a Louisville Slugger.

"Damn you, Dorian, fight me!" Kane stepped on his wrist breaking it. The *crunch* of bone filled the store.

A single, bloody tear escaped Deirdre's eye and ran down her cheek. I thought of Juliana for a moment. Kane kicked Dorian repeatedly in the ribs, shattering them one by one. Finally, he lifted him above his head and snapped his spine. Dorian cried out, choked as the blood he'd taken from Erik gurgled in his mouth. Kane dropped him on the floor, broken and useless. Then he looked at me.

Deirdre went to her brother, cradled his form in her arms and rocked him softly, singing something, I assumed, was Gaelic. Kane approached me, dragging his feet through the mist that was Erik as a child would do through a puddle. It was Kane's final insult to Erik, my friend. Kane's neck still had vicious claw marks on it from Dorian's earlier attack. A little bit deeper and Dorian would have found his mark.

"What's it to be, Elvis?" His voice was raspier now. "Be one of us or die by all of us." Kane raised his arms and all the other vampires flocked to his side.

"Guess I only have one choice." I grabbed the stake from Lauren's chest and stuck it deep into Kane's.

He grasped at it, falling backwards. Deirdre ran to him, got a hold on it and readied to tug.

"Stop it right there, bitch." I walked up to her and kicked her off Kane's prone form.

His eyes were filled with hatred and rage.

"I won the fight. I'm king of the vampires now, the whole damn bloodsucker nation," I announced. I jumped up and down on Kane's chest to emphasize the point.

On the floor, Lauren stirred, groaning and clutching the hole in her chest where the stake used to be. I saw Dorian not too far from her, bent back like a damn pretzel.

"He's your fucking brother, you whore," I said. "Help him out."

Deirdre rushed to his side, whether from my words or her own sympathy for Dorian. I watched the last of the mist from Erik dissipate into cracks in the floor. Now it was truly finished.

I walked over to Lauren, straddled her chest, and pushed back a lock of her hair. She sure was pretty—would have been more so if not for the burn scars. If Daddy were here, he'd say that since she fucked me over, I should do the same to her—whip out the captain and thrust it into the chest wound. I had more efficient plans. From my pants pocket, I pulled out my cross. Lauren tried to cover her eyes, but I had her arms under my knees. Thankfully, she was weak from the staking. I kissed the cross, said a prayer for Erik, Momma, and Daddy and dropped it into the hole, jumping quickly off her. It wouldn't last long. Her chest glowed like a light inside. She wailed as fire shot out from her chest. There was an unearthly *howl*. She burst into flames and exploded. The flames spread out across the floor, filling the aisles. I dove under Kane's chair as the fire danced overhead. The flames ceased, and smoke rose slowly. The other vampires began to disperse.

"Wait," I shouted standing on Kane's chair. "There will be no damn vampire leader. Just go back to what you were doing. Don't ever fucking cross my path, because if you do, you're all fucking dead." I hopped off, kicked the chair over, and went to Dorian.

His eyes had rolled up and bloody foam oozed between his lips. Kane had done him good.

"What can we do?" I asked.

Deirdre turned, crying and looking to me for help. "It's like he's lost the will to live. He's not healing," Deirdre said. Her eyes went wide and I saw the words get stuck on her lips—a warning.

I hadn't see Kane sit up or pull the stake from his chest. Jonathan Kane strode over to us, kicked me off the stairs, and picked up and tossed Dorian across the room. Dorian collided with and fell into a display of mannequins almost as pale as he. Deirdre was his target, she knew it and screamed as he bit into her neck. The blood flowed down her slender throat and leaked out from his lips. A cry slowly escaped her. Kane released her, and she fell lifeless once again at his feet. Her features changed, morphing back to her original form—soft eyes, gentle features, but pale and lifeless. He wiped his lips headed for me.

I did the only thing I could. I ran through the aisles and past display cases, and headed for the loading docks, looking for anything to use as a weapon. The other vampires started to come back and fill the room. Kane was in front of me in a heart-beat, swatting me back into the main room with his massive claws. I grabbed a broken piece of glass. It cut into my hand, but I jumped on Kane and thrust it into his forehead, leaving the jagged piece lodged in his skull. Blood dripped down from between my fingers, staining the floor. Kane cried out and tore the glass from his face. The wound healed instantly.

"We could have been such a team, Elvis, but now because of you, they're all dead, or soon to die."

I got hold of Deirdre's pipe and bashed Kane's head with it a few times. It resounded with a hollow metallic *ring* on each hit, but it didn't even phase him. I dropped the pipe, leaving my bloody handprint on it.

"Hurts, doesn't it? I can put an end to the pain, Elvis."

"Fuck you, bloodsucker!" I closed my eyes as Kane moved in for the kill.

But there was a scream—one I recognized. Claws and fangs bared, Dorian sailed out from the tangle of mannequin parts where I could see two legs sticking out—presumably one of the thralls that had gone to check on Dorian to see if he were really dead. His first blow caught Kane in the eye, ripping it from the socket. Kane howled, grew claws and thrust them down into my gut, ripping, tearing. The pain was the worst I ever felt. I tasted my blood and my vision started to haze over. I toppled over near where Erik went down and started praying.

I watched Dorian deliver so many fast vicious blows it seemed incredible and improbable, but Kane shrugged them off like annoying bug bites, still covering his empty eye socket. The other vampires held back Kane's thralls. This was no longer a political struggle but a personal one. They would not interfere with this. Personal feuds always took precedence in the bloodsucker world.

Kane staggered a little. Dorian kept up his furious onslaught and sliced into Kane's face, practically carving off his ear. He grabbed Kane's arm and dislocated his shoulder so his arm hung loose exposing his bleeding vacant socket. I crawled over to Lauren's ashes, leaving a trail of gore in back of me. The pain subsided and a coldness started to fall over me.

I fumbled through the ash, looking for the cross. With my last bit of strength, I threw it to Dorian. He caught it in the air, screaming as it burned his flesh. I started to pray again amidst the *screams* and *howls*. Kane popped his arm back in, ripped one of Dorian's off, and tossed it into the awaiting crowds.

Dorian fell to his knees, cradling the cross burning through his hand. He waited for Kane to approach, and when he did, Dorian jammed the cross into Kane's eye socket.

Dorian dove for cover, trying to shield me from the firestorm that followed. All of Kane's power and life exploded outward. Those in close proximity were vaporized from the blast. The store windows blew out, showering the sidewalk and street with glass. The sunlight streamed in, coating and covering the other vampires in a blanket of fiery death. I coughed up blood and watched a whirlwind of flame circle Kane, envelop him, and swallow him into its center. The only thing that remained of him, was my cross, lying on the floor in a pile of ash.

The other vampires tried to flee from the sun. Some made it, but most didn't. They cried and screamed as the fires claimed them. The dying fell, burning about us. I heard Dorian groan. Blood flowed from his torn socket, and beneath his weakening fingers, I saw pink tissue and the white of shattered bone. At last it ended. Nothing moved.

"We're going to die now, Elvis." He rolled me over onto my back, looked at my wound, and smiled.

"It was one hell of a fight," I said, blood staining my teeth and gums.

"It was that, Elvis—*one hell of a fight*." Dorian sat down beside me.

I lay back staring at the sun-traced shadows of parking meters and parked cars on the wall. Heard the *wail* of sirens and the *chatter* and *cries* of people on the street. I would have loved to read the police report on this one. Dorian's face hovered over mine.

"Elvis, I cannot give up. There's still too much to be done."

Through the white haze that stole all my thoughts, I saw my mother's face—and then my father's. I was going home. My time was up. I tried to focus on Dorian, but his face was blurry. I did see the fangs slipping free.

"No," I wheezed. "Please don't do it Dorian. Let me die."

He bit into my neck and began sucking out what I had left in me. It felt painful yet sexual, terrible, and wonderful all at the same time.

"It's the only way, Elvis, to save us both. We cannot die here like this," Dorian said. He chewed away at the skin at his wrist, tore out the veins and arteries and pressed his blood spewing hand into my mouth. It was bitter and warm. My own blood was being fed back into me. It was sweet yet somehow natural. I felt strength returning. I wrapped my hands around his and drank greedily from his wrist until at last he pulled it away and fell backwards.

Dorian let go of his shoulder and the flow of blood slowed and stopped. New skin formed over the terrible wound. I watched the deep gashes in my gut scab over and start to heal. Fresh pink flesh appeared where intestines had peeked out moments earlier. I tried sitting up, caught a sunbeam, and my skin started to burn.

"No, Elvis, Jesus no." He dragged me away to the loading dock.

Already, the police cars had started to arrive. Someone had called in a bomb blast. No way to cover this up. I pulled free of Dorian, staggered back, and found my cross. It didn't burn me. I slid it into my pocket and retreated to him. We went past the offices and through the break room. Finally, we filed into a small room where Dorian felt along the stones for a switch, tripped it, and slipped through. I followed him and we were again in the tunnels. We collapsed on the floor in the darkness, only it wasn't dark anymore. Everything was lit up like it was daytime. I heard the police searching through the other parts of the store looking for survivors. All they found was Dorian's arm and a whole shit-load of blood and ashes. They'd never know what happened. Never find out the truth.

"So," I asked, turning to Dorian. "When can I turn into a bat?"

About the Author
Scott T. Goudsward

Scott T. Goudsward is the author of numerous short stories, screen plays and novels. He has an avid interest in the horror genre since seeing the horror classic, Friday the 13th, when he was only 13. By total accident he hails for the same odd New England town—Haverhill, Massachusetts—that has produced the likes of Colonial axe murderess, Hannah Dustin, bellowed Abolitionist poet, John Greenleaf Whittier, TV Host, Tom Bergeron, and heavy metal rocker/movie director, Rob Zombie.

Visit Scott's web site at:

www.goudsward.com/scott

Made in the USA
Charleston, SC
10 October 2013